"ONE TOUGH HOMBRE...
Hunter's excursions into bone-breaking and face-crumpling are frequent and explicit—so, for that matter, are his sexual exploits...Morse has written a book that is at once in the genre of the old-fashioned pulp magazine detective yarn and a send-up of the genre...and it works."
TORONTO STAR

"HUNTER IS
A LOS ANGELES PRIVATE EYE,
content to knee groins, smash noses, crack arms and, when push comes to shove, blow magnum-sized holes through unpleasant people ...Morse's writing crackles with witty toughness, a hard-boiled prose always faithful to the genre. And it's fun."
OTTAWA CITIZEN

"THE PEOPLE WHO USED TO ATTACK MICKEY SPILLANE FOR SEX AND VIOLENCE SHOULD READ THIS."
*THE ARMCHAIR
DETECTIVE*

"A CONSIDERABLE FORCE IN THE 'TOUGH DETECTIVE' GAME...The story is carefully plotted, well told and both enthralls and entertains."
QUILL & QUIRE

Other Avon Books by
L. A. Morse

THE BIG ENCHILADA
THE OLD DICK

SLEAZE

A SAM HUNTER MYSTERY

L. A. MORSE

◆ **AVON**
PUBLISHERS OF BARD, CAMELOT, DISCUS AND FLARE BOOKS

AVON BOOKS
A division of
The Hearst Corporation
1790 Broadway
New York, New York 10019

Copyright © 1985 by L. A. Morse, Inc.
Published by arrangement with the author
Library of Congress Catalog Card Number: 84-91195
ISBN: 0-380-89227-8

First Avon Printing, February, 1985

AVON TRADEMARK REG. U.S. PAT. OFF. AND IN OTHER COUNTRIES, MARCA REGISTRADA, HECHO EN U.S.A.

Printed in the U.S.A.

WFH 10 9 8 7 6 5 4 3 2 1

This book contains numerous scenes of gratuitous sex and violence, as well as a lot of bad language and worse jokes. If you don't like that sort of thing, this is a good place to stop.

e letters were Day-Glo yellow and ten feet high. They

ONE

SLEAZE.

The letters were Day-Glo yellow and ten feet high. They took up the entire width of the top floor of the six-story brick building that had been painted glossy black.

Below, five-foot letters spelled out ". . . For Men Who Know What They Like."

I parked in front of a Korean ginseng parlor, walked past a triple-X bookstore and into the lobby of the elegant Sleaze Building. A skinny old guy with sunken cheeks and a sallow complexion was listlessly pushing a string mop over the speckled-green linoleum-tile floor, leaving muddy brown streaks as he went. A spiffy dude sporting a pencil-line mustache and wearing something that looked like a zoot suit was leaning against the wall, whistling as he cleaned his fingernails with a six-inch switchblade. In the corner, a sweaty big guy and a smiling little guy were having a friendly discussion as to which would occur first, the big guy paying off what he owed, or his ending up in a green plastic garbage bag. No question, this was one of fashionable East Hollywood's prestige addresses.

I rode the elevator up to the sixth floor. As I stepped out, there was a frosted-glass door bearing the same message as the front of the building. I opened it and went in. The reception area had phony wood paneling and was filled with the usual Scandinavian shit. It could've been a dentist's waiting room.

Well, almost.

The wall opposite the entrance was covered with what I first thought was an abstract painting. Then I realized it was one of the close-up gynecological studies that were the main feature of the magazine, only blown up wall size.

7

Tasteful.

The model had a tattoo of a butterfly very high up on her inner thigh. The actual tattoo must have been quite small, but in the enlargement it had a twelve-inch wingspan and resembled one of the giant tree moths of Malaysia.

"You like it?" a voice to the side of me asked.

It was the receptionist. If her goal was to look like a cheap Vegas hooker, she'd succeeded pretty well. She had a tangled mane of thick black hair. Her eyes were so darkly and heavily made up that they looked like the after effects of a broken nose. She was a good twenty pounds overweight, and her maroon sweater had been made for someone much smaller. It was stretched so tautly over her huge breasts that her nipples showed through the gaps in the weave.

"You like it?" she repeated, motioning to the mural.

"Oh, yeah. It's swell."

"That's me. I was 'Slit of the Month' for last June," she said with a cheerful smile.

I looked again at the gigantic picture and nodded. "Nice tattoo," I said.

"You like it? Want to see it?" She stood up and moved around the desk, hoisting her already short skirt to display a pair of thighs that could have come from the Pittsburgh Steelers' offensive line. She propped herself up on the edge of the desk and gave me just about the same angle of view as that of the photograph.

"Yeah. Real nice," I said.

"Oh, you can't see it from there. Get closer."

I sighed, but held my ground. I asked her to tell Mr. Orlov that I was here.

She looked at me for a minute, then said, "Oh, all right," and hopped off the desk. She went through a door, the outlines of which were cleverly hidden in the dark curls of the mural. The opening itself was just about where you'd expect it to be.

I shook my head, lit up a cigarette, and looked around. There wasn't a hell of a lot to see, just a few more photographs in the same style, though smaller, barely life-size, and three framed documents on the wall behind the receptionist's desk. There was an Award of Merit from *Screw* magazine for the October issue of SLEAZE, which had regis-

tered 94 on the Peter Meter. There was a certificate for
"Significant Contributions" from the California League of
Indecency. And there was a letter of praise from a Mid-
western local of the Teamsters. It's always nice to know
that your efforts are appreciated.

Tiny Butterfly came back and told me I could go in. Feeling a little like a character in some nervous preadolescent
dirty joke, I went through the door and down a long corridor until I came to the office of N. E. Orlov, editor of
SLEAZE. The door was open, and I went into a large, bright
corner room with windows on two walls—what might be
called, under the circumstances, a womb with a view.

A woman was standing at a light table, examining large-
format transparencies with a magnifier. When she looked up
I said, "I'm Sam Hunter. I'm looking for Mr. Orlov."

"So am I, pal." She stared levelly at me, a smile forming
at the corners of her broad mouth.

"On the other hand," I said, "maybe I'm looking for Ms.
Orlov?"

"Got it in one." She came over to me, smiling, and held
out her hand. "I'm Natalie Orlov, known professionally as
N. E., for fairly obvious reasons."

I took her hand. It was warm and smooth, and her grip
was firm, but not trying to make a big deal out of it. In fact,
nothing about her seemed to be trying for a big deal. She
looked twenty-five, but I figured she was somewhere in her
thirties. Her brown hair was cut functionally short and
shaggy, her makeup was minimal, and she wore a man's
large blue oxford-cloth shirt tucked into baggy chinos.
Still, even an apparent lack of effort couldn't disguise the
fact that her eyes were a spectacular green, that her
mouth was wide, full, and sensual, and that there seemed
to be a pretty fine body beneath her loose clothes. She'd
never be considered pretty, but I had the feeling that if she
wanted to, she could make herself stunningly beautiful
with about five minutes' effort.

"Then who's the guy who poses as N. E. Orlov in those
picture spreads depicting the SLEAZE lifestyle?" I said.

"Oh, shit! Don't tell me you're a loyal reader?"

I shook my head. "Afraid not. But when your secretary,
or whoever, called for an appointment, I looked through
some back issues."

"And?"

"You put out a classy publication, lady. Sure lives up to its name."

"Yeah, doesn't it?" She laughed. "It was going to be called *Hot and Juicy,* but I said that sounded like a chile relleno burrito. Besides, I've always believed in truth in packaging." She gave me a smile, and I started to think this was a woman who might give me trouble. "Anyway," she said, "the guy in those pictures really is N. E. Orlov."

"Huh?"

"My brother, Norman Edward. One of the last refugees from the sixties—you know, brain lightly sautéed in acid, at one with the cosmos. He lives up north in a cabin without electricity or running water. Grows enough sinsemilla to stay happy through the year. If Norman was brighter, he'd grow a little extra and make enough to retire in luxury, but that's not his style. So I bring him down twice a year, clean him up, and pose him with a lot of tits drooping over him. For this I give him enough to keep him in Oreos and tortilla chips, which he says are all that he requires from civilization." She shrugged. "It's an arrangement that suits both of us. He gets what he needs, and I don't have to worry about having my cover blown."

"Yeah. I guess it wouldn't be very good for business if it got out that you were the man behind SLEAZE."

"Exactly. All those men who know what they like might not like it a whole lot if they knew a woman was dishing it up. Probably make 'em a touch nervous. At a minimum, our sincerity would be questioned."

I had to laugh. "And not without reason, I'd say."

She looked at me for a minute before replying. "Let's just say that a degree of cynicism isn't exactly a handicap—as I suspect you already know very well, Mr. Hunter."

She continued to look at me, smiling slightly, and I nodded in acknowledgment. In this town, in this job, cynicism—about my clients, about their motives, about what they wanted me to do, about almost everything—was not exactly a handicap. In fact, I'd found that contempt wasn't necessarily inappropriate either, since a lot of my clients turned out to be pretty contemptible. On the other hand, they probably wouldn't hire me if they weren't, so I suppose it worked out okay for everyone concerned. At least, as long as I didn't give more of a shit about my clients than they gave about me, I usually did all right. And if one of the bastards who hired me tried to get cute, I saw to it that he ended up with a surprised expression on his face. I didn't figure to be a candidate for the Nobel Peace Prize in the near future, but who the fuck wants to go to Sweden anyway. The weather stinks.

I had a feeling, though, that Natalie Orlov wouldn't turn out to be one of the assholes. I saw no reason for contempt, only curiosity. After just a few minutes, I found her to be an impressive—and very unexpected—woman. Obviously tough, shrewd, and smart. I thought she could handle just about anything that came up, and I was wondering what she wanted me to do.

I was about to ask her when a tall thin guy with a mustache like a blond caterpillar hurried in, a large manila envelope in his hand.

"The stuff for Miss September just arrived," he said.

"Well, it's about time. Let's see it."

The guy spread out a couple dozen transparencies on the light table, and Natalie Orlov bent to study them. After quickly going over them, she straightened up. "Christ! What the fuck are they doing? We want slick and slippery. How many goddamn times do I have to say it? Slick and slippery and ready for action. If what's-her-name can't manage to juice herself up, then have Hank use glycerine or Vaseline or something. Christ! Our guys get enough of this dry hole stuff when they roll on top of their wives after about three whole seconds of warm-up. They don't want to see it laid out over a double page. Shit! Look at this!"

As they huddled to discuss labial technicalities, I looked around the office. It was simple, uncluttered, and totally functional, just large pine worktables and gray metal filing cabinets. It was all business, but nothing to indicate what that business was, much like Natalie Orlov herself. And there was none of that bullshit—leather couches, coffee tables, a small bar, a nifty little collection of ancient pottery—that was supposed to turn an office into a living room and impress the hell out of a visitor. The only decorations were a page torn from an old *National Geographic* and stuck up on the white wall with masking tape—a pic-

ture of a large white Victorian wooden building overlooking what appeared to be a South Pacific beach—and a
framed certificate behind her metal desk. This one wasn't
about the magazine, though, but a diploma from the Uni-
versity of California awarding Natalie Elizabeth Orlov a
Ph.D. in medieval lit about six years before. Yeah, a most
unexpected woman.

After the guy left with instructions to schedule another
photo session, and this time make sure it was glistening,
she turned back to me, shaking her head. "Swell job,
huh?"

"A lot of guys'd think so."

"A lot of guys are fourteen . . . forever. What about
you?"

I shook my head. "Maybe I was never fourteen. At least,
I never found women in pieces to be all that interesting."

"Hmmm." She looked at me for a bit, speculatively. "I
think we might get along."

I looked back into her large, clear green eyes, and felt an
odd pressure begin to form at the base of my spine. I shook
it off. "Maybe. Now, what can I do for you?"

She gave me a long, hard look, then nodded with a smile.
She went around behind her desk, waved for me to sit in
the chair in front, and sat down herself. She wrinkled her
forehead and fiddled for a while with a blue felt-tip
marker. Then she looked up, apparently having decided
how to proceed.

"Have you ever heard of a group—or something—called
the Sword of Truth?"

"No. What is it?"

She shook her head. "I'm not really sure. Until a month
ago, I'd never heard of them. Neither has anyone else I've
asked."

"Sounds like one of those fringe religious groups."

"That's what it seems like. They say they're the tenth
and last Crusade. Originally, you may know, there were
nine Crusades, between the eleventh and fourteenth centuries. Their ostensible purpose was to rescue the holy
city of Jerusalem, to recapture it from the Moslem
hordes."

"Maybe this bunch has the same idea."

"They do. Or at least that's what they write."

"You're getting letters?" I was beginning to see what this was about. "Go on."

"Yeah. They started arriving about a month ago. Went on and on about redeeming the New Jerusalem from the New Infidels."

"Meaning people like you?"

"That seemed to be the implication. I really didn't pay that much attention to the first couple. There are a lot of cranks around, and a magazine like this is a convenient target for them."

"Then what happened?"

"The messages started to get more explicit. Said we were 'befouling the Holy City,' something like that. And that we must be removed."

"The Holy City? They couldn't mean Hollywood, could they?" I laughed. "Hell, you get rid of the heathens here, it'll be deserted. Look like a neutron bomb hit the place."

She smiled. "I have a feeling they were speaking metaphorically." Then she grew more serious. "I'm just not certain how metaphorical the threats are."

"Do you have any of the letters?"

She opened a drawer, took out a file folder, and handed me some papers. "They're all there except for the first few."

There were seven letter-size sheets, all the same, fairly good-quality ivory stationery. "Sword of Truth" was printed at the top in fancy lettering and dark red ink. The first "T" in Truth was formed out of a drawing of a large sword, pointing down, with a bloody, dripping tip.

The front side of each sheet was covered with a spidery scrawl in brighter red ink. The letters were undated and they weren't addressed to anyone specific, but started off with friendly salutations like "YOU are a vile, Godless creature, a stain of corruption upon the Waters of our Purity, a belching, demon TOAD." The writing continued in the same vein: repetitious, rambling, and near-hysterical. It was the usual fire-and-brimstone fundamentalist masturbatory bullshit, neither original nor interesting. The only real difference among the letters was that they grew progressively more violent. They changed from "You should be excised from the HOLY BODY like a Cancerous Growth" to "You *will* be smote with Flaming Swords and

Thunder." It seemed as if the writer's dementia was feeding upon itself, getting angrier the more it screeched,
working up to a fevered, frothing pitch. It was probably
nothing but bad-smelling wind. The problem was, you
could never be entirely sure what one of these self-
righteous assholes was liable to do.

"How were these addressed?" I asked after I'd gone
through the lot.

"To N. E. Orlov, Editor of SLEAZE."

"Do you still have any of the envelopes?"

"Just three." She took them out of the folder and handed
them to me.

They were ordinary white number 10's, the kind that
are sold all over in packets of twenty-five. The writing was
the same spidery scrawl that could have come from an old
witch of either sex. They all had L.A. postmarks and, not
surprisingly, none had a return address.

I pushed everything back to her. "Forget about it. Like
you said, there are a lot of cranks around. This is probably
just some old bat in an attic in Pasadena, cackling to herself and getting off on this shit. It's like an obscene phone
call. By reacting at all, you're doing just what this person
wants. I usually don't try to talk myself out of a job, but I
don't think there's anything here to bother about."

"That's what I thought. Until two days ago." She took
one last envelope out of the folder. "This came to my
home."

She handed it across to me. The name on the front was
"Natalie Orlov," at an address that I recognized as one of
the few nice residential neighborhoods left in Hollywood.
The letter inside was the same as the others, though
maybe a bit more menacing. It closed by saying, "We know
where you are. You cannot escape from your FATE."

I looked up at her and nodded. I could see why she was
starting to get upset. It was getting closer, becoming personal.

"You mean someone made the connection between Natalie and N. E. Orlov?" I said.

"That's right. And it's not that easy a connection to
make. I've made sure of that—both for business and personal reasons. As far as I know, I've never been identified

publicly as N. E. And I'm not listed in the phone book at all."

"So you think someone went to some trouble to track you down?"

"Yes."

"And that indicates a degree of seriousness that wasn't necessarily present before?"

She nodded, looking very serious herself.

"That's one possibility," I said.

"One possibility? What else could it be?"

I shrugged. "It could be someone who already knows you."

She looked at me disbelievingly, then slowly shook her head in denial. That was to be expected. This kind of stuff—anonymous letters, nasty phone calls—was so ugly, no one wanted to believe that the source might be an acquaintance. But it often was. This was a cheap, easy way for someone to get even for a grudge, or to exercise power in the only way he could.

"Anyone you consider an enemy?" I asked. "Or that might consider you one?"

She shook her head.

"Anyone you had a fight with lately? Anyone you cheated or screwed?"

"No, no, no." She sighed and looked straight at me. "I don't pretend that this is the nicest business in the world—and there are a hell of a lot of slimy creeps floating around in it—but I try not to be one. And it is a business. I figure in the long run it's not good for business to screw and cheat people. And even if it were, I wouldn't do it."

She stared at me, eyes flashing, as though expecting a challenge, but I just looked back. "Okay." I had the feeling she was as straight as she sounded, but at this point it didn't matter either way. "But what about some of those slimy creeps?"

"I don't deal with them. Period. I don't deal with pimps or boyfriends or so-called managers. I deal only with the girls that we use. I don't use them if I think that they don't really want to do it, that maybe someone's making them. I pay them good money to spread their legs while a camera looks up their crotch, and I pay the money to *them*. If they decide to give the money to someone else afterwards—well,

I think they're stupid, but I can't do anything about it. And they get paid for one thing only. Nobody gropes them. They don't have to suck or fuck anyone, or do *anything* except pose. Now some people may think that these are meaningless distinctions—and ultimately they may be right—but they make a difference to me." She paused, as if she was surprised at having made a speech, then shook her head and gave me an ironic smile. "How about that, Mr. Hunter? A principled pornographer."

How about it? I didn't know. Most people are pretty apparent right from the beginning, but I couldn't quite figure Natalie Orlov. Not that I had to; but the more she talked, the more intrigued I got.

"Okay. Nobody pissed off at you that you know about. What about old boyfriends? . . . or girlfriends?"

Again she shook her head, and her short hair bounced. "And it's boyfriends, if you're interested," she said with a smile.

I looked at her but didn't smile back. I *was* interested. Shit. Did I need this? The hell with it. I'd worry about it later.

"Why don't you go to the cops with this?" I said, for some reason still trying to talk myself out of a job.

"The last time I called the police it was three A.M., and someone about seven feet tall wearing a black cape was scratching around my front door like the Curse of the Vampire. It took them forty-five minutes to get to my place, by which time the guy was gone and I'd gone back to sleep. After waking me up, they told me they couldn't find anyone, and acted as if they were pissed at me for not being a mutilated corpse. No, I figure the cops'll get real interested if I get smote with fire and thunder, but not before. Besides, how concerned do you think they'd be about the editor of SLEAZE?"

"Oh, I don't know. A lot of 'em are probably loyal readers."

"Exactly," she said.

I shook my head. "They'll be real disappointed, you know, missing the opportunity to get their hands on your files with all the addresses and phone numbers of your girls. Not to mention the chance to see what's her name's tattoo."

"Claudia? Is she still doing that? I'll have to talk to her again. Christ! What a bimbo!"

We both considered Claudia's bimbosity for a while, then I asked her just exactly what it was she wanted me to do.

"You're probably right that all the threats are bullshit, but I'd like to know for sure. Even though I don't intend to do this forever"—she gestured at her office—"I sure as hell don't want some crazy to excise me from the Holy City. I have a more graceful exit in mind. Nobody needs this kind of grief, and I don't like feeling nervous all the time. But most of all, I don't like shit like this, someone passing judgments on me, intruding into my life. Mr. Hunter, I want you to try and find out who's doing it."

"And if I manage to?"

She looked at me for a long minute. "I've heard you have a way with assholes," she said finally.

I grinned at her. "I guess I've got a new client."

"I'm glad."

I looked at her wide, full mouth smiling back at me, and felt that pressure return to my lower back. "As long as you pay your bills."

Her eyes widened momentarily, then she opened her mouth and laughed, a sound of genuine amusement. It sounded pretty good.

She got out a current-account checkbook, filled in a check, and handed it across. "Is this enough?"

I looked at it. "To start with." I folded the check and put it in my pocket. Ah—Sam Hunter, Private Eye to SLEAZE. Pretty fucking classy.

I stood up and told Natalie Orlov I'd see what I could do. As I was heading to the door, she called, "Thanks."

I turned. "I haven't done anything yet."

"No. I mean thanks for not making any dumb remarks. A lot of people who come in here make some joke about a 'womb with a view,' something like that."

I tried to keep my face very straight as I looked at her, but I guess I didn't, since she laughed and said, "That's okay. I still think the same thing myself sometimes."

I decided this was a woman I'd have to be very careful with. Much too sharp.

I went out the door, then looked back in. "Just out of curiosity, what would you have said if I'd been the one who called what's her name—Claudia—a bimbo?"

"I'd have given you a lecture, of course. Then thrown you out."

"That's what I thought." I turned to go.

"Oh, Mr. Hunter."

I looked back. "Yeah?"

"A word of advice."

"What's that?"

"If Claudia offers to show you her goldfish, give it a miss." She smiled sweetly.

I went down the hall and into the reception area. As I headed to the outer door, Claudia bounced over to me.

"Want to see my goldfish?" she said.

I smiled and hurried on.

What a bimbo.

TWO

A mutant with slightly greenish skin, a pale pink Mohawk haircut, and black leather overalls covered with metal studs cruised up on two-hundred-buck rollerskates. He handed me a flyer for Helga's House of Perversions—"43 Varieties." I watched as he rolled away, eyes drooping shut, head nodding, wired to one of those miniature recorders, and 'luded as flat as the Gobi Desert. Hooray for Hollywood.

I was sitting at a scarred picnic table in front of a ten-by-ten shack at an intersection not too far from the SLEAZE offices. The place looked like something out of a Third World slum—tattered awning, listing walls, every inch covered with hard-edged Chicano Gothic graffiti, layer upon layer like a densely worked abstract painting. Not exactly an upscale sidewalk café frequented by the Beautiful People, but it did serve some of the most potent Mexican shit around.

I'd just put away a couple of soft tacos piled with carnitas—little bits of roast pork covered with chopped radishes, cilantro, and a killer green sauce hot enough to make my forehead sweat and my eyes blur. Then I had another pair with machacha, a spicy dry stew the texture of shoelaces, doused with a homemade salsa known locally as Red Lightning.

I drained the second can of Tecate and pulled on a cigarette. I considered how I should proceed as I watched a scruffy group troop down the sidewalk single file. There were eight of them, all barefoot and dressed in burlap robes, and each was beating the person in front with a knotted piece of cord. At first I thought they were another promotion for the House of Perversions, then I noticed that

the last one in line carried a sign that identified them as
"The Children of Misery—a tax-deductible religious foun-
dation." Except for the guy in front ringing a bell, who was
a Gabby Hayes look-alike, the Children were just that, no
more than fourteen or fifteen. The expressions on their
pimply faces were beatific as they wailed about how miser-
able they were. At the corner, the blissed-out zombies got
on a bus heading toward West L.A., still single file, still
moaning, still flailing the person in front.

This was the town, all right. Cults, sects, whatever you
wanted to call them, they flourished here like mushrooms
in bullshit, showing the way to the lost, the blind, and the
lame, promising easy answers to people who didn't even
know what the fucking questions were. This was the land
of sunshine and palm trees and golden opportunity waiting to be plucked like a juicy orange; if you couldn't make
it here, you were in deep shit, because there was nowhere
else to go. This was the edge, the last frontier, the end of
the goddamn line. There'd never been any shortage of
dime-store gurus here, or of terminal losers looking for the
magic mantra that would let them put it all together. A
few groups had some staying power, but most sprouted at
night, bloomed under the full moon, and scattered to the
wind when the Ultimate Solution turned out to be just one
more scam in the City of Angles.

Given that most of these flocks of turkeys vanished before they even got noticed, I was trying to figure how I
might get a line on one particular flock. Despite Natalie
Orlov's denials, I still thought there would turn out to be a
connection between her and whoever was threatening her.
But since she couldn't give me a place to start, that only
left the bunch calling itself the Sword of Truth.

In a place where every other waiter or gas jockey was in-
corporated and had fancy embossed calling cards, the fact
that this group had an insignia and stationery didn't necessarily mean anything. On the other hand, they might be
organized enough for someone to have picked up on them.
Hell, for all I knew, they had a press agent and turned up
on afternoon talk shows.

I got some change from the woman running the taco
stand and went over to the office building across the street,
where I spent the next hour in a lobby phonebooth. I called

everyone I could think of who might know something, or who might know someone who'd know something. It wasn't a big success. A reporter I knew named Harold Ace had never heard of them, but said he'd run a computer check on his paper's stories. A guy in the D.A.'s office had the idea that he might once have seen the name, but didn't have a clue where; reluctantly—too reluctantly, I thought, considering he owed me a bunch of favors—he also agreed to run a search of the files. A psychologist who specialized in deprogramming middle-class cult kids said the name rang distant bells, but he had the feeling they hadn't been around for a long time. And that was about it. As I'd half expected, the Sword of Truth was somewhere in the mists of never-never land, and nobody knew anything.

Finally, though, as I was just about through a roll of dimes, I got a little luckier with a guy named Eberhardt. He'd been a presidential speechwriter, then switched to become the religion editor for one of those scummy tabloids that supermarkets peddle. He'd once said it was a good career move; he didn't have to lie so much, and he had more time to drink.

"I think I may have something for you," Eberhardt said. "From a couple years back when I ran a series on the local scene. Maybe you saw it. 'L.A.'s Leading Lunatics Tell Us How It Is.' Or maybe 'Ten Hot New Cults in Tinseltown.' "

"Sorry. I must've missed it."

"Too bad. It was good stuff. I was the one who broke the story about the Neo-Aztecs, just before one of their ritual sacrifices got out of hand and landed them all in the joint. And I did a good piece on the Anaconda Brotherhood. I think they broke up after their leader became their god's dinner."

"I'm surprised you didn't get a Pulitzer. What about the Sword of Truth?"

"Give me a minute. I have to check the files."

He put me on hold. Instead of the usual musical interlude, there was a tape of the publisher saying he paid top dollar for photos of extraterrestrials and for accounts of sexual encounters with aliens from outer space. I'd have to keep it in mind.

Eberhardt's return cut off the publisher's promo for the

miracle diet that would be featured in the next issue.
Something to do with bat guano and the Shroud of Turin.

"Not much, I'm afraid," he said. "When I was working
on the series, I put out feelers soliciting statements of prin-
ciple from all those practicing what we call alternate theology. You wouldn't believe some of the things we got
back—four-color glossies that looked like the annual report of General Motors. Not so the Sword of Truth. There
was just a piece of paper with their name across the top."

"The T made out of an upside-down sword?"

"That's the one. Dripping blood."

"What was their message?"

"Very short, badly typed, and barely literate. It's your
basic us-and-them: everyone but us is screwed, and we've
got all the answers. I quote: 'We are a Tribe wandering in
the wilderness. Our great leader Joshua will take us to the
Promised Land. We have the Truth. The Truth is a Sword.
We must destroy everybody who's fucked up so we can
make a better world.' "

"That's what it said?"

"Yeah. The Gospel According to Joshua."

"And that's it?"

"That was it, and I think it was tough for them to put
that much down."

"Did you follow it up?"

"Actually, I did, a little. It was so dumb I was kind of curious. Also, I thought maybe I'd lucked onto a band of genuine crazies roaming the countryside. That can make
awfully good copy. You know—'Joshua, the Last Prophet,'
'Is This Man the Messiah?' Stuff like that."

"That's swell, Eberhardt. What'd you find out?"

"Not very much, in fact, because I never managed to
catch up with them. But it just sounded like the usual
thing: dumb kids with no place else to go and social misfits
looking for a context for their anger."

"Were they dangerous? Violent?"

"I don't know, but they could've been. One of my notes
says that Joshua's role model was Charlie Manson."

Swell. Joshua's hero was Manson, and Manson's hero
was Hitler. Maybe Natalie Orlov really did have something to worry about.

"Go on," I said.

"That's about it. I remember wondering what I should do. I mean, we could get an awful lot of mileage out of a new Charlie Manson, front-page stuff for a long time. It was tempting. But on the other hand, did I really want to get involved with somebody like that? The guy in the White House was bad enough. . . . Anyway, journalism won out—not to mention the bonus I'd get—and I decided to go after the story. Only there was no more story."

"What do you mean?"

"The Sword of Truth was gone. I couldn't get a line on them. I couldn't even get a line on what had happened."

That checked with what the psychologist had told me. Lot of good it did me.

"When was this?"

"About three years ago, I guess," Eberhardt said.

"What do you think happened?"

"Probably nothing. At any one time there must be a couple hundred groups like that wandering around. They come and go."

"Yeah. Only this one seems to have come back."

"Huh?"

"A client of mine has been getting letters from the Sword of Truth. Not exactly fan mail."

"Really?"

"What do you think's going on? Any guesses?"

Eberhardt paused. "Not many. When one of these groups folds up, that's usually it. Whatever dynamic there was, is broken. I suppose they could have gone underground and then resurfaced, but that would be pretty uncommon. Or maybe Joshua was out of circulation a while—jail or something—and started up again when he got back. From the little I heard, it sounded like he was a pretty powerful personality. I couldn't tell if he was a hustler, or a total psycho, or a combination; but he sure knew how to exert a strong influence on people. Strong enough, at least, to get thirty or so followers at one time. Guys like that have a way of turning up again."

"Well, something's turned up. Anything more?"

"I don't think so. But if you come up with anything, Sam, let me know. We pay pretty good dough for tips we can use."

"Even if it doesn't involve flying saucers?"

He laughed. "Well, we can work it in."

"Maybe that's what it is."

"What?"

"That's where Joshua's been for three years—circling Venus."

"What a terrific concept!"

"You like it, Eberhardt? It's all yours."

"What do you think? 'Cult Leader Returns After Alien Sojourn.' I think it could work."

I hung up.

I had to start working.

THREE

There was a message from the D.A.'s office with my answering service, suggesting I try to get hold of a girl named Chrysanthemum who worked for an outfit called Heaven on Wheels. She'd been picked up in an investigation the guy there had run a while back. It was about something else, but in the interrogation, she told them she had once belonged to the Sword of Truth. That was why he'd recognized the name.

For a couple of quarters I got one of the sex tabloids that are sold on nearly every street corner. On the cover, a pair of bovine honeys smiled inanely as they showed off some not especially newsworthy tits. Boldfaced type covered their lower halves, announcing that issue's feature story—"Twelve Things You Never Thought Of To Do With Vibrators." I bet Eberhardt wished he'd come up with that one.

I found the ad for Heaven on Wheels, which billed itself as L.A.'s first radio-dispatched modeling service. Their slogan was "We'll come to you, then you'll come with us." Pretty snappy.

I called and asked for Chrysanthemum, not really expecting she'd still be with them, but I got lucky again. A woman with a husky bedroom voice gave me a corner on Sunset where Chrysanthemum would pick me up in half an hour.

I didn't have far to go, so I went back across the street, got another beer, and sat in the sun. It was one of those rare days you sometimes get in the early spring in L.A. when the air is actually clear—the kind of day when you can for once see the mountains that ring the city, and when little kids get scared because they hadn't known that the sky is supposed to be blue. It was the kind of day that made you wonder why you weren't living someplace else.

I got over to Sunset a little ahead of time and propped myself against a lamppost. It was still early enough in the afternoon that there wasn't much traffic—or anything else. Just a few palm trees lining the wide street, some low-rise office buildings, and a small shopping center that provided everything necessary to sustain life: a Thai grocery, a sushi bar, a video arcade, a massage parlor, and an adult bookstore. There was a dingy hooker bar on the side street, and across from me was a run-down motel that rented rooms by the hour and changed the sheets every week whether they needed it or not.

This used to be the heart of working Hollywood, with all the big studios close by, but that was long before my time. Now most of the business was curb service, conducted by girls wearing tight shorts and small price tags.

A thin girl in a black spaghetti-strap prom dress walked slowly by, looking at me, hoping to see some sign of interest. She teetered slightly on her spiked heels and had a couple of small pimples between her bare, bony shoulders. She was maybe fifteen, though rapidly growing older.

A bleached blonde wearing too much makeup approached me. She was packed into a red spandex bodysuit that, if it had been any tighter, would have been under her skin.

"Are you waiting for me, honey?"

"Are you Chrysanthemum?"

She rolled her eyes and made a face. "Honey, I'll be a whole fucking garden if that's what you want. A whole goddamn arboretum." She put her hands under her breasts, pushing them up and out against the already straining fabric, and stepped close to me. "Baby, get a load of these blossoms. We're talking American Beauties, pal, not some pitiful little buds." She moved even closer, pushing her breasts and belly against me. "Come on, honey. What do you say? How about dropping your pollen on me?"

Swell. Just what I needed. The Queen of Latex cracking botanical jokes.

She was starting to run her hand up my leg toward my stamen when a van turned onto the side street and pulled up with a squeal. It was black, with a voluptuous nude airbrushed on the side. A girl with a halo of curly light brown hair was driving. She rolled down her window and called over.

"I'm Chrysanthemum. You John?"

I said I was, and she told me to get in the back. As I pulled the door shut, I heard Red Rose say to the girl driving, "You better watch yourself, honey. I think he's weird."

I sat on a thick cushion and leaned against the rear door. A heavy striped curtain separated the driver from the back of the van. There was a piece of orange synthetic carpet on the floor, a mattress with a purple bedspread, a Formica bedside table, and a picture of a nude, all tits and ass, painted on black velvet. It reminded me of a furnished apartment I'd once lived in.

We drove for a few minutes, making a couple of turns, before we stopped and the motor was turned off. The girl pulled the curtain open, climbed through, and sat cross-legged on the bed.

She was about twenty, I thought, but she could—and probably did—pass for much younger. She had one of those round, open faces usually associated with innocence, smooth, lightly tanned skin, and a spray of freckles across a button nose. Her dark lipstick was smeared a little at the corners of her pouty mouth, like she hadn't had much practice putting it on, but from the shrewd look in her clear blue eyes, I figured it had been no accident. Her body was sleek and slender. With her plaid cotton shirt tied in a knot beneath small breasts, and frayed cutoff jeans with the side seams split almost to the waistband, Chrysanthemum looked like an adolescent farm girl ready for a roll in the hay.

"Where are we?" I asked.

"Parking lot. It's cheaper than a room. . . . Which means you have more money to spend on me," she added, and gave me a smile that might have been genuine. "The fat bitch said you're weird. Are you?"

I shook my head.

"Good. I'm getting tired of weirdness. Well, what's it to be?"

I took out two twenties and handed them to her. She tucked them in the pocket of her shorts. She pulled at the knot in her shirt, and it fell open, revealing small but

shapely breasts with soft pink nipples that were starting
to pucker.

She nodded toward my pants. "Well? The meter's running. Get 'em off."

"Actually, what I'd really like is some conversation."

"Oh, shit!" She sounded fed up, and looked half disappointed. "Conversation's extra," she said, retying her
shirt.

I handed her another twenty, but it didn't seem to please
her.

"Christ! Whatever happened to sex? You're right,
sport—you're not weird. You're right in the mainstream.
Shit! Between the guys who want to talk, and the ones who
want to be spanked, and the ones who want to play a little
dress-up, and the ones who want to be pissed on, it doesn't
seem like anybody wants to ball anymore. Hell, if I wanted
to be a therapist, I'd go work for a clinic." She stopped and
shook her head. "Sorry, sweetie. It's not your fault. I just
figured a big guy like you would be into fucking, but whatever you need . . . What's it to be? Is this an ego boost or a
humiliation? Or do you have a script?"

"What I'd like is some information about the Sword of
Truth."

Her eyes grew round with an expression I couldn't quite
read. Surprise, combined with anger, maybe a touch of fear.

"Who are you? The Ghost of Christmas Past?"

I showed her my I.D., which she examined closely, then
she looked at a few other cards in my wallet to make sure
the name matched. I'd had the feeling she had something
on the ball, and her caution confirmed it.

She handed the wallet back and said, "I haven't thought
about them for a long time, and if I never do again, it'll be
too soon."

I took another twenty out and handed it across. She
looked at it for a minute, then shrugged and took it.

"I take it that you did belong?"

She gave me a disgusted look, then turned a hip to me
and pulled back the split shorts, revealing a big piece of a
nice rear end. High up, there was a tattoo of a sword, the
bloody tip pointing down.

"Branded like the rest of the herd," she said, sitting

back down. "But the Sword's real old news, man. Long gone."

"So I've heard. What makes you so sure?"

"I made it my business to be sure." She paused, then explained. "I ran out on them. Joshua didn't like it when his girls did that. I guess he thought it cut his authority. Or maybe he was afraid it would give the other girls ideas. Let's just say it was discouraged. A couple tried it before me, but he found them and brought them back. It wasn't nice." She hunched her shoulders as a shiver went through her body. "No way did I want that to happen to me. So after I made my break, I spent about a year looking over my shoulder. Scared, man, real shit-scared. I didn't know if the next corner I'd turn, I'd run into one of his goons—Soldiers of Truth, he called them—and that would be it."

"But you didn't?"

"No. Instead, I ran into one of the other girls. I asked her how she got away. She said she didn't. One day, Joshua and a few others just weren't there anymore, and that was that. No more Joshua. No more Sword of Truth."

"When was this?"

She thought a minute, counting off on her fingers. "Maybe three years ago."

"Is this girl still around?"

"No. Back east somewhere, I think. But what's your interest in this?"

I looked at her, but didn't say anything.

She smiled and nodded. "Gotcha. You're not paying me to ask the questions. Okay. What do you want to know?"

"Whatever you can tell me. Who was in the Sword. What they did. Where they operated. What their line was. It was some kind of religious thing, right?"

Chrysanthemum barked out a laugh.

"What's so funny?"

"Man! The Sword was religious like the mob's a social club." She shook her head. "Shit! Where do you think I got my job training?"

I looked at her. This was starting to turn strange. First everyone says the Sword of Truth has packed it in, now the little mobile hooker tells me it was where she learned her trade.

My reaction must have showed, because she said, "You

really don't know anything about them, do you?. . . Okay,
let's get this over with. They had a year of my life, and another year when I was scared. As far as I'm concerned,
that's more than enough time, so I'm going to go through
this fast. Who was in it? It was mostly girls like I was—
young, scared runaways, scuffling to survive, and not
doing a very good job of it. So fucked up and desperate that
they'll believe any cheap line that looks like it offers them
something—anything—else. And when they bite, they find
out just how bad things can get. Half the girls on the
Boulevard'll have the same story. Shit! It's been a movie
on TV a dozen times."

"You're saying Joshua was a pimp?"

"Got it in one, man. Oh, he didn't look like those spiffy
dudes with custom cars. And his patter was different. And
maybe he didn't even think of himself that way. But the
bottom line was the same."

"What was the pitch?"

Chrysanthemum looked at me and shook her head. "At
this point, it's hard for me to say. I can remember thinking
it sounded pretty good. Like most pimps, he could talk a
good line. And besides, we were so wasted most of the time,
and so hungry to belong to something, that we would've
believed almost anything. . . . He *was* a kind of preacher, I
guess. He wore these robes—you know, like in one of those
biblical movies—and he had a big beard and long hair.
He'd go on and on, talking to us, hour after hour. It was
like he was hypnotizing us, and it got so the easiest thing
was just to flow with it."

"What'd he talk about?"

"Nothing very original, I now realize, not that it made any
difference. He went on about how we were a lost tribe, and he
was going to lead us to the Promised Land. He knew the way
because he had the truth. And we would destroy all our ene-
mies, get even with everyone who put us down, and be the
rulers of a new world. And all we had to do was obey him.
Real plausible, huh? But we were lost, all right, and we'd
sure had a lot of people put us down, so I guess it sounded
pretty good. I hope I'm never that stupid again."

I shrugged. "You aren't the first to get suckered. But
this Joshua just sounds like another bargain basement
messiah. What's the rest of it?"

Chrysanthemum laughed. "Suckered is the word, man. For all that shit about truth being a sword and so on, when it came down to it, there was only one sword that mattered." She gestured. "The one between your legs. Joshua said—now get this—that the closest a guy ever gets to heaven is a good blowjob. And that women were created to lead men to heaven. And that the way we were going to get guys to believe in us and follow us is to show 'em a glimpse of heaven. Can you believe it? Sweet fucking Jesus!"

I could believe it. Very easily. Like I told her, she wasn't the first. "So . . ."

"So, we went around in this old school bus, and we'd stop at every raunchy bar in Southern California. And everybody in the bar would come out, and we'd give 'em all a glimpse of heaven, and Joshua would collect five or ten bucks a pop. 'Sucking for God,' he called it. Selling it cheap, I call it. Sometimes we had fifty guys lined up. Fifteen girls, no waiting. Suckers for God. The Sword of Truth Special. Shit! And when we weren't doing that, we did whatever Joshua and his boys told us to. Promised Land, my ass!"

"Why'd you put up with it?"

"Told you—no choice. There were these guys, six or eight, Joshua's soldiers. Together I don't think they were bright enough to light a match, but they were big, and they sure as hell were mean. Joshua told you to do something, you might refuse one time." Chrysanthemum shook her head. "But that was all. You learned better than to do it again."

"But you got out?"

"It wasn't a big deal, man. I just decided that I'd get out or I'd get dead, and it didn't much matter which. Either one would be an improvement. It was probably the first smart thing I ever did, and it worked. I'm doing okay now. I keep most of the money I earn. I'm saving some. I'm going to school. One of these days, I may even get my shit together."

I looked at her. Her eyes were clear and her jaw was set, and I thought that maybe she would. On the other hand, I didn't know what the hell I was going to do with all the shit I was collecting. There didn't seem to be much connec-

tion between what Eberhardt and Chrysanthemum had
told me and Natalie Orlov's letters.

"Tell me about Joshua," I said. "Did he believe what he
preached, or what?"

The girl thought a while. "I don't know. With whatever
smarts I've picked up since then, I'd say he didn't. It was
just a power trip, and it could have been anything. The
only thing he believed in was looking out for himself, and
the thing he really got off on wasn't the sex, it was the
control—having people scared of him. And believe me, he
was scary. I've seen my share of creepos, but I've never run
into anybody like that. He talked in this low voice, and he
had the weirdest eyes I've ever seen. They were kind of yellow, and crossed, so it always seemed like he was looking
through you, like you weren't there. Real cold. Snake's
eyes. Like he'd just as soon kill you as spit. Sometimes in
nightmares I still see those eyes. . . . I think maybe I'll
have one tonight."

I took out another twenty and handed it to her.

"That wasn't what I meant."

"I know," I said. "Take it. It's expenses."

She shrugged and took the bill.

"Besides what you told me, what else did the Sword do?
Did you send threatening letters to people, anything like
that?"

She looked puzzled, and laughed. "Hell, I don't think
anybody could write. Or those that could were too wasted.
Why?"

I waved it off. "What did the girl tell you about when
Joshua disappeared?"

"I told you. One day Joshua, and a couple of his goons,
and Alice—that was the girl who was his private property—just weren't there. That's it."

That's it? Shit. It sure didn't leave me much to go on. A
crazy, and a three-year-old dead trail. Swell.

I grabbed at a straw. "Would anyone but Joshua use the
name Sword of Truth?"

"No one. No way." Chrysanthemum looked hard at me.
"What's up? What's this all about? They're back, aren't
they?"

"Well, somebody using paper with 'Sword of Truth' on it

is sending threatening letters. The line's different, but the feeling's the same."

"Oh, shit."

"I'm going to make whoever it is stop," I said, "but I have to find 'em first. That's the point of these questions. Now, do you have another name for this Joshua? Do you know anything about what he did before the Sword?"

"No, no names. Only Joshua, though I doubt that was his real name. He probably changed names so often he couldn't keep track himself. And I don't know what he did before, but I guarantee it wasn't anything straight. I have the idea he pimped Alice, or Alana, as I guess she's called now. I think she was with him before the Sword. I don't know how she got caught, but he treated her worst of all. It was too bad, she was a nice kid. So I'm glad to see that she got away and is doing okay for herself . . . . Meanwhile," the girl laughed, "I'm a nice kid, and I'm still turning tricks in a fuckmobile. It's just not fair."

"Maybe you didn't suck hard enough?"

She laughed again. "Tell me about it," she said.

I was going to ask her about the other girl when she got up on her knees and once again untied her shirt.

"What're you doing?"

She moved across to me. "Joshua's evil, man, a complete snake. My one real regret is that I didn't cut his head off before I left." She moved closer, to the end of the mattress, about two feet from me. "If you ever see him, I want you to do something bad to him. Do it for me, for Alice, for all of us. Hurt the son of a bitch." Her eyes were bright and hard, and her hands had formed tight fists. "You guys usually get a retainer up front, don't you?"

"Yeah, just like you guys."

"Then that's what this is." She opened the top button of her shorts and gave me a big wink. "Incentive."

The zipper going down seemed very loud inside the small space of the van.

"Maybe I won't find him."

She moved the final two feet. Her hand touched my cheek, my shoulder, my bicep. "I don't know—I have the feeling you're lucky." She took my hand and looked at it. "And I've got the idea you'll know what to do."

"I've had some experience with snakes," I said.

"Mmm."

She took my hand and put it up to her breast. It was small but firm, and nicely filled my cupped hand. She smelled clean and warm.

She raised herself and straddled my legs. She brushed my face with the tip of a swelling nipple—eyebrows, cheekbone, lips—as her fingers opened my shirt, belt, zipper.

She moved forward, pushing her breast into my mouth, holding my head tight as my tongue tasted her scent and my teeth felt the firmness of her flesh, the resilient tautness of her nipple.

Her breathing quickened. She moved back, then ducked her head and nipped at my neck, my shoulders, my chest, moving lower, moving slowly.

An image of Natalie Orlov, standing hand on hip, wide mouth smiling, popped into my mind.

Christ! The hell with that shit!

I put my hands under Chrysanthemum's round ass, picking her up as I moved forward, then laid her on the mattress. One quick movement and I pulled her shorts from her smooth tan legs. One more movement and I was inside her, hard.

Her eyes opened wide, surprised. "Oh, we're angry about something," she said. "Good."

She repeated the word again and again as I pounded into her, harder, faster, wet skin slapping against wet skin, until the word became a growl deep in her throat. Her hips rose up to meet me and her teeth closed on my shoulder and her body shook, two, three, four times, then relaxed with a sigh as I finished off.

I probably didn't have any more questions to ask her anyway.

FOUR

After I staggered out of the van into the afternoon sunlight, I called the answering service for messages.

There was the usual collection—somebody selling magazine subscriptions, a guy who ran an appliance store out of the back of a moving van offering me a great deal on a gross of video recorders, a janitorial service telling me they had a special this week on steam cleaning. It was tough to decide which I needed most. Steam cleaning probably, unless that was what Chrysanthemum had just done.

Harold Ace had called to tell me he'd only managed to find one article. It wasn't much, he said, but it was being held for me at the reception desk and I could pick it up anytime.

There was also a message from someone called either Philip Prince or Prince Philip—the operator had gotten confused and wasn't sure which—asking me to meet him at the Kava Klub at five o'clock. He said he had a night's work for me that would pay well.

Since I kind of doubted that I'd get hired by both SLEAZE and the Royal Family on the same day, I made a wild guess that the name was Philip Prince. That sounded vaguely familiar, but I couldn't place it. After half a minute's consideration, I figured I might as well see what he had for me.

I had some time before five, so I decided to go downtown and pick up the article Harold Ace had pulled for me. I walked to my car, a beat-up old Checker that I'd gotten in barter for some work I did for the owner of a hack company. Even though he'd thrown in a dark blue paint job, the car still looked like what it was—an old taxi with a quarter million miles on it. But it ran okay, and it took abuse, so who cared.

When I got to the newspaper building, there was an envelope with my name on it waiting for me. Inside there was a single sheet of paper, a photocopy of a four-inch-long story that had appeared a little over three years before. "Joshua Loses Battle of Jericho," the snappy headline ran.

There were no trumpets yesterday, but Jericho Canyon, located near the Ventura County Line, avenged its historical namesake when a self-styled prophet calling himself Joshua was evicted from a ranch in which he had taken up unlawful residence.

Answering a complaint, County Sheriff's officers removed Joshua and his band of followers known as the Sword of Truth. They were charged with trespassing, vagrancy, and possession of firearms, and then released.

Upon leaving the station, Joshua, bearded and wearing a robe and sandals, said the officers were all Philistines and swore that he would pull their temple down.

He must have gotten his stories confused. However, astronomers have been notified to be on the alert in case the sun and moon stop in the heavens.

Real funny, no doubt the work of a bored comedian on the late-night rewrite desk. Had the canyon had a different name, the item would never have gotten in.

For all the good it did, it might just as well not have. If I didn't come up with anything else, I supposed I would follow it up, but it was the kind of thing that almost never got you anywhere. I went out to the car and headed back to Hollywood.

I got to the Kava Klub a few minutes early. It had been a while since I'd been there, but nothing had changed. It was one of those places that the guidebooks referred to as a "Hollywood institution," meaning that it had seen better days. The decor was phony Polynesian, forty-something years old and showing it. The walls were covered with framed caricatures of celebrities, most of whom were unknown and unrecognizable. I didn't like the joint, but at least it didn't smell as bad as some of the places clients had asked me to meet them.

On one side of the dimly lit room, there were a lot of bald old guys, big-bellied, smoking fat cigars, wearing heavy

pinkie rings, plaid jackets, and white shoes. On the other
side were the younger guys, lean, dark, hungry, in sunglasses, shirts open to their waists, little gold coke spoons
on chains around their necks. Each side eyed the other,
greedily, jealously, each wanting what they thought the
other had.

I looked at one side, then the other, then sat in the middle. Two tables away there was a pair of yokels whispering
excitedly, trying to figure out which famous people were
there.

I was halfway through a beer when a guy in a nicely cut
gray suit entered, looked around, then came over to me. He
was middle-aged, medium height, and well maintained.
He had sleek, silvery hair brushed back, large, very white
teeth that looked capped, and one of those Hollywood tans
that are just a little too dark and even. I knew I hadn't met
him, but I had the idea I'd seen him someplace before.

"Are you Mr. Hunter?" he asked. His voice was as
smooth as the rest of him.

I said I was, and he sat down and handed me a card. It
identified him as Philip Prince, Attorney-at-Law, with an
office at an address in West Hollywood. It fit. The name
was familiar because I must have come across it before,
and I'd probably seen the man himself at a courthouse or a
cop station.

I waited and watched while he ordered the currently
fashionable aperitif, something that looked like carbona-
ted cat piss with a couple of peeled grapes dropped in it.

Philip Prince was slick all right, with about as much appeal as an oil spill. Maybe it was just that I disliked guys
who spent more on manicures than I did on shirts. Or
maybe there was something about lawyers that made me
want to make sure I still had my wallet.

After tasting his drink and looking around, he finally
got down to what he wanted. "I have a small errand that
I'd like you to handle. Nothing very difficult, but it must
be done tonight. I'll pay you, say, two hundred dollars now,
and a similar amount upon completion. That seems gener-
ous for a night's work, don't you think?" I must have
looked like I didn't, because he added, "Plus, of course, rea-
sonable expenses," and showed me a lot of his teeth.

"What sort of an errand?"

"You'll pick up a small package and deliver it to me."

"Where do I have to go?"

"I'll give you the address. It's in Tijuana."

Shit!

"Come on, Prince! Just what's in this 'small package'?"

He looked puzzled for a second, then surprised, then shook his head. "Oh, it's nothing like that, I can assure you. There's nothing illegal here. It's more—shall we say—of an embarrassing nature."

"Blackmail?"

"Yes."

"Pictures?"

Prince shook his head. "Letters, actually . . . and some other papers."

"You know that if I go down there, I'm going to make sure that that's all I'm carrying back across the border."

"Of course. In fact, you'll have to examine them to make certain that it's the correct material."

"How will I know it's the right stuff?"

"Once you're there, you'll call me. You'll describe the material to me, and I'll know if it's genuine or not."

"Why don't you just go down yourself?"

Prince shook his head. "Because I'll be handling the payment up here. When I know that you've seen the correct material, I'll release the money. Shortly thereafter, the person with the money will call to say that he's not been followed, and you'll get the material. That's all. What do you say, Mr. Hunter? Are we agreed?" He gave me another look at his expensive teeth.

I lit up a cigarette. It was a nice arrangement for the blackmailers. Being on opposite sides of the border made an already secure setup nearly airtight. The deal looked a hell of a lot less sweet at the other end.

"Look, if the stuff is going to be down there, why don't I just take it and forget all this other bullshit?"

Prince shook his head again. "Those are not my client's wishes."

"Then your client's a jerk and so are you. These people will be back in two months and you'll have to go through the whole number again."

"I don't believe that will be necessary if you do your job. Will you, Mr. Hunter?"

Prince looked like he was going a little rancid around
the edges. Beads of sweat dotted his hairline, and an anxious expression appeared in his eyes. He obviously wanted
me to go, but if everything was as nice and simple as he
tried to make out, he didn't need me. A messenger service
could do as good a job. No, I figured Prince for the kind of
guy who wouldn't tell you the time without trying to work
an edge for himself out of it. So I acted accordingly.

"Seven fifty now," I said, "and seven fifty when I deliver." I didn't know what Prince's angle was, but that was
probably enough to smooth it out. He went sort of green,
and I grinned at him. "But I'll pick up my own expenses."

"That's too much."

"That's too bad." I stood up. "See you around."

"Wait!"

I looked down at him. He was sweating more heavily.

"Five hundred now," he said, "and a thousand on delivery."

"No good."

"That's all I've got on me."

"Show it."

He pulled eight new fifties out of a slender billfold and
some wrinkled tens and twenties out of his jacket pocket. I
looked at the dough, then scooped it up and sat down.
"You've got an errand boy." I grinned again.

Prince had gone pale. Shit. You'd think he'd opened a
vein instead of just his client's wallet. He gulped down the
rest of his drink and mopped his forehead. A few more minutes and his color had returned and he was again more or
less composed.

He gave me the address I was to go to, and the phone
number of the restaurant where he would hand over the
money. At least he had enough sense to do it in a public
place, and not some isolated dirt road.

I tried to get some info about his client and the nature of
the material, but Prince was evasive. That was okay. It
was none of my business. We discussed the arrangements
again, then I pushed my chair back to stand up.

"Oh, by the way, Mr. Hunter," Prince said, like something had just occurred to him. "You will be taking a gun
with you, won't you? I mean, I'm sure it won't be necessary, but just to . . . you know . . . a precaution . . ."

He looked off to my right and fluttered his manicured hands to indicate the inconsequentiality of it all. Christ! What an asshole! I'd been waiting for this shoe to drop. A small errand, nothing difficult. Right. I thought about asking him just what precautions he had in mind, but decided I didn't really care about his answer.

Instead I stood up, leaned over, and gave him another grin. He cringed, then went pale and started sweating again.

Golly! My smile seemed to have lost its insouciant charm. I'd have to work on it.

I was halfway to the door when Prince caught up with me.

"Mr. Hunter, this is rather embarrassing, but you've got all my money. Do you think you could . . ." He motioned toward the bar.

"Sorry, Prince. The first rule they teach us in private-eye school is that the client always buys the drinks. Talk to you tonight."

I left him standing in the middle of the Kava Klub, counting his change and laughing nervously to no one in particular.

On the way out, I looked into the mirror in the foyer and smiled.

Nope. Looked okay to me.

FIVE

It wasn't like I was sleepwalking into this thing. Anytime someone says, "Oh, by the way, bring a gun," I tend to perk up my ears. But since I'd assumed that Prince wasn't being entirely straight with me about what I might run into, and since I'd never go into a deal like this anyway without carrying some metal, I wasn't too concerned. I had to figure I could take care of myself. Besides, I didn't tend to get a lot of calls to do, say, a review of corporate security procedures at IBM, so if I started to get too squeamish, I'd start to be out of business.

The way I saw it, I'd gotten five bills to go down and take a look. If it was more or less what Prince had indicated, he'd get his job done. If not . . . Well, I'd be pretty fucking stupid to give more of a shit about the welfare of Prince and whatever sleazeball he represented than they gave about mine.

And some people said I didn't have any principles. Screw 'em.

The meeting wasn't set until midnight, so I had plenty of time to drive down. I went through all those little towns that are strung along the lower part of California, all picture-postcard pretty, tucked into the hills overlooking the sea, dripping with bougainvillea and smelling of money. They had Spanish names, six-figure average incomes, and politics that were somewhere to the right of Attila the Hun.

About halfway to the border I pulled into an open-air, tin-roofed place on the edge of a cliff above a rock beach. The small hand-painted sign, lit by a forty-watt bulb, said "Gus's Chili."

Gus looked like one of those guys who rode the rails in

41

the thirties. He was tall and scrawny and wore faded overalls over an old striped T-shirt. He had a long narrow head,
eyes like a pair of black pebbles, and a dead, hand-rolled
cigarette permanently stuck to his lower lip. The story was
that Gus had done twenty hard ones in West Texas for
feeding his wife to the hogs. His defense had been that
she'd kept after him and after him to feed the damn hogs,
so he did.

The menu at Gus's was the same as the sign, and the
only choice was whether to have a cup, bowl, bucket, or
barrel of the stuff. I thought I should be prepared to move
quickly if necessary, so I settled for a bucket.

I watched as Gus ladled it up from a cast-iron pot the size
of a garbage can. The same batch of chili had been simmering on the stove for at least fifteen years. Gus said it
took at least ten years for a chili to develop character. His
had that, all right. It smelled of cumin and tasted like mol-
ten lava. Gus used a lot of different kinds of chiles in his
brew—ancho, pasilla, mulato, chipotle, pequín, chile de
arbol, and a few others—but the real killers were the fresh
habaneros that he had flown in every week from the
Yucatán. Those were strong enough to blister paint.

Gus served his chili under an inch-thick layer of bubbling mozzarella, along with sourdough garlic bread and a
salsa cruda of chopped onions, tomatoes, and pickled ser-
rano chiles. It took two mouthfuls before my toes started to
tingle, and another two before my throat went numb.
Damn! It was good shit.

After I finished, I had a third icy San Miguel beer and a
couple of cigarettes as I listened to the waves crash on the
rocks below. Eventually, feeling started to return to various parts of my body, and I reluctantly moved on.

It was about eleven when I finally rolled over the bridge
into Baja California. As I'd expected, I needn't have bothered hiding my gun in the trunk. There was very little
traffic going in my direction, and the uniformed Mexicans
waved me through. The only thing they were concerned
about people bringing into their country was sufficient dollars.

Tijuana used to be your typical border town—small,
sleazy, and selling vice to gringos. Now it was bigger.

The address I was looking for was on Calle Esperanza. I

didn't know where that was, so I followed my ears to where
the action was. Mariachi music and rock 'n' roll blasted
out of the bars and junky souvenir shops. Marquees and
flashing lights and flickering neon colored the air, turning
everything red and gold and acid green. Garbage filled the
gutters, and predators of various sorts prowled the sidewalks or waited in doorways. The air was heavy with the
smells of charcoal smoke and decay, piss and the cheap
perfume of hookers. It was Hollywood Boulevard and
Times Square stripped down to the hungry essence, a
world of buyers and sellers and nothing else.

High school boys from Pomona strolled the avenue trying to look cool, and sailors from the naval base in San
Diego tried to look sober. They were all there for the same
thing—to cut loose, to get drunk, to get laid. And, if they
didn't watch themselves, maybe get sick and rolled and
need a lot of penicillin in the bargain. Sometimes it was
tough to tell just who was taking advantage of whom.

I found a place to park, got out, stood next to the car, and
waited. It didn't take long. A kid about ten years old came
over. He had shaggy black hair, a round Indian face, and
dark shiny eyes. He introduced himself as Hector, and offered to take me to his sister, who, he assured me, was a
virgin. Before I had a chance to explain that his line was a
bit dated, he hurried on. Sounding like someone selling
kitchen appliances door-to-door, he proposed his brothers,
his mother, twin cousins, and other members of his ex-
tended family, all of whom were pure, untouched, and in-
tact.

"Even your mother?" I asked.

"Yes, señor. Especially my mother. I swear—" Then he
looked at me, grinned, and started to giggle. For the first
time he looked his age. He was a cute kid.

I asked him if he knew Calle Esperanza. He thought for
a minute, then said he did. When I agreed without argu-
ment to the exorbitant fee he quoted to direct me there,
Hector looked surprised.

It took about ten minutes to locate the street. As we pro-
ceeded, each block grew darker, quieter, shabbier. Hector
said there wasn't anything to interest me in this place. I
had a feeling he was right.

After we found Esperanza, I took Hector back to his

hunting ground, then returned alone. There was only the
occasional dim streetlight, but the neighborhood looked to
be mostly warehouses or small factories. A few were
burned out, a few more had boarded-up windows. The
pavement was mostly potholes under a lace of asphalt.
Maybe it looked better during the day, but at midnight
Calle Esperanza didn't seem to have a whole lot to be hopeful about.

I parked a couple of blocks away from where I guessed
the address would be. I got a flashlight out of the glove
compartment and took my gun from the trunk. I hooked
the holster to my belt in the small of my back, where it
would be easy to get at but still be covered by my jacket.

There was no one else around. Besides my own footsteps,
the only sounds were some dogs fighting a few streets over.

The building I wanted was a one-story rectangle taking
up about half of the small block. The crumbling plaster
walls were covered with torn posters advertising old bull-
fights and wrestling matches. There were a couple of small
windows at the front, but no light showed through them. It
was not what you'd call real promising.

I went down the side street, and again no lights. Finally,
down a small alleyway at the rear, a light was showing at
the far corner of the building. I went down to take a look,
but the inside of the window had been covered with brown
wrapping paper. I listened, but heard nothing.

I went back to the front and stood outside the door. I
can't say I was thrilled with the way things looked. I considered going back to the car, then shrugged and tried the
door. It opened, and I stepped inside.

It was completely dark, with no sign of the light I had
seen outside. It smelled damp and musty. The only sound
was the plink of a dripping water tap.

I took two steps forward and turned on the flashlight.
Before I had the chance to see more than the dirty concrete
floor in front of me, there was the sound of movement to
my right. As I whirled toward it, I was hit from the left. A
metal pipe struck me on the forearm. From my shoulder to
my fingertips, it felt like my arm had exploded, and a
bright flash of pain burst behind my eyes. I howled, and
the light dropped to the floor.

I started to reach for my gun, but a fist the size of a bowling ball clubbed me on the chest and sent me sprawling to one knee.

In the darkness I saw a darker shadow coming toward me. As it reached down to grab me, I rose to meet it and buried my fist into its belly. It felt good.

I heard a grunt of surprise, then a gasp. Before I could follow it up, though, I was grabbed from behind by someone even bigger than I was, and my arms were pinned to my sides. I smelled sour sweat. A husky voice close to my ear said, "Hurry up!"

I did. I lifted my foot and brought the edge of my heel down hard on the foot of the ape holding me. He screamed in pain and released his grip enough for me to slam my right elbow into his ribs as hard as I could. I heard a satisfying cracking sound, and I was free.

I reached again for my gun, and this time managed to touch it before my wrist was grabbed and my arm twisted in a fierce hammerlock. My hand was almost up to my neck, and my shoulder felt like it was going to pop from the socket. I tried to reach back with my left arm, but it didn't respond, just hung at my side, limp with a vibrating numbness.

I got a whiff of lime-scented after-shave, then something wet and intensely cold closed over my nose and mouth. There was a sickly sweet metallic smell that made my skin crawl and the nerves in my teeth ache. I held my breath and tried to twist and squirm away. No good. Eventually I had to take a breath.

When I did, I began a slow spinning descent. I tried to stop it, tried to pull my head away, but the cloth was tight against my face.

I started to spin faster . . . faster . . . down into a soft black vortex.

SIX

It felt like my skull had been turned inside out and used to wipe out latrines. My tongue had the texture of a bath towel and seemed about as large. Wasps had built a nest in my sinuses and were buzzing angrily. Chloroform or ether or whatever had been used can really fuck you up.

I was lying on my front, the side of my face pressed against the concrete floor. I thought about moving, and decided to start with an eyelid.

Wherever I was, there was a light on. I saw a crumpled potato-chip bag about six inches away. It moved. A cockroach the size of a hot dog emerged. It looked at me, antennae twitching.

I focused a bit further away. I saw a pair of brown shoes. From my angle, I couldn't see if anyone was in them.

I managed to raise my upper body. I saw a pair of wrinkled beige pant legs rising above the shoes, and I figured there was a connection.

A couple of minutes more and I was on my knees. According to my watch, I'd been out about twenty minutes. My left arm was throbbing, but it seemed to work. So did everything else. I was sore and kind of sick, but I'd make it.

Which was more than I could say for the guy inside the shoes. He was sitting in a straight-backed metal chair. His wrists were securely tied to the chair legs. He had on a jacket that matched his pants, and a stained blue shirt open at the neck. He was short and fat and balding, with a ratty little mustache. I'd never seen him before, but it didn't look like I'd missed much. His face was cut and bruised, like he'd been pretty thoroughly worked over. His

46

eyes were open in an expression of surprise. A bullet hole in the forehead'll do that to you.

I got to my feet, swayed a bit, and looked around as I waited for everything to settle back into place. The room was about ten by ten, lit with a bare bulb hanging from the low ceiling. The one window was covered with brown paper, so this must have been what I'd seen in the alley. I hadn't seen any light when I'd entered the building because the room was partitioned off with unpainted plywood. There was a cheap wooden desk, a couple of chairs, and some cardboard boxes. That was all.

Well, almost.

Lying among the garbage that littered the floor, I spotted my gun. Bending very carefully, I picked it up. It had been fired. It wasn't too tough to guess where the bullet had gone. I put it back in my holster.

In the guy's jacket pocket I found a wallet. It had some pesos and some dollars in it, the usual credit cards, and a California driver's license that identified the body as Edward Flight. That meant nothing to me, and I put the wallet back.

I went over and looked in the cardboard boxes. They held magazines for a somewhat specialized audience. Cheaply printed and badly photographed, they were mostly pictures of not very attractive women having things done to them with whips and chains and ugly-looking implements. This wasn't any of that high gloss sado-chic stuff that was used to sell perfume and underwear. From the expressions on the women's faces, this was the real thing. There were about ten different magazines with maybe a hundred copies of each—probably ten grand worth of merchandise on the street. One box held videotapes and eight-millimeter films with titles like *Gang Bang* and *The Pain Master*. If the dead asshole was connected with this shit, I didn't imagine there'd be a lot of mourners at the funeral. If there was a funeral. Letting rats eat him would be too nice.

I didn't particularly want to hang around, so I quickly went over to the desk to see what was there. Again, there wasn't much, just some office supplies and a stack of cheap paper with a rubber-stamped letterhead that said "EF Distributing," with a Tijuana post-office box. The large bottom drawer, though, was locked.

Two quick kicks split the thin wood at the back of the desk enough for me to pry it off. One more kick to the rear of the drawer sent it flying out the front. Maybe not a hell of a lot of finesse, but after being clubbed, slugged, and drugged, it sure felt good to kick something and have it break.

Just as well I hadn't farted around trying to be neat. As the drawer broke free, I heard sirens and the squeal of tires. They were close. There was no way I had enough time to make it through the front. A glance told me that the window was the kind that didn't open.

I didn't even have to think about what to do. I went around the desk, picked up the loose drawer, and hurled it through the window. With one motion I stepped onto a chair, onto the windowsill, and out into the alley. I scooped up the papers that were in the drawer, and was a block away by the time I heard the cars screech to a stop. I got to my car and put some more distance between me and Calle Esperanza.

When I was far enough away, I found an open grocery store and pulled up. I went in, bought a quarter liter of Cuervo Gold, and took it back to the car. The good tequila helped cut the throbbing in my arm and cleared away the awful taste in my mouth.

As I pulled on the bottle, I looked through the papers I'd picked up. They seemed to be concerned with the material I'd seen in the office—queries about content, requests for samples, orders, and so on. It looked like Edward Flight had a nice little business going. Even in the porno shops his kind of stuff was strictly under-the-counter goods, sold only to known clients. But that just made the price higher. Operating out of Tijuana, he could keep up his supplies without having to worry much about the police. Apparently, though, there were some other folks he should have worried about.

Nothing in the papers looked to have any blackmail potential; I wondered if there ever had been anything. That was just one of the questions I would ask Mr. Philip Prince in the morning. I felt my lips pull back in a smile. I was already looking forward to our little chat.

SLEAZE   49

I unclipped the holster from my belt, took out the gun,
and put the holster in the glove compartment. I unloaded
the gun, carefully wiped it off, wrapped it in an old newspaper that was in the back of the car, and put the package
inside a paper bag. Then I looked, spotted a suitable trash
can at the end of the block, and buried the bag in the middle of the garbage. There was little chance it would be
found, and less chance the police would ever see it. Even if
they did, there was no way to trace it back to me, since I'd
taken it off a four-hundred-pound sociopath named Twee-
tie. Somehow I'd never gotten around to registering it.

As much fun as it had been, I figured I'd spent enough
time south of the border, and started back. The guard at
the U.S. side wanted to know what I was bringing in. I told
him I had a kilo of Mexican brown in the glove compartment, six Kalashnikov AKMs under the seat, and two wet-
backs in the trunk. He said that as long as I didn't have
any citrus fruit, I could go on through.

After I was across I found a pay phone and called the
number Prince had given me. It was a restaurant, all
right, but they'd never heard of him, and he didn't
answer the page. All things considered, I wasn't too surprised.

I still felt like shit, but didn't think I was ready for sleep,
so I opened all the windows and pressed on the accelerator.
Cruising north on the nearly deserted highway, I thought
about the night's events.

Actually, there wasn't a whole lot to think about. It
looked like the two thugs had been expecting me. Or expecting someone. They'd been waiting by the door, and
they'd had chloroform with them. That certainly suggested preparation. Had I been set up? Or had I just
walked into something? Was this connected with the
blackmail, and therefore with Prince and Prince's client?
Or was it something else that I—and maybe even Prince—
knew nothing about? Maybe even Prince was being used
by whoever he represented? And there were still lots more
possibilities, but at this point it was all empty speculation.
I'd have to see what Prince had to say before deciding what
I'd do. Maybe I still had a job. Maybe it was all just a fuck-
up—thieves falling out, or something—and I'd write it off,
figure I'd been paid for a few lumps, and that was that. Or

maybe someone was trying to jerk me around, and then I'd
have a different kind of job to do.

The one thing that was clear was that I was pretty lucky
to be where I was instead of being kicked about in a Tijuana jail. I didn't know when Flight was shot or when the
cops were called, but if they'd gotten there a little earlier
or if I'd come to a little later, I'd be feeling a lot worse than
I did. No matter that I might have been unconscious; being
found with a gun and a dead body wasn't exactly a swell
position from which to start discussions with the Mexican
cops. They weren't much known for their subtlety. I'd
probably have gotten out of it in the end, but not before
they'd had a lot of fun with me. No, I never thought I'd be
happy to be riding the San Diego Freeway, but there it
was.

It was well after four by the time I got back to my place. I
was staying in a four-room stucco shack on the Valley side
of the hills, far enough up to have what they called a view.
That meant I looked down on a Safeway parking lot and up
at an incipient mud slide; on a clear night, I could see the
sign for a Mercedes dealership. The only good feature was
the sauna that the current owner had put in just after he'd
sold a screenplay and just before he was indicted for selling
counterfeit Superbowl tickets. The guy was now a guest of
the state—you don't fuck with the NFL—and I got the
place cheap.

As soon as I was through the door I stripped and headed
for the sauna. I hoped half an hour at two hundred degrees
would sweat out the aftereffects of my successful evening.
It did. After my third rinse under an icy shower, I was back
in the sauna, sitting on the cedar bench, simmering gently
and watching my sweat drip onto the floor. With it went
the residue of the drug. The soreness started to dissipate,
my muscles started to relax, and I finally began to feel
okay again.

I hardly reacted when the door opened. It was the girl
who lived across the street. I had the idea she'd said her
name was Tawny, but maybe that was just the shade of
hair coloring she used. She was about nineteen, tall and
slender except for her full breasts and an ass like a pair of

honeydew melons. A typical graduate of Xanadu High, she
seemed to divide her time between sunbathing and roller-
skating. I'd once asked her what she did, and she'd said,
"Mostly grass, sometimes a few 'ludes." For formal occasions she put on tight satin gym shorts. This morning she
was casual, and wore only a thin gold chain around her
curving hips. She had a nice tan.

"Hi," she said brightly, showing me some good teeth and
shaking her thick mane of hair. "I saw you come in and
thought you might like some company."

"I don't."

"Okay." She shrugged, and her breasts bounced gently.
"Then you want to fuck?"

"It's two hundred degrees in here."

"Yeah, far out. We'll just slip and ooze all over the
place."

I shook my head. Tawny shrugged again and sat at the
opposite end of the bench, assuming a lotus position that
showed off the triangle of light brown curls between her
legs. The temperature seemed to rise to 210 degrees. After
a few more minutes, I went out and let the shower pour
cold water on me until I started to shiver. I dried off with a
rough towel, then lay down on a padded bench covered
with terry cloth.

I don't know how long I was asleep before I started
dreaming, but the subject was Natalie Orlov. This was
starting to be a drag. I didn't know what it was about her,
but she seemed to have gotten very deeply into me in a
very short time.

Like a lot of early-morning dreams, this one started off
vague and shadowy, then soon turned bluntly sexual. The
focus was Natalie Orlov's wide, full mouth. It moved
slowly over me. I was erect and hugely hard . . . tense . . .
waiting . . . straining to be encompassed by her . . . to feel
her warmth closing over . . .

I opened my eyes. The towel that had been around my
waist was on the floor. Tawny was on her knees, bending
over me, her hair softly brushing my stomach. Her tongue
licked the length of my cock, and when she got to the top,
she looked at me and smiled.

She knew she wasn't the girl of my dreams, but she didn't care.

I reached out and closed my hand around a firm breast. I pressed the nipple between my thumb and forefinger. It grew hard, and I heard her inhale sharply.

I guess I didn't care much either.

SEVEN

I slept later than I'd planned, but it was still morning when I got up. Tawny was gone, but there was a piece of paper on the bed with a drawing of a happy face on it. That was probably her idea of literacy. Oh well, she gave a great oral report.

I brewed up some extra strong coffee with beans from Surakarta in Central Java while I had a long hot shower. A survey of the damage showed that things could easily have been a lot worse. I had some twinges of pain in my right shoulder and a nice sore bruise on my left forearm, but I was sure they'd both be all right in another day or so. If I ever ran into the goons who did it, I'd make certain they hurt for a whole lot longer.

I fried up four eggs and some slices of spicy chorizo sausage, and covered it all with half a jar of salsa ranchera. On the label there was a picture of a thermometer that indicated the degree of hotness of the salsa. This one had exploded at the top. I ate the mess with a stack of warm tortillas while I enjoyed my view. Down in the supermarket parking lot a group of thirteen-year-old smash-and-grabbers were running off with the loaded shopping carts of women wearing curlers and Bermuda shorts. And they said the young had no entrepreneurial spirit.

By the time I'd finished my third cup of coffee and my second cigarette, the system was functioning. I pulled on some clothes and headed out.

The sun was bright but just pleasantly warm, and the sky was uncharacteristically blue. It was the kind of day that held a lot of promise. Everything looked new and gleaming, birds were singing happily in the eucalyptus

trees, and I was looking forward to scaring the shit out of
Philip Prince.

It took me about half an hour to get over the hill and find
his office. It was in a small building just off the Strip, in
an area where most everything was connected in some
way with show business—promoters, managers, bookers,
agents, producers, that kind of thing.

The street-level storefront in Prince's building held an
outfit called "Psychofantasia—Rent-an-Entourage." Their
sign announced they could provide toadies, lackeys, and
hangers-on for all occasions. There were a lot of people
milling around who lit up as I appeared, then looked disappointed when I went by the door. Things must've been
rough: in hard times, toadies were frequently among the
first to feel the pinch.

The directory in the lobby said Prince was on the third
floor. I went up the stairs, down a narrow corridor, and entered a small reception area. There were a couple of
chrome and fake-leather director's chairs, a chrome and
glass corner table with copies of *Variety* and *Billboard* on
it, and one door leading to what I assumed was Prince's office. The girl at the desk was young and pudgy, with a
wide, flat face and the look of a Guernsey cow wearing lip
gloss. She was reading a tabloid and sucking on a straw
from a can of diet cola. She looked surprised when I came
in, and I had the feeling that despite Prince's prosperous
personal appearance, the office didn't see a lot of custom-
ers.

I motioned to the door. "Is he in there?"

"Who shall I say is here?" She had a high chirpy voice.

"Montezuma's revenge."

I flung the door open hard enough for it to bounce
against the wall, then slam shut with a nice loud bang.

"All right, Prince," I growled, "just what kind of dumb
asshole do you take me for?"

Maybe I was being unnecessarily dramatic, but I figured
that with a guy like Prince, if I could push him off guard, I
had a better chance of getting something out of him. It was
a good idea . . . except it didn't work. He was standing behind his desk, looking out the window. He flinched when
the door slammed, but waited until I finished speaking before he slowly turned around.

"I don't know," he said. "What choices do I have?"

I was all set to continue with the angry-barbarian line, but I came to a crashing halt. It wasn't the same guy. He was about the same age and had roughly the same build. His silvery hair was combed the same, and he had the same kind of smugly detached attitude that lawyers liked to affect. He was a lot like the guy who hired me, all right, and I figured he was just as much of a shifty sleazeball. Only he was a different shifty sleazeball. The other one had seemed vaguely familiar, but I'd never seen this one before.

"Who the fuck are you?" I said. It was probably not the most probing question, but it was all I could come up with.

"Considering that you came into *my* office, shouting *my* name, I'd think that should be my question, don't you? Who the fuck are *you?*"

"I take it you are Philip Prince?"

He rolled his eyes toward the ceiling.

"Then I'm one very dumb asshole."

"Oh, really?"

I looked at him, but couldn't say much. "And I owe you an apology. My name is Hunter. I'm a P.I. I don't suppose that means anything to you?"

He shook his head, looking not very interested.

"And I don't suppose you know anything about the fact that someone hired me yesterday to do a job—someone who used your name?"

"What?"

That got his attention. He looked puzzled, then slowly sat down behind his desk, and I sat in front. I showed him the card I'd been given. It was his, but, not surprisingly, he had no idea who he'd given it to. I quickly went over the meeting at the Kava Klub. When I finished, he shook his head.

"How very strange. And you say this person looked like me?"

I nodded. Actually, now that I had a chance to examine Prince more closely, the guy yesterday looked more like what Prince probably wished he was. This one was not nearly so sleek and shiny. His complexion was sallow, and his fingernails were dirty and bitten. His suit was a decent one, but his white shirt was in its second day of use, and

the cuffs were a bit frayed. From a distance he might look
okay, but not up close. There was a nervousness in his eyes
and a scent of desperation and failure that gave the lie to
his confident manner. On the basis of the bare worktable
against one wall and the absence of other signs of activity,
I again had the feeling that business was not exactly brisk.

"And this had something to do with blackmail?" he
asked, like he was wondering how he could get a piece of
the action.

"So he said. Any of your clients in trouble?"

"Not that I know of."

Of course not. If he had clients, and they had trouble, he
wouldn't.

"Can I assume that everything did not go as it was supposed to last night, and that's why you burst in as you did a
few minutes ago?" He gave me a smile remarkably similar
to the impostor's, only his teeth weren't nearly as nice.

"Yeah, you can assume that." He was obviously fishing
to find out what the story was, but I didn't much feel like
biting. This was a different guy, but I had the same sense
of having my pocket picked. "So you have no idea who it
might have been?"

Prince shook his head. "None at all, but I'd like to know.
It sounds actionable to me. If you find out, give me a call.
You already have my card."

"Yeah."

I stood up. I didn't care for Prince, but I was pretty sure
he was being straight, at least in this instance, so there
was no point in continuing. I apologized again for coming
in like an asshole, and started for the door. Then I stopped
and turned back, and asked the only other thing I could
think of—if by any chance he'd ever heard of someone
called Edward Flight.

He slowly shook his head and said no, but I thought I'd
noticed a momentary squint when I said the name. I had
the idea he might have recognized it, but you can never
tell with lawyers. If they didn't know anything they acted
like they did, and if they did, they acted like they didn't. It
was kind of a reflex.

"Operates out of Tijuana. Probably deals in ugly porn," I
said, but Prince was still shaking his head from side to
side.

"Is this man connected with your mystery?"

I shrugged. "Not anymore."

"What do you mean?"

"He's not connected to anything anymore. Someone put a .38 slug through his head."

This time there was no question. Prince flinched violently, then made a face and said, "How terrible!"

Was it just a reaction to my bluntness, or did he know something about Edward Flight? I had the feeling he did, but I couldn't be sure. More to the point, I wasn't sure I could get anything by pursuing it just then, so I decided to let it slide. I could always get back to him. After all, as he said, I had his card.

I settled for one small push. "I don't think it was so terrible. He got off easy. A piece of shit like Flight probably should've been strangled with his own intestines. Slowly."

Prince's face turned the same dingy white as his shirt. As I went out the door, I heard him trying on a laugh, but it sounded more like the rattle of a consumptive.

Before I got to the outer door, the bovine receptionist called out, "Shall I make another appointment, Mr. Montezuma?"

I looked at her. "No, I don't think that's necessary. Why don't you just tell Mr. Prince that I'll be back. Real soon," I added with a grin.

EIGHT

Goddamnit! Was I ever one fucking stupid son of a bitch! Talk about being played for a sucker. Shit!

Bouncing down the stairs two at a time, I couldn't tell if I was more pissed at myself or the guy who had set me up. Me, probably, but it hardly mattered. All I knew was that I felt like I wanted to smash and rip things into little tiny pieces.

I must've looked that way as well, because when I hit the sidewalk three would-be toadies took one look at my face and scattered like mad to get out of the way.

I got to my car, only to find that a shiny Mercedes with a personalized license plate saying "STUD 1" had parked illegally behind me, sealing me in. The guy probably did this all the time, figuring that because he had a fancy car, he was the center of the fucking solar system. Well, not today, pal. You just met an alternate universe.

There were a couple of things I really liked about my old Checker—one, I didn't care what happened to it, and two, about the only thing heavier and more solid was an armored personnel carrier. I got behind the wheel and pulled as far forward as I could. I put it into neutral, floored the accelerator, then threw it into reverse. There was an encouraging sound of breaking glass and bending metal, and the Mercedes moved back about a foot. I repeated the procedure, causing an even louder crash and moving the car a little further. Once more, and I had enough room to get out, and STUD 1 looked like it'd tried to hump a brick wall.

The third time I'd rammed it, an old pickup truck packed with three beefy, beer-guzzling country boys cruised by. They saw what I was doing, let out some joyful whoops, and pulled a U-turn. They hit the Mercedes broadside, pushing it into an alley, where an enormous garbage truck doing about forty plowed into the other side and continued on without slowing down.

I checked the mirror as I pulled away. STUD 1 was now L-shaped. Happy motoring, pal. I was feeling better already.

I thought back to my meeting with the phony Prince, but couldn't find anything to go on. I now realized that just because the guy yesterday was an asshole, I'd been wrong to take that as confirmation that he was a lawyer. Live and learn. At least my instincts about his not being straight had been correct. Yeah, big deal. That and the five-buck entry fee would put me up for Chump of the Month.

Other than the fact that I now knew why we'd met after office hours in a bar, nothing else made sense—not the impersonation, not why he looked familiar, not the way he acted, not the money, not what I was hired to do, not what happened. Nothing. Generally, things don't just "happen"—there are reasons—but sometimes in my business they did, and I was beginning to get the feeling that maybe this was one of those times.

Thirty minutes later I found I was even wrong about that.

I pulled up close to a pay phone and called the service. The guy with the moving van had left a message that I was too late for the video machines, but that he could give me a really good price on a truckload of cameras. My reputation wasn't exactly one of unblemished virtue, but I still didn't know where he got the idea I was into that kind of action. On the other hand, considering the dazzling expertise I'd been displaying, I wondered if maybe I shouldn't give some thought to moving hot Nikons.

Natalie Orlov had also called. Half a dozen times, apparently, and the operator said she'd sounded worried or upset.

I could've called, but I decided I wanted to see her. In fact, I realized I'd been looking for a reason to see her since I got up. Shit. Something was happening, and I wasn't entirely sure I wanted it. Then again, I wasn't entirely sure that I didn't. Shit.

When I entered the office, the bimbo receptionist was perched on her desk while a guy with a shiny red bald spot, a limp wash-and-wear shirt, and a clip-on bow tie was taking a good close look at the butterfly tattoo. When the girl spotted me, she said, "Ooh!" and hopped off the desk in a way that gave the lepidopterologist a nifty little neck flip that threw him to the floor, leaving him dazed and stunned.

The bimbo opened the door to the .main office and shouted down the corridor, "He's here!"

About thirty seconds later, Natalie Orlov ran out, stopped in the doorway, looked at me, and then gave a big sigh that caused her shoulders to sag in relaxation. "Thank God!" she said.

She was flushed and seemed a bit distracted, but on her I thought it looked good, as did the pale, loose-fitting raw silk shirt that draped in interesting ways. My jaw started to ache.

"What's the problem?" I said.

"Are you all right?"

"Sure. I'm fine."

"When you didn't return my calls, I got worried."

"I didn't get in until late, and I only just checked with the service."

"You mean—"

"Why don't you tell me what's going on."

The guy on the floor groaned. Natalie Orlov glanced at him, looked puzzled, then shook her head and said, "Come on."

I followed her back to her office. When I was seated in front of her desk, she handed an envelope across to me, her expression very serious. "I found this this morning. It had been pushed under the door."

Natalie Orlov's name was typed on the outside, but nothing else. Inside, there was another sheet with "Sword of Truth" across the top, only this time the letter was typed, and the message was much shorter.

"You will not be permitted to destroy the reputation of a fine Christian lady," it read. "We have taken care of the man you hired, and we will take care of you if you persist. We are all-powerful because we possess the TRUTH, and we will prevail. Cease and repent, or be destroyed. This is your final warning."

I read through it twice, and looked up.

"What does it—"

I held up a hand to silence her, then read it one more time. It certainly put a different perspective on a lot of things.

I took a notepad and a pen from her desk, wrote "Go along with me," and showed it to her.

"What—"

I made a face and pointed insistently at the pad until she shrugged and nodded agreement.

"It looks to me like it's just more of the same," I said. "I don't think it's anything to worry about. On the other hand, why make trouble for yourself? Since whoever this is seems to think it's such a big deal, maybe you should just forget all about it. It doesn't really matter all that much, does it?"

Natalie Orlov was looking at me like I was crazy, and I motioned that she should carry on.

"I suppose you're right," she said hesitantly, and I continued to motion. "Maybe I should just let it drop."

I nodded. "Yeah. I think that might be best all around."

She looked all sorts of questions at me, and I held up my hands again, trying to tell her to be patient. She shrugged, shook her head, and made a face, but shut up.

I looked at the letter again. One thing that was now clear was that the letters and the threats were not simply because some crackpots didn't like SLEAZE. No, the aim was not necessarily to stop the magazine, but rather to stop the magazine from doing one specific thing—apparently, publishing certain pictures, or something like that.

There were also a couple of other things that were clear.

"I've been meaning to ask you," I said. "What's that picture all about?" I indicated the photograph of the South Pacific hotel taped on the wall.

"What?"

I pointed to the note I'd written, and repeated the question.

Natalie Orlov looked completely confused, but at least she didn't freeze up. "That's what this is all about. That's the end of the line."

"What do you mean?" I motioned that I wanted her to keep talking.

"That's what keeps me going—the idea that one day I'm

going to get out of here, maybe get myself a run-down hotel
on a speck of sand in the South Pacific. Set up shop
someplace clean and fresh and a hundred years behind the
times." She laughed. "Become a living legend, known to
every displaced drifter between the Tropics. 'Orlov of the
Islands.' " She laughed again, and affected a deep, rough
voice. " 'That tough old broad on Ponape—she don't take
no bullshit, but she serves honest food and stiff drinks, and
she'll help a fella if he's between ships.' How about that?
Just shows what happens if you come upon Maugham and
Conrad at too impressionable an age. Terminal romanti-
cism."

"Whatever does the job."

She shrugged. "I guess. At least it gives me something
to look at that's not hot and juicy."

I again motioned that she should keep talking. She
started telling me about some little island where there was
no electricity, and I focused on the letter and thought
things through.

"We have taken care of the man you hired." That could
only refer to last night's adventure. And that meant that it
wasn't a mix-up, or an accident, or something that just
happened. It was deliberate, designed to get and keep me
out of the way. That I wasn't currently being sweated in a
Tijuana jail was due only to dumb luck—with the emphasis
on *dumb*—and probably to the fact that the only call Mexican cops responded to quickly was one of nature.

Okay, so it was a setup and it was connected with this.
Somehow that made me feel better, gave me reason to
think I had more of a chance of eventually getting to the
guys who were responsible.

And if it was a setup . . . that meant . . .

I looked up at Natalie Orlov. She stopped talking, and
looked back. I took the notepad and wrote, "Who knows
you hired me?"

She shook her head. No one.

That could only mean what I suspected the first time I
read the letter.

I looked around. Why be fancy? I decided to start with
the obvious place, and there it was.

Natalie Orlov was again looking at me like I was crazy. I

put my finger to my lips to tell her to be quiet, then showed her the bug inside the mouthpiece of the telephone.

She looked puzzled. When she understood what she was seeing, her mouth dropped open, but she had enough control not to say anything. I liked that.

"There were some papers you were going to show me," I said. "In the other room?"

She picked up on it right away. "Oh, yeah. Come on."

I followed her into the corridor. She turned and started to say something, but I took her by an upper arm and hustled her through the reception area. The butterfly fancier was stretched out on the couch, still groaning. I steered Natalie Orlov out to the elevators. Her arm felt nice and strong, and her body seemed solid yet limber. Her hair smelled like sun at the beach.

"Hunter, what the fuck is going on? First those letters, and now my office is bugged! And I don't know what that letter's talking about. What lady? What reputation? And it sounded like something happened to you. That's why I was worried when I couldn't get you. And how'd you know there was a bug? What kind of son of a bitch is fucking around with me? Who is this creep?. . ."

She kept on for a while, getting hotter, hands forming fists, green eyes flashing, short hair bouncing. All in all, it was quite appealing. Eventually, though, she began to slow down, then abruptly stopped. She rolled her eyes, looking embarrassed. "Don't mind me. I'm just hysterical."

"No, you're just angry. Actually, under the circumstances, I think you're showing a lot of restraint."

She laughed. "What I really want is to rip out that fucking asshole's liver."

I stared at her, and she looked back. "Maybe that can be arranged," I said.

Natalie Orlov sighed. "Hunter, do you understand any of this?"

"A few things are getting clearer."

I then gave her a quick rundown on the little I'd learned about the Sword of Truth, and how everyone said it had folded years ago. Then I told her about the meeting yesterday afternoon and the trip to TJ. That really upset her, which I thought was kind of nice. And finally I told her about my meeting with Prince.

"As soon as I saw the latest letter, I realized that what happened in Tijuana was connected with your problem. I also realized that whoever fixed it up had to know you hired me. That meant that either someone told him, or he had some other way of knowing. I figured there was a bug, but I first wanted to think things through. That's why I wanted you to talk. If someone was listening, maybe they wouldn't catch on that we were catching on."

"Why not just pull the goddamn thing out? Shit! It spooks me to think that it's there."

I shook my head. "Don't be too quick. I'm a long way from putting this together. Let's not push the wrong things. If we know it's there—but whoever's at the other end doesn't know we know—maybe we'll get a chance to use it to our advantage. If you figure you can live with it for a while, it might be worth it."

Natalie Orlov closed her eyes and hugged herself, then looked at me and sighed. "I hate it. I hate the idea that it's there, that someone's listening . . . been listening for who knows how long. It's an invasion. I feel violated, used." Her eyes grew hard. "But if you think we can use it to get that fucking creep, then I'll live with it."

"Good. It won't be so bad. I'll get someone in to sweep the other offices. That way you'll know exactly where you can be secure and where you can't. If you want to call me, either watch what you say or use a pay phone."

She nodded grimly. "How long is this going to go on?"

"Don't know. It looks like things are heating up. Yesterday it didn't seem that I had anything to go on. Now they've handed us a few lines to follow."

"Like?"

"Like we now know there's a focus. It's not just foaming at the mouth."

"Yeah, I realized that right away, too. You mean the reputation of 'the fine Christian lady'?"

"Exactly. Any idea who it might be?"

Natalie Orlov shook her head, her wide mouth curled into an ironic expression. "Hunter, we check out their crotches, not their church attendance."

"That's what I figured. Yesterday you said that you

never used girls who weren't willing, who you thought
were being coerced into it."

"That's right."

"What about the other way 'round? Girls who are perfectly willing, but who have someone who's really opposed
to it—boyfriends or husbands, fathers, brothers, whatever?
Someone who somehow thinks *his* reputation will be destroyed if the girl appears in SLEAZE?"

"You think that's what this is?"

I shrugged. "It's a possibility."

"Then why didn't I hear directly? What's all this Sword
of Truth stuff?"

I shrugged again. "Everybody says the group disappeared, but maybe they didn't. Or maybe they reformed,
and whoever's behind this is a member. Or he was a member and decided this was a good way to go about it—either a
way to hide, or a way to appear to have more power."

"But it doesn't make any sense. Up until this morning, I
didn't even know it was about someone specific."

"I know that, but just because the guy has a reason
doesn't mean he's rational. Besides, he seems to assume
you'll know who he's talking about."

"I wish I did, but I don't."

"Nothing special in the works? Something that would
stand out?"

"No, nothing. Just the usual Vaginas on Parade."

"Nothing you can think of? Nothing anyone said? Other
letters that you got? Some reference? Anything to make a
connection?"

Natalie Orlov shook her head. "No. It's probably just
that this guy is so obsessed with this that he assumes
everyone else is as well. He doesn't realize we use six or
seven girls a month, and that I have no way of knowing
who he's concerned about if he doesn't tell me."

"You may be right, but that doesn't help us. There is one
thing, though."

"This is something that hasn't happened yet. He says,
'You will not be permitted . . .' The point is to keep something from happening. How far ahead do you work here?"

"Pretty far. One issue is at the printers, the next is
about to go, and the following three are in different
stages."

Swell. This was starting to look like just the kind of thing that I hated—a lot of slogging through the mud looking for something I wasn't even sure I'd recognize. The fact that the letters had started about a month ago didn't really narrow things. Maybe it meant the girl was selected about then, or maybe it meant the guy just found out about it then.

"How many girls have you got for those issues?" I asked.

"About thirty, as of now."

"Shit. All local?"

"No, from all over. Only about ten or twelve are Southern California."

I shook my head. "Well it's better than thirty."

"Are you going to see them?"

"Yeah. It seems to offer the best shot as of now. I'll see—maybe I can make a connection to the Sword of Truth. Or maybe pick up something else."

"What do you think the chances are?"

"Don't know. What's clear is that this is awfully important to somebody. Important enough to bug your office. Important enough to rig that setup yesterday, and to give me five hundred bucks. Apparently, even important enough to erase that piece of shit in TJ. So it's really a big deal—maybe, like you said, as an obsession, or maybe in some other way. I don't have a clue, but I've got to figure anything that matters that much has left a few signs."

"I hope," Natalie Orlov said. "It was bad enough before. This new stuff . . . I don't know how much I can handle. You know, Hunter, I might act tough, but I'm not, not really."

"Hey! You'll do fine. Just remember—you're Orlov of the Islands."

She laughed, and gave me a nice little smile as she momentarily put her hand on my forearm.

"Besides," I said, "there's one other thing."

"What's that?"

"They made one very big mistake."

"They did? What?"

"Lady, they got me real pissed off."

NINE

I talked a bit more with Natalie Orlov. She said she doubted that she'd ever heard of either Edward Flight or Philip Prince, and she was certain she'd never had any contact with them. The name Joshua meant nothing to her, nor did his description ring any bells.

Then I went through the material she had on the girls who'd be appearing in SLEAZE. Beyond names—most of which were probably phony—addresses, and brief bios that seemed largely wishful fantasies, there was nothing that looked like it'd be any help. With a couple of exceptions, they more or less looked like the receptionist—overweight and trying to look as sluttish as possible. Most succeeded pretty well. They all seemed undecided as to whether they should make their careers in show business or in something less demanding, like surgery or computer programming. From the expressions on their faces—in the few shots where their faces were visible—I figured most would have trouble spelling "computer."

Before I left, Natalie Orlov gave me a letter of introduction asking the girls to cooperate with me. She said she didn't know how some of them would take that, but if I didn't watch it, I might—so to speak—have my hands full.

"I'll keep it in mind," I said.

"Yeah. I imagine you will."

She tried to sound casual, but I thought I noticed an edge underneath. I was smiling as I left the office.

I gave a call to a guy I knew who had an electronic security service. Even though it was a small operation, he was doing pretty well, since there now seemed to be a lot of people who wouldn't order lunch unless the table was swept first. Some of them were probably right to be cautious, but

I figured most of them grossly overestimated the value or
the interest of their conversation. I asked him to go over
the SLEAZE offices, but only to find out what was there, not
to remove it, and he said that he would get right on it.

I thought about trying to locate the receiver. The bug I'd
found was an FM transmitter with a very limited range,
and it had to be close by. But it could be hidden in the basement, or in a nearby building, or in the trunk of a parked
car. No, trying to find it sounded even worse than trying to
get a lead from the models, so that was where I'd start.

The closest girl was Candi Labamba, who worked at a
place on Santa Monica called Celebrity Blow Job. Considering this was Hollywood, I guessed it had to happen
sooner or later, and in the ten minutes it took to drive over,
I tried to decide whether the celebrities were giving or receiving. There was probably a good market for both. I
thought it was only a matter of time until the operation
was franchised across the country—the perfect service in-
dustry for the eighties.

When I pulled up outside, I saw that it was only a new
hair salon, its name an example of classy Hollywood wit.
And I'd been envisioning coupon books, two-for-one sales,
and Certificates of Performance. What a letdown.

Inside it was all black and white high tech, with loud
music blasting and people moving quickly about, shouting
to be heard. Close by, a woman who looked like a molting
cockatoo was critically studying her reflection as a pale
young man hovered anxiously behind her shoulder. "It's
still not quite right," she said, touching her feathery
orange crest. "Maybe if we tipped it green."

After a couple of minutes a graying Peter Pan floated
over to me. "Thank goodness you're finally here! I can't
tell you how badly I need you. Follow me. We can do it in
the back."

"What?"

"Didn't they tell you? I'm all blocked up."

"What?"

"I can hardly stand it. I've been waiting all morning to
get reamed."

"What?" I must've growled, because he leaped backwards.

"Aren't you here about the drains?"

"No. I'm looking for Candi Labamba."

"Oh, dear. What am I going to do?"

"Is she here?"

He pointed toward the rear. "You see those enormous tits? Well, far in the distance behind them, that's Candi."

As I moved off, the guy clucked his tongue and said, "Some people have all the luck. . . . Now, where is that man?"

Candi Labamba was seated on a stool next to a sink that was half filled with gray, soapy water. She was wearing tight hot-pink jeans and a T-shirt that said "I'll curl your hair." Even though the shirt was large, it was stretched taut over breasts that stuck out far enough to require warning flags. They jiggled in time to the fast music.

"Oh, good," she said. "But didn't you bring your—what do you call it?—your snake?" She looked in the direction of my crotch, then giggled and turned the color of her jeans.

I didn't want to get into another of those discussions, so I introduced myself and showed her Natalie Orlov's letter. Since I couldn't see any way to casually work around to what I wanted, and since there probably wasn't much point anyway in trying to do that, I decided to be direct. More or less.

"It seems that some of the girls who've posed for SLEAZE have been getting hassled lately, and I've been asked to look into it. Have you had any trouble?"

"What kind?"

I shrugged. "Letters, phone calls, threats? Anything?"

Candi shook her head. Actually, that was not all Candi shook.

"Is anybody upset that you posed?"

Her breasts again swung from side to side.

"What about your boyfriend? Didn't he mind?"

"Johnny? Why should he? Oh, if I showed it to you here, he'd beat the shit out of me. But he knows I don't fool around, so he doesn't care who sees me in the magazine. He's real proud of me, and he kind of likes the idea of other guys knowing what he's got. Besides, we used the money I made to put a down payment on an RV."

"An RV?"

"Yeah. We're going touring. By this time next year,

we'll have visited every camp in the Southwest. Great, huh?"

"Great. So there wasn't anybody—not your family or anyone else—who was bothered about your posing?"

"Well, Armando was kind of angry."

"Armando?"

"That's the guy you talked to when you came in. Actually, his name is really Arnold, but don't say I told you."

"He was angry?"

"Well, maybe not really angry. He just didn't like the idea that I said I was a model. He thinks I should have said that I worked here. But I thought it sounded better to say I was a model. Don't you? Besides, by the time it comes out, Johnny and I will be in Tucson. Or is it Tulsa? I forget. So it wouldn't do Arnold—I mean, Armando—any good, would it?"

I agreed that it wouldn't, and asked if she'd ever heard of the Sword of Truth.

"Sword!" Her eyes went round. "You mean a real sword, or . . ." She again looked at my crotch, and again blushed and giggled. "Oh, dear! Johnny says I've got just one thing on my mind."

I suspected that Johnny was right, and that she had trouble holding onto even that. I told her I hoped that she and Johnny had a swell time, and she let her tits wave goodbye.

On the way out, I heard a harried Armando say to a tall, cadaverous, serious-looking woman, "It's terrible! I'm all stopped up."

"Have you tried prunes?" she asked.

TEN

The address I had for Conchinita Samosa was a surprisingly fancy one up in the hills in an area known as Valhalla, a real estate development that only the gods could afford. The house was a low, sprawling affair of redwood and marble, with oversize columns and plaster statues, a style the glossy promotional brochure called Parthenon Ranch. Taste and money have never had anything to do with one another, as that house made perfectly clear, but I still wondered what someone who lived there was doing spreading her thighs for SLEAZE.

The door was opened by a Mexican maid, and I was led through to the rear of the house, where a large room opening onto the patio and pool had been fixed up as a gym. Loud music was pounding out of an expensive sound system, and Conchinita was in front of a wall of mirrors, working hard, if not very gracefully, at a Vegas-style dance routine. She was very short and very plump, with an enormous mane of bleached blond hair. She was sweating profusely as she bounced around, and in her bright red tights, she looked like a boiled sausage about to burst its casing.

The music finished about six beats before Conchinita did, then she came over to me, panting and dripping and smiling the way they teach you in dance class.

I told her my name and said I was there because of the pictures in SLEAZE.

"Terrific! It's just like Manny said. Only I'm surprised— the magazine hasn't come out yet. Did you see an advance copy? Or what? Which studio are you from?"

"What? Who's Manny? I think you've—"

"Or are you from a network? I may not be quite ready for my own special, but I figure after a couple of guest shots,

71

maybe a late-night or two, it'll be right. Or do you think we
should go right to prime-time? You know, just burst out of
nowhere—'Conchinita Samosa, the Bolivian Fireball.' Of
course, you know I'm not really from Bolivia, but Manny
says you've got to have a shtick, and nobody knows where
Bolivia is anyway, so I guess it doesn't matter."

I was about to clamp my hand over her mouth in order to
shut her up long enough to say a couple of sentences, but a
bell went off.

"Whoops! Time for my sun. I do twenty minutes every
morning and every afternoon. Gotta keep up that golden
glow. Right? Come on out. We'll keep talking by the pool."

She headed for the glass doors, peeling off her tights as
she went. She was fat but firm, with bursting breasts over
a round belly, broad hips, and a dimpled ass. With all those
solid bulges, it looked like she was inflated—the wife of the
Michelin Tire Man.

She stretched out face down on a chaise and indicated I
should take a nearby chair. Before she had a chance to
start in again, I explained who I was and what I was doing.
I even got her to listen, which must have been an unusual
experience for her. When I finished, Conchinita shook her
head.

"No, there's been no trouble, nothing like that. In fact,
nothing at all. But Manny says all that'll change once the
magazine comes out. Manny's my publicist. Axel—that's
my husband, maybe you know him—Axel Samosa, 'The
Auto Parts King'? Well, Axel thinks I've got the stuff to be
a big star, and he hired Manny to plan out my career
moves. That's why they've got me on this tight schedule,
with dancing lessons, and singing lessons, and acting lessons, and you name it. About the only time I get a chance
to stop is when I have sun time. Well, anyway, Manny says
that in order to make things happen you have to get expo-
sure, and he says with SLEAZE, I'll really get a lot of that.
After all, that's the way Marilyn Monroe and Jayne
Mansfield started. Manny says as soon as that magazine is
out, everybody's going to be talking about me."

"You mean like herpes?"

"What?"

"Nothing. So, as far as you know, no one is upset about
your posing."

"Of course not. Manny says that when those pictures come out, I'm well on my way to becoming a major star. And that's what it's all about, isn't it?"

I'd seen the shots, and either Manny was bullshitting them or else he was as self-deluded as Conchinita and the Auto Parts King. About all those pictures might get her would be a ribbon at a livestock show.

"I don't suppose you ever heard of the Sword of Truth?"

"Is that the new group that's playing at the Hollywood Bowl next month? What do you think? Should I have them open for me at Vegas?"

"Good idea."

Just then the bell rang again.

"Time to do my front," she said, and I figured that was a good time to leave.

As I went out, she treated me to the same view that a million loyal SLEAZE readers would see spread over two pages.

A star is born.

ELEVEN

I'd hardly begun, and I was already starting to get fed up. I
didn't mind it if things got hot, but doing the same thing
over and over, to no purpose, tended to make me crazy. I
tried to con myself by saying, "Well, just do one more, then
maybe you'll come up with another approach." I didn't believe it, but I went on to the next address.

This was a small thirties apartment building in West
Hollywood, Spanish-style, old brick with ceramic tile decorations, built around a shaded courtyard. Apartment 10
belonged to someone who called herself Strawberry Sunday. I wondered what both of us were doing in a nice place
like this.

For a SLEAZE girl, Strawberry Sunday had seemed uncharacteristically attractive in her pictures. She was tall,
with a lot of copper-colored hair, and a body like something
drawn by a feverish cartoonist: all long legs, large pointy
breasts, and an ass like a cleft marshmallow. According to
her short bio, she was planning on an academic career.
Right. Nuclear physics, no doubt.

I rang the bell, and after a bit the door was opened
partway by a woman wearing dark green army fatigue
shorts and a Hawaiian shirt patterned with parrots and
palm trees. She looked to be the right height, and from
what I could see, it could have been the same body, but her
hair was light brown and fell straight to her shoulders
from a center part. She didn't have any makeup on, and
she gave me a no-nonsense look through her oversize
glasses. I wasn't at all sure it was the same woman who'd
been photographed gazing lustfully at a peeled banana.

"Strawberry Sunday?"

"Who are you?"

I handed her Natalie Orlov's letter. She read it, then said, "Just a minute," and shut the door. A couple of minutes later, the door was opened wider, and she said, "Come in."

"You checked?"

"Yeah."

I followed her into a small, bright living room. There was a comfortable-looking couch, a couple of matching armchairs, a few large plants in clay pots, and lots of shelves overflowing with books. There was a desk with a typewriter on it, and stacks of paper and note cards, and still more books, some with strips of colored paper marking places. Stuck to the wall above the desk was a neatly lettered sign that said "Screw principles—take the cash."

I sat down on the couch and laughed. "You really are going to have an academic career."

"Maybe not. It looks like my thesis might be sold to Hollywood."

"You're kidding. What's it about?"

"Economics. An historical analysis."

"Huh?"

" 'Sex As a Small Business.' "

"Oh. Midgets?"

She laughed. "Probably, by the time they're through with it."

"Is that why you posed for SLEAZE? Research?"

"Only partly. Mostly it was because it would cover tuition for a year. Which is not bad for a day's work."

"Have you had any problems as a result?"

"What do you mean?"

"I don't know. Phone calls? Letters? Any kind of hassle? That's what this is about. Anyone upset about your doing it?"

"Shit! No one—I mean *no one*—knows. Why do you think I wore that wig and used that name?"

Just then the phone rang, and I noticed there were two on the desk, one red, one beige. Strawberry Sunday picked up the red one and said, "Audio Erotic—what's your pleasure?" She listened for a minute, then said, "Sure, I remember you. Can you hold on a sec?" She covered the mouthpiece and turned to me. "Can you wait? This won't take long."

I nodded and leaned back. Strawberry Sunday looked in a metal file box and pulled out a three-by-five card. "Honey, this going to be on the same credit card as before?. . . Okay. Hold on." She made some notations on the card, then took off her glasses and leaned back in her chair. When she started talking again, her voice was low and sultry.

"You know, Jimmy, I've been hoping you'd call. The last time was so good—I mean *sooo* goood—that I've been waiting to hear from you. . . . What am I wearing? Well, I've got on a shirt and some shorts. . . . You know I never wear anything underneath. I like to feel free and ready. And this shirt is kind of loose, you know, so it brushes my nipples. . . . Oh, yes. They're getting so hard. Oh, Jimmy, I wish you were here to see them. They're just sticking right out against the fabric. I don't think I can wait any longer, Jimmy. I'm going to open up my shirt now. One button, two buttons. Just enough to get my hand in."

I watched as she stretched back in her chair, eyes closed, her voice a husky whisper. As she spoke, she did what she said, opening her shirt, then putting a hand in and caressing her breast.

"Oh, Jimmy, it feels so good to touch my breast. It feels like it's swelling and growing hot, and when I squeeze my nipple I can feel tingles all through my body. Oh, Jimmy, if you were only here. I can imagine what that would be like."

Still with her eyes closed, Strawberry Sunday picked up the phone and started to move slowly around the room. She held the receiver against her head with her shoulder, leaving her with a hand free to slowly caress her body, cupping and squeezing her breasts, first outside her shirt, then inside, all the while talking softly, persistently, hypnotically. Finally, she was standing in front of me, shirt half open, chest heaving, breasts full and covered with a film of perspiration, nipples hard and pointed like small dark brown cones.

"Oh, Jimmy, I can imagine what it would be like if you were here. . . . You'd put your hands up to the front of my shirt. . . ." She took my right hand and brought it up to her shirt. "Then you'd slowly, so very slowly, undo each button, one by one, until my shirt hung open. And you wouldn't touch me, not yet, just look at me, and just your looking at my breasts would make them swell and send shivers through me. Then I'd lift my shoulders, and the shirt would drop to the floor."

Her shirt dropped to the floor. Then she lowered herself until she was straddling my left leg, gripping my knee with her strong thighs.

"Oh, Jimmy, I know what it would feel like when your hands finally touch my breasts. Your hands are big and strong and feel slightly rough against my smooth skin. You'd squeeze, softly at first, and then harder . . . harder . . . harder. Oh, yes! Yes! And my nipples are burning into your palms. Yes! Then you put your mouth on my breast and take the nipple between your teeth. Oh, God! Then you strum it with your tongue. Oh, I can hardly stand it, Jimmy! I'm so damp! I've got to get my shorts off. Oh, Jimmy! They've got buttons down the front. Help me!"

I put my hands at her waistband, pulled it with one quick motion, and buttons went flying.

"Oh, Jimmy!"

She stood up, and her shorts dropped to the floor and she stepped out of them. Her triangle of pale curls was glistening. Still with her eyes closed, still talking into the receiver, she bent over and undid my belt and pulled at my zipper, working frantically to expose me. When she did, her eyes finally opened.

"Oh, Jimmy, I can see you now. You're enormous! You're huge! Oh, Jimmy, I'm just streaming. I can't *wait* any longer."

Strawberry Sunday straddled both my legs, then slowly lowered herself onto me and gasped.

"Oh, God, Jimmy! That feels so good!" Her thighs gripped my hips, and she began to thrust and rock with her pelvis, moving faster, more desperately, each movement accompanied by a gasp, each gasp rising higher and higher in pitch.

"Oh! Oh! Oh! Oh, Jimmy, I can feel you biting my shoulder. Oh, yes! Harder! I want you to leave a mark. Yes! Yes! Oh, yes! Jimmy! Jimmy! I'm coming. Oh, oh, oh. I want to feel you explode! Ohhh! Yesssss . . ."

The last word was a hiss of expelled breath, and she relaxed, deflated, against me. After a minute I heard a small sound coming from the phone receiver.

"Oh, yes, Jimmy," she answered. "It was wonderful. Was it good for you?. . . Oh, I'm so glad. . . . No, thank *you*. . . . Now, don't wait so long until the next time. . . . Okay. Bye-bye."

She leaned down and hung up the receiver. Then she eased herself off me and stood, picking up her shirt, shorts, and the telephone. She carried the phone back to the desk. She stepped into her shorts, which no longer closed, put on the shirt, and sat down again.

"Thanks." She put on her glasses. "Now, where were we?"

"What was that? Dial-An-Obscene Phone Call?"

Strawberry Sunday laughed. "Just about."

"More research?"

"Again, only partly. It also pays the bills. Actually, it's a perfect income supplement. I can work at home, it doesn't take much time, and I provide a useful service. Poor little Jimmy, for instance, has a few dysfunctions, but he still likes to think he can give a woman pleasure. So he pays me fifty dollars to have an orgasm."

"And you deliver."

"Sure. Why would I want to rip off Jimmy?. . . Now, what else can I tell you about my posing for SLEAZE?"

I shook my head. "If you're positive that no one knows you did, there's probably nothing you can tell me."

"I'm positive."

"Does the Sword of Truth mean anything to you?"

She gave me a look, part surprised, part skeptical. "This isn't about girls being hassled, is it? There's something else."

"Maybe. You know something?"

She shrugged. "Nothing recent. A few years ago I was doing some work on the fringe religions. More economics."

"Small business?"

"No. More the way a lot of these groups use religion as a front to keep from paying taxes, and to keep anyone from looking too closely into just what they're doing. Along the way, I heard some things about the guy who headed up the Sword. What did he call himself?"

"Joshua?"

"That's it. You know anything about him?"

"A little. Sounds like a real charmer."

"I'll say! Quite an interesting career. Seems he either started as a low-level con man and then became a used-car salesman, or the other way around. I don't remember which, but whatever it was, it was real small-time. Then, in what seems to be a fairly common progression, he started to use his talents to sell religion. Or rather, he started to use religion to make a buck for himself. He became one of those road-show preachers—self-ordained, apparently. One of those fire-and-brimstone, hate-your-enemies kind. Then, moving onward and upward, he did a little pimping, did a little porn. But again in a real small way. For all the ability he had to control and manipulate people—and I gathered it was considerable—he was fundamentally not very smart. You know: too greedy in the short run to really set up a good score."

I knew the type. This town was full of them. "And the Sword?"

She shrugged. "The perfect combination of everything he'd previously done—fraud, religion, power, and pimping. No longer satisfied selling God, Joshua was going to become God."

"Yeah. I heard he modeled himself on Charlie Manson."

"Shit! It figures."

"What happened to him? I haven't been able to find out."

"Don't know. Not sure that I want to."

I looked at her. There was something disturbing her. "Where'd you hear all this stuff?"

"From someone who was one of Joshua's lieutenants—a so-called soldier—until he decided that even unlimited sex with the girls that Joshua collected couldn't compensate for all of Joshua's craziness. It seemed he liked to go around heavily armed, and one of the things that really got him off was taking a gun and jamming it into somebody's mouth, and saying, 'I hold your life in my hands. You are nothing and I am everything.' Something like that, all the time playing with the trigger, pulling it slowly back. Every once in a while, he'd pull it all the way, only the chamber would be empty. The victim, of course,

wouldn't know that, and would scream or faint, and
Joshua thought that that was really funny. Nice, huh?"

"What's the name of the guy who told you this? Any idea
where he is?"

She nodded. "Oh, yeah. After I heard all this, I got interested, and started asking around about Joshua. Not making a big deal, but since I was going around anyway . . .
Only no one seemed to know anything. I had the feeling
that maybe some people did, but they were afraid to say
anything. Which I came to understand."

"Oh?"

"Yeah. One day I got a letter with 'Sword of Truth'
printed at the top. It told me to stop asking questions about
Joshua or very bad things would happen to me. There was
also a clipping about the guy who'd talked to me. Seems
he'd accidentally shot and killed himself while playing
with a gun. Someone had written at the bottom, 'It was no
accident.' I stopped asking questions, but that's the reason
I remember all this. Things like that do tend to stick."

"How long ago was this?"

"Maybe three years, or a little less. Is this any help?"

"I have no idea," I said, standing up. "Give me a call if
you remember anything else."

"Okay." The red phone rang, and Strawberry Sunday
looked at me. "You want to wait?"

I shook my head. "I might be a bit dysfunctional myself
right now."

"Well, then, I'll manage on my own."

"I'm sure you will."

TWELVE

I was only about ten minutes away from Philip Prince's office, and decided to make that my next stop. Since I now knew the murder in Tijuana was somehow connected with SLEAZE, and since I strongly suspected that the lawyer knew something about the dead asshole, I thought it might be worthwhile to drop in on him again, just to see how he was getting on. He could probably stand to stew a bit longer, but I was at least reasonably certain that he'd keep his clothes on.

A large grease spot was all that remained of the Mercedes. Or maybe that was all that was left of its owner. Too bad.

As I was going in the building entrance, a big guy came out of Psychofantasia. He had long, pure white hair and wore a spotless white suit. A white velvet cape hung from his shoulders, and he carried a cane with a large gold eagle as a handle. I recognized him as the current local arch-villain of wrestling. He had a good dozen toadies, lackeys, and hangers-on happily trailing behind him like Cub Scouts on a field trip. "Straighten up," he growled, and they straightened right up. Being a toady was serious business.

When I opened the door to Prince's office, I was treated to a view of Miss Guernsey's hindquarters. She was burrowing under her desk, and her short skirt had flipped up to reveal straining panty hose over green-and-white-striped bikini briefs. I had been thinking I'd get a hamburger for lunch, but changed my mind.

"Got it!" she said in her squeaky voice, and backed out from beneath the desk. She stood up and seemed surprised to find me standing there, but recognized me right away.

"Mr. Montezuma! I lost my eyelash," she explained, sounding like it had been her spaniel, then held out a pudgy little hand to show me something that looked like a soggy caterpillar resting on her palm.

"Better keep it away from the philodendron," I said, and continued on into Prince's office.

He wasn't there. A drawer on the file cabinet was pulled partway out, as were a couple of desk drawers.

"Where is he?" I asked Miss Guernsey, who was standing in the doorway looking confused.

"I don't know. About ten minutes after you left, Mr. Montezuma, Mr. Prince hurried out of here. He looked real worried. I didn't even get a chance to give him your message. I'm sorry."

"That's okay. Do you know where he went?"

"Yes. I wrote it down." She went back to her desk and rummaged through some papers. "Here it is. Mr. Prince said that if anyone asked for him, I was to say that he was in Timbuktu and wouldn't be back until next spring. That must be a very big case he's got."

"Yeah, must be. Do you have a home phone or address for him?"

"Gee, I don't know. This is only my second week here."

The third time through the Rolodex, after I explained to her how it worked, Miss Guernsey came up with a phone number, which I copied down. Then I got out one of my cards, added my home address to the front, and wrote on the back, "If you've got trouble, maybe I can help."

"Leave this on his desk for him, in case he comes back."

"Okay. Who's Mr. Hunter?"

"One real dumb son of a bitch."

"This is all very perplexing."

"Yeah, I know what you mean."

"What do you think I should do, Mr. Montezuma?"

"About what?"

"Well, when Mr. Prince was going out, I asked him what I should do. And he said, anything I damn well wanted."

"Okay. What do you want to do?"

"I don't know."

"Has he paid you yet?"

"No, not yet."

"Then I think you should take that typewriter there and

sell it, and use that for your salary. And if there's anything left over, buy yourself something nice."

"Do you think that's what Mr. Prince meant?"

"Is that what you'd like to do?"

"Sure."

"Then, that's what he meant."

"Okay. Thanks."

"My pleasure," I said, heading for the door.

"Oh, Mr. Montezuma. Where's Timbuktu? Is that close to Fresno?"

"Not quite as remote."

"Oh."

THIRTEEN

Well, it looked like my instincts were still okay. I'd pegged
Prince for some connection with Flight, and his hasty departure seemed to confirm that.

Only my timing sucked.

I was sitting in the back booth of a joint called the Terminus Grill, located in one of the barrios between Hollywood and downtown. Despite its name, it wasn't close to
any train or bus stations. It was just the end of the line.

At one time, it'd had a reputation as the toughest bar in
town. They liked to tell stories in the Terminus about ser-
vicemen who'd swagger in, laughing and self-important,
and be rolled, stripped, and put out with the garbage in the
back alley, bare-assed and beaten flat, in under six minutes. But those were the good old days.

Now the place was home to a handful of losers who
draped themselves over the bar and spent their afternoons
watching the soaps through bloodshot eyes. The floor was
sticky from four decades of spilled beer, and the smell of
defeat mingled with those of stale draft and old piss.

The Terminus had all the ambience of a Roach Motel,
but it was also one of the few places in town where you
could still get decent fried chicken. I'd decided that
chicken, country biscuits, and a big mound of dirty rice
was what it would take to make me feel slightly less like a
jerk.

While I was waiting for my food, I called my friend with
the security service. He'd finished the sweep of the SLEAZE
offices and had found only the one bug. He said he'd looked
at it and it was your basic little transmitter, with a range
of under five hundred yards and a battery life of about five
days. It could be picked up without much trouble for a cou-

ple hundred bucks, and while he didn't recognize the work, he could give me the names of about twenty-five guys in town and another twenty-five out of town who might have done it if I wanted to check it out. "Of course," he added, "there are probably a lot more guys doing this that I don't know about. And besides, anyone with a soldering iron and a ten-buck set of plans could put one together without too much trouble."

Which was what I had figured. Which was the reason I told him I'd pass. Which turned out to be another mistake.

Then again, I was on a roll.

I called the number I'd gotten from Miss Guernsey. It turned out to belong to *Mrs.* Prince. Or rather the ex-Mrs. Prince.

"No, I haven't seen the son of a bitch. And I don't know where he is. And I don't really give a shit. But if *you* see him, tell the creep that he'd better fork over the money he owes me pronto, or I'm going to hire an out-of-work Haitian to repossess his fucking life."

Somehow, I got the feeling that their romance had lost its bloom. About all I managed to learn from the gracious Mrs. Prince was the address and phone number where Prince now lived.

I tried the number, but there was no answer, and then lunch arrived.

An enormous bald black man with a gold front tooth and two fingers missing on his left hand deposited a platter of backs and thighs on the table, and added a big bowl of rice and a basket of biscuits. I asked him to bring me three bottles of Dos Equis.

He brought the beer. "That's six *equis,* man," he said with a laugh as thick and bubbling as the lard he used to fry the chicken.

The food was as good as ever. The chicken pieces were dusted with a combination of garlic and chili powder and just a touch of nutmeg, then dipped in an egg-milk mixture, then rolled in flour, and dropped into a huge pot of boiling lard until they were crispy golden on the outside and juicy and tender on the inside. The rice was fried with lentils, tomatoes, onions, and bits of spicy sausage, then everything was coated with a sauce of smoky chipotle

chiles. The biscuits steamed when you broke them, and the
butter melted right away. Not bad.

By the time there was only a pile of bones and a few
small crumbs left, I was feeling pretty good.

By the time I had a cigarette, the last half bottle of beer,
and gave some thought to what I'd do next, I was feeling a
little less good. Between the guys who'd pulled vanishing
acts, and whoever was writing the letters, and whoever
was behind the bug, and whoever had iced Flight, and
whatever it was all about, I felt like I was in the middle of
a shadow dance. I was chasing insubstantial figures who
were moving to a tune I couldn't hear, images circling a
light source I couldn't see. For all the action that was
going on, there seemed to be very little to follow up, and
less that looked like it had any chance of paying off. The
girls who'd be appearing in SLEAZE were still the best bet,
but the feeling was growing that I was wasting my time
there. Ordinarily, I'd have dropped it and tried something
else, but everything else looked even worse. I badly needed
to get something solid. Something I could put my hands on.

Something I could kick the shit out of.

Speaking of which, I heard a voice behind me say ear-
nestly, "You know, Mrs. Banks, for really *fast* relief from
constipation, most doctors recommend DynaLax, the twen-
ty-minute miracle."

Maybe that was what I needed.

I started to get up, then froze. Goddamnit! That voice
sounded familiar, smooth and smug and self-confident, as
round and full as a DynaLax turd.

I turned around and there he was, on the old TV above
the bar. He looked a few years younger, a bit more orange
and green than I remembered, but there was no mistaking
that sleek silvery hair and that oily manner. This time he
was playing a pharmacist in a nifty white nylon jacket instead of a lawyer, but he was just as much of an asshole.

Goddamnit! He was a fucking actor! No wonder I'd
thought he'd looked familiar. At some point I must've seen
that commercial, or something else he was in.

In this little drama, the fake Prince was called Mr.
Crocker. He was standing behind a counter in a drugstore
set, talking to a scrawny woman who, from the expression
on her face, was stopped up worse than the drains at Celeb-

rity Blow Job. "Mr. Crocker" held out a package with a
graphic of an explosion on it and said, "You can't buy a
more powerful laxative without a prescription." Then he
flashed all those pretty teeth of his.

Right! Gotcha!

It just goes to show you—if you live clean and eat up all
your rice and biscuits, everything'll work out okay. Shit.

I went back to the phone and called a tough broad named
Adrienne Benedict, who ran a small casting service. I'd
done some work for her when she'd been an agent, getting
a couple of clients out of some minor jams, and she was always good for a little info if it didn't take much of her time.
Of all the people I knew, she might get a line on this guy
the quickest.

I explained to her who I was trying to locate.

"Oh, sure. I know who you mean."

"You know who he is?"

"No, but it'll only take me a couple of calls. What do you
want?"

"His name and how to find him."

"No problem, Sam. Do I assume you're not going to offer
him a job?"

"Not quite."

"So I guess I shouldn't use your name."

It was a pleasure dealing with Adrienne. You didn't
have to draw pictures, and she was never nosy. "You guess
right."

"Okay. Call me in an hour. I'll have whatever there is."

I used the time to check out Trixie Quick, another
SLEAZE girl. Along with her husband, she ran a blue-collar
bar called Hank and Trixie's Hideaway. He was short, and
with his huge arms and bigger belly, he looked like he'd escaped from the primate house at the Griffith Park Zoo.
Trixie might've been the twin sister of the butterflied
bimbo in the SLEAZE office, and in a couple of months, she
too was going to get the coveted centerfold. Rather, about
nine square inches of her would.

Far from anyone being bothered about this, they were
all excited, because they figured it would really pick up
business. Hank said that in honor of their Canadian
friends, they were going to rename the bar "Trixie Quick's
Beaver Valley."

I used their phone to call Adrienne.

"His name is Hugo Depina," she said. "He's currently working in a shoe store on Rodeo Drive, and he's expecting you."

"What?"

"Well, I thought you wanted to get hold of him, so after I found out where he was, I gave him a call and told him George Lucas admired his work as the DynaLax Man and wanted to send someone over to talk to him about the possibility of a featured role."

"And he believed it?"

"He's an unemployed actor, Sam. Of course he believed it. My guess is he'll stay right where he is for at least the next week, without even going to the bathroom for fear of missing you. So there's no hurry in your getting over there."

I laughed. "Thanks. That's great, though I won't make him wait too long. You find out anything else about him?"

"Other than the fact that he's got a real dumb agent, not much."

"What do you mean?"

"Well, he had a fairly decent career a few years back. Nothing spectacular, but he did some summer theater, and got the occasional bit part. It wasn't enough to live on, but he was working, which meant that there was always the chance something better would come along. Then his agent got him that commercial. Probably thought it would bring in a few bucks and help to get him known. Right? Well, he got known—as the asshole in the DynaLax ads— and he hasn't worked since. I mean, who the hell is going to hire the guy who's identified as the spokesman for the world's strongest laxative? A real good move, right? Talk about going down the toilet! He should've fed his agent a box of the stuff. What a jerk!"

"I'll pass the advice along," I said, and told her I owed her one.

I went out to my car, smiling. I finally had something definite to do. My fingers were curling involuntarily, as though around a neck. I smiled again. Hugo Depina's system was in for a bigger shock than he'd ever get from DynaLax.

FOURTEEN

Rodeo Drive is the kind of place where it costs $2.50 to park for twenty minutes, and they don't let you in if they think your car might lower the tone of the lot. I found a place on the street a couple of blocks away and walked back.

This was hardly one of my favorite parts of the city. It liked to think it was the most exclusive shopping area in the world, but it was only the most expensive, home of the 10,000 percent markup. On Rodeo Drive they didn't sell goods and services. They sold labels and addresses to people who thought those meant something, which in turn meant that business was always brisk. Talk about one being born every minute. The sidewalks were littered with them, dressed in pastel-colored designer sportswear and calling each other "darling." Goddamn! You could probably sell cat shit on Rodeo Drive, as long as you put it in a fancy little box and said it was imported from Switzerland. In fact, I was surprised someone hadn't thought of it: "Crapper and Sons, Purveyors of Excrement to the Crowned Heads of Europe." Better yet, "Purveyors of Excrement *of* the Crowned Heads of Europe." It was a natural.

The joint where Depina worked was called Carissimo, a pinkish-brown pseudoclassical building that I supposed was intended to convey the impression of Old World elegance, but that looked more like a small-town mortuary. I headed for a door that would have been more appropriate on a bank vault, but I was blocked by a thug dressed like a Roman centurion.

"Do you have an appointment?"

Shit. What a racket. You had to make an appointment to hand 'em your money. And they probably had an unlisted phone number.

"It's a fucking shoe store," I said.

The guy looked me up and down and sneered. "No admittance without an appointment. Now shove off, pal. You're blocking the sidewalk."

He turned away, like I'd already taken up too much of his valuable time. I was tempted to grab his pikestaff and give him a couple of extra orifices, but I decided to save it all for friend Hugo.

"I'm from George Lucas. I'm here to see Hugo Depina."

The centurion's mouth dropped open, the color drained from his face, and you'd have thought I *had* stuck him, the way he started oozing before my eyes.

"Oh! I am sorry! I didn't realize. Please forgive me, sir. You should have said so right away."

I started again for the door, but he continued to stand in front of it.

"Uh . . . you know, sir, I don't do this all the time," he said. "This is just filling in. I'm really an actor. If I say so myself, I'm really much better than Hugo. I've got terrific range. Do you think there might be something. . . ? Shall I have my agent call you? If you just give me a minute, I could do something for you right here. . . . Please. How about a break?"

I slowly looked him over, nodding, then paused as I got to his bare legs. "No," I finally said, "your knees stink." I brushed by him and went inside. As the heavy door closed I heard him say, "I can have them fixed."

Right, pal. Have 'em removed.

Inside, it was more like the library in an English manor house than a place of business. Rather, it was more like a Hollywood set of a library in an English manor house. The walls were paneled with dark wood, and large dreary oils in heavy gilt frames hung between bookshelves filled with leather-bound volumes purchased by the yard. A cheery fire blazed in the stone fireplace, which meant that the air conditioner had to strain to keep the temperature down to a comfortable level. Instead of anything as mundane and functional as a row of chairs for the clients, there were various so-called conversation areas discreetly placed around the large room.

Since this was Rodeo Drive, shoes weren't brought out in boxes to be tried on. They were wheeled out on an ornate trolley, one pair at a time, artfully perched on a plastic pedestal like a piece of sculpture or some fancy pastry. It was swell. The suckers really got their money's worth here.

About all that was missing was a string quartet, but there was a guy padding around with a silver tray carrying delicate little cups and a china coffeepot. He wore an expensive gray suit, had sleek silvery hair, and moved so silently he might have been greased. It was my favorite character actor, fresh from triumphs as a smarmy pharmacist and a slick lawyer, currently appearing as a deferential family retainer. Now *there* was terrific range.

I watched as Hugo Depina coasted up to a woman with an elaborate lacquered hairdo that resembled a trumpeter swan in full flight. I recognized her as one of those celebrities who only appeared on the cheap talk shows, and whose main talent seemed to be for marrying wealthy men. She hadn't had as many husbands as she'd had face lifts, but it was close.

As Hugo was pouring a tiny cup of coffee for the woman, he glanced over his shoulder toward the door, no doubt checking for George Lucas's representative. When he saw me, I heard him say "Oh, shit!" and he froze. A hot black stream of coffee went onto the woman's head. The swan collapsed, as though dropped by a shotgun blast. The woman screamed and leaped to her feet. The clerk who'd been trying to ease her swim fin of a foot into a miniature slipper was kicked in the face and sent sprawling. He jumped up and charged Hugo, demanding to know what he thought he was doing. Hugo responded by whirling around and smashing the Spode coffeepot against the guy's head.

Ah, Hunter, you spread gaiety wherever you go.

Hugo took off for the back of the store and I started after him. Then he paused and turned back toward me with a motion I recognized quite well. Shit. He faced me, holding a .22 automatic in his hand. "Oh, Hugo," I muttered, "you're making a big mistake." As a weapon it was a piece of junk—the coffeepot was probably more dangerous—but it kind of pissed me off when people pointed guns in my direction, and I intended to make sure Hugo understood this.

He threw a slug at me, but it went way wide. A gun like that's barely accurate even at point-blank range. Just then a guy with all the appeal of Richard Nixon on a scruffy day stumbled out from a door marked "Private." He was stumbling because his trousers were around his ankles, and he was followed by a body builder wearing a T-shirt with the word "Hunk" on it. Hunk was just zipping up. They both looked confused, though I suspected that was the body builder's natural expression.

Hugo fired another shot in my direction. It didn't get any closer, but it did blast a pair of gold-colored shoes to bits. The guy who looked like Nixon howled as though he'd been shot and cried, "My pumps!" In an effort to prevent further terrible carnage, he threw his body over a pair of purple sandals that were lying unprotected.

Meanwhile, all the fancy ladies were yelling their fancy heads off and diving for cover behind the leather armchairs. But the clerks, who were paid peanuts to be daily shat upon by the rich bitches, must have decided that there was some stuff that even they wouldn't put up with, and they grabbed the armchairs for themselves, shoving their barefooted clients out into the field of fire.

The front door flew open and the centurion ran in. He must've thought it was part of the audition, because he started shouting, "Back, you Vandals. Back, you Goths! Away from the gates of Rome!" With all his might he hurled the pikestaff at Hugo. It wasn't any more accurate than the gun. After a wobbly flight of about ten feet, it came to rest, point first, in the pale pimply butt of the Nixon look-alike. The guy howled again, but at least the sandals were safe.

Hugo Depina disappeared out the back, and I went after him. Hunk scratched his head and said "Hey!" as I ran by.

I went through the back of the store where the shoes were kept, boxes neatly stacked like piles of five-hundred-dollar bills, and out into the alley. Even on Rodeo Drive they produced garbage, and their back alley looked like any back alley, though they did have higher-quality dogs rooting around the trash cans. In Beverly Hills, even the strays had to have papers.

Hugo was about a hundred feet ahead, running hard, continually glancing over his shoulder and nearly stumbling every time he did. I followed easily behind him, but saw no reason to close the gap just yet. Hugo turned down an intersecting lane, I sped up, and when I turned the corner, I had cut the distance in half. Hugo looked around and saw how close I was, did a little panicked jump, and promptly ran into the rear of a parked delivery van. He bounced back, stunned, and I closed to about fifteen feet. He waved the gun at me, still thinking that would be enough to make me back off.

"Don't be stupid," I said. "I only wanted to ask you a few questions."

His long silver hair hung down in front of his face, his glossy white shirt was dirty and stained, and one sleeve of his fancy suit was half ripped out of the socket. "I have nothing to say." Then he fired again, this time hitting the garbage can next to me.

I grabbed the lid and hurled it like a Frisbee. It hit him in the rib cage and smashed him back against the van. He started to run as I moved toward him. I grabbed for him and got the collar of his jacket, but he kept moving, and the back of the jacket tore in a large V pattern down to the vent. As I spun him around, he tried to bring the gun down on my head, but only managed to hit my shoulder.

"Is this the way you want to do it?" I said. "Fine."

I buried my hand in his belly almost far enough to grab his spine and crashed him into the side of the van.

Goddamn! It felt good.

As he doubled up, he fired the gun again, this time awfully close to my ear. The sound was like a green flash of pain, but I wasn't going to be the only one hurting. I whirled him around, grabbed a handful of his pretty hair, and rammed his face into the side of the van. "Drop the fucking gun!" I said, then said it four more times, each time punctuating the request by bouncing his face against the vehicle.

Finally, Hugo caught on and dropped the gun. I turned him around. His forehead was scraped raw, his nose was flat and squishy, like something on a rag doll, and his million-dollar smile needed a lot of Polyfilla.

"Talk," I said. "What was that number you ran on me?"

He shook his head. "I can't."

I grabbed the front of his shirt and twisted hard. "What is it? You like pain?"

He shook his head. "I can't. He told me he'd kill me if I ever said anything."

I nodded, then let go of his shirt and smoothed him down. I spoke very softly. "You know, Hugo, I understand you have some trouble determining what's really in your best interest. Let me explain it to you in a way that might help you see things clearly. Now, on one side, you've got some guy, someplace, who may or may not do something to you. And on the other side, you've got a guy right here who's really pissed at you because you've caused him a lot of trouble, not to mention the fact that you tried to put a slug in him. And this guy has already made your face look like something a buzzard might refuse. Got it so far? And if you don't start talking, like in the next two seconds, this guy"—I'd been moving closer to his face, all the while talking very quietly, then suddenly shouted—"IS GOING TO RIP YOUR FUCKING EARS OFF!" I grabbed a lobe in each hand and started to yank up.

"Okay, okay, okay!" Hugo said.

"You see, Hugo. They said you were real stupid, but I figured all you needed was to have the matter explained the right way. Now start talking."

"Okay, I'll talk, but I'm telling you, I don't know anything. I was just hired."

"To do what?"

"To play that lawyer, Prince. My part was to hire you to go down to Tijuana."

"Didn't that seem strange to you?"

"He said it was just for fun. Kind of a practical joke."

"And you believed it?"

Hugo shrugged. "I needed the money. Those women come into that place and drop a couple grand on shoes at one time, and they barely pay me enough to keep my suit pressed." He looked at the rag that was now hanging down from his wrists. "This suit was my meal ticket. What am I going to do now?"

"Give up eating. Go on."

"That's it. I needed the money. Besides, it was the first acting job I'd been offered in a couple of years, ever since I

did that damn laxative commercial. I wanted to act. . . .
He said it was just a joke!'' Hugo was starting to whine.

"It was pretty funny. I got beat up and chloroformed.''

"Oh?''

"Who's Edward Flight?''

"I don't know. I've never heard of him. Who is he?''

"He's the guy who was killed at the address you sent me
down to—with the gun you told me to bring.''

"Oh, shit.''

"Shit is right. Was that part of the deal? That I bring a
gun?''

"Yes.''

"Who hired you?''

"I don't know. Honest. He never told me his name.''

"Come on.'' I brushed a finger across an earlobe.

"Really! I just got a call a couple of days ago. The guy on
the phone said I'd be paid two and a half bills for a little
work. I never got a name.''

"A couple of days ago? When?''

"I don't know. Monday, I guess. The day before I saw
you.''

That was the day I made the appointment to see N. E.
Orlov. Interesting. They hadn't even waited until I'd been
hired. Something was strange in that, but I'd think about
it later.

"Why were you called?'' I asked.

"I don't know. He must've seen my picture in the directory. Maybe I look like this Prince. How do I know?''

"You met somebody?''

"Yeah, in one of those hooker bars off of Sunset.''

"Who'd you meet?''

"There were two guys. One was really big, but he never
said anything, just sat there, you know, like a bodyguard.
The other one did all the talking.''

"Is that the guy who called you?''

"I guess.''

"What was he like?''

Hugo shrugged. "You know those guys in the Kava
Klub? The hustlers? He was kind of like that, only not
quite so young.''

"More.''

"He was sort of short, thin. He had dark hair, a thin mustache. He was pale, very pale . . ." He paused.

"And?"

"And he was scary. Real scary."

"In what way?"

"It's hard to say. His head was real narrow, with high cheekbones and a big forehead. With his white skin, it made me think of a skull. He talked very quietly, almost a whisper, like he was forcing you to pay attention. But most of all, he had these weird eyes."

"Weird eyes?"

"Yeah. They were almost yellow, and slightly cross-eyed or something, so you were never sure if he was looking at you or not. It was really creepy."

Cross-eyed, huh? I'd heard that before. It didn't figure that there'd be more than one guy with yellow crossed eyes in this deal, so it could only be Joshua, the leader of the Sword of Truth. Another connection. The loose ends were starting to form a nice little ball of yarn.

"What did he say at your meeting?"

"What he wanted me to do. He gave me the lawyer's card and told me how I should play it. Then he gave me two fifty to give to you, and another two fifty for me."

I laughed. "No wonder you were sweating it. You were paying me out of your pocket."

"Yeah," he said sadly.

"Why'd you do it?"

Hugo shook his head. "He told me there'd be a bonus if I got you to go, and that he'd make it up to me if I had to pay you more. Which sounded okay. But then he said—talking real low so I had to lean to hear him—that if I screwed up, if I couldn't get you to take the job, I was a dead man."

"Come on!"

"Hey! You didn't see this guy. He reached down beneath the table, like to his foot, and came up with this long thin knife. He started playing with it, and smiling in this funny way. Like one of those crazies Richard Widmark always played, only this was no act. Let me tell you, I believed him."

"How were you supposed to get your bonus?"

"I was supposed to meet him at that bar at noon today."

"I gather that he didn't show."

"No. What am I going to do? He said he'd gut me like a dead fish if I ever told anyone about it. I'm scared."

"Is that why you had a gun?"

"Yeah. Since I saw that guy, I've been jumping every time I hear a noise. I should have left the money and walked away."

He should've, but he didn't. Instead, he had no money, probably no job, and a new face. What a stone loser. I guess Hugo Depina was pathetic, but somehow I couldn't work up the energy to feel much of anything for him. He had two eyes like the rest of us, and supposedly something gray and soft between his ears. So if he insisted upon wading over his head into a lake of shit, I didn't see any reason to dive in after him.

"And the worst of it," he went on, "is that I'd finally gotten a break. I was all set for a part in George Lucas's new movie. Now look at me."

I sighed. I could've told him, but I didn't think it would make any difference. This was a town where Santa Claus was alive and well and hustling tricks on Santa Monica Boulevard, and everybody was going to run into him one day. If the word ever went out that he'd been busted by Vice, this place would come to a grinding halt.

"Look at it this way," I said. "You don't look like the DynaLax Man anymore."

He brightened up. "You're right! I don't! I'm going to call my agent."

Ah, Hunter—Santa's little helper.

FIFTEEN

I took one of the canyons over the hill back to my place. As the old Checker lumbered along, I went over the last few hours. If not a hundred percent successful, the day had at least given me something to think about. There were still just shadows out there, but their edges seemed to be growing sharper, less fuzzy.

Central—and maybe dead center—was Joshua, though I doubted he called himself that these days. The letters had come from the Sword of Truth, and he'd been the leader. I still didn't see the point of the letters, but maybe they were supposed to create an atmosphere of fear, throw Natalie Orlov off balance, so she'd become more amenable to whatever he wanted. Or maybe they were supposed to be a kind of cover: say Natalie Orlov was not amenable, and something happened to her, it would—or could—be blamed on the violent, hysterical, lunatic religious outfit who had sent all those threatening letters. Except the Sword of Truth had disappeared years before, and with it the so-called Joshua. Who, according to what Strawberry Sunday had told me, seemed quite determined to stay disappeared. Maybe he was afraid of something catching up to him, or maybe he was into something else and didn't want to be connected to the Sword.

Then he turns up, looking like your basic Hollywood sharpie and nothing like a spaced-out Old Testament prophet, and hires a washed-up actor to send me down to Mexico. Where I'm supposed to be framed for murdering Edward Flight. Who was a porn dealer. And Strawberry Sunday had heard that at one time Joshua had been involved with porn. Had he been involved with Flight? There must have been something, because the guy was dead.

And then there was the real Philip Prince. Obviously, Hugo Depina's role had not been chosen at random, or because Joshua just happened to have that business card. After he heard about Flight, Prince took off like he had a firecracker up his ass. So there was a connection. But did that mean there was also a connection to Joshua? It looked like Prince was scared, and everyone said Joshua was one scary dude. Was that what had started him running?

There were still a hell of a lot of spaces, but patterns did seem to be forming. Of course, I still didn't know what this was all about, but it was starting to look awfully important. To me, it was starting to smell like money. Where, and whose, and how, and for what, I couldn't see, but as I'd told Natalie Orlov, things were definitely heating up, and I expected it to become a lot clearer pretty quickly. I just had to make sure that I made out the pattern in time to keep it from enveloping Natalie Orlov any further.

Edward Flight and Philip Prince were maybe the next line I'd follow. I knew nothing about them apart from their roles as pieces in the puzzle, but I'd make a few calls the next day to see what I could find out.

There was one call, though, I didn't have to wait for. By this point I was on Ventura, and I pulled into a gas station to use the phone booth. I didn't expect to find Prince at home, but it didn't hurt to try. I let it ring ten times. No answer. I hung up and dialed again. On the fifth ring, it was picked up, and a husky voice said, "Yeah?"

"Is Philip Prince there?"

"Wrong number," the voice said, and hung up.

I put another dime in, redialed. I let it ring a long time. Again there was no answer, but the ring had exactly the same sound as the times before, and I was pretty sure I hadn't previously misdialed.

The address I had for Prince was out in the West Valley, about twenty-five minutes from where I was. Was it worth it? Probably not, but I headed west anyway, away from the hot shower and the glass of tequila I'd been looking forward to. What dedication.

The place turned out to be a two-story, dark brown stucco apartment building. Like most Valley apartment houses, the basic design was that of a roadside motel, about thirty units built around a swimming pool the size of a bathroom sink.

Prince's apartment was on the second floor. The drapes were drawn and I couldn't see if a light was on or not. I walked by on the balcony that circled the courtyard, but couldn't hear anything either. I went back downstairs and settled myself at a metal table under an umbrella with "Cinzano" printed on it. I was mostly hidden, but I could keep my eye on the door to Prince's apartment. I figured I was wasting my time, but that wouldn't exactly be a new experience.

The only other person in the courtyard was a skinny kid of about nineteen lying by the edge of the pool. He wore baggy trunks, had long greasy hair, and a complexion like a gravel road. Every couple of minutes he stuck some kind of inhaler up his nose and went "Whoo!" Next to his head there was a giant portable tape machine playing something that sounded like the 747 Overture to the Airport Symphony. I was about thirty feet away, and it was still loud enough to make the table rattle. Shit.

I strolled over to him. "How about turning it down a little."

He looked up at me with eyes that displayed all the liveliness and intelligence of a pair of eight balls. "Nah. I like it like this."

"But there are other people here."

He looked around. "I don't see anyone. Oh—*you* don't like it. Leave."

I nodded at the wisdom of this, then knelt down to admire the machine. "Looks like a good one. It must've cost a lot."

"Nah. Got it from a friend of a friend. Didn't cost me nothing. You know—Midnight Hi-Fi." He laughed a couple of times, then took a pull on his inhaler and went "Whoo!"

I stood up, reached in my pocket, took out a dime, and handed it to him.

"What's this for?" the kid said, taking the dime and looking even stupider than before.

"Give your friend another call."

I picked up the ghetto blaster, lifted it overhead, and tossed it into the deep end of the pool. Sparks flew, and

there were a couple of stutters of static as it hit the water,
then nothing as it settled to the bottom.

The kid jumped up, his loose lips flapping silently, looking like he couldn't believe what'd just happened. He
started to snarl something, but I said, "You don't like it?
Leave," and smiled at him.

He looked at my smile. Then he looked at my hands,
which were twitching a little.

Then he left.

I went back under the umbrella. I told myself that I'd
give it until six, which would be just about an hour, then
I'd go for the shower and tequila, and the hell with it.

At a quarter to six, Prince's door opened and a guy the
shape and size of a large refrigerator came out. He was
about six-six, probably well over two fifty, and built like a
defensive lineman. In fact, the guy by himself could've
replaced the entire line of some teams. With his square
massive body, his head—neckless and with close-cropped
hair—looked like a wart on the tip of a large thumb.

He shut the door and lumbered along the balcony. He
was limping, walking on his right heel, not letting the ball
of his foot touch the ground. When I saw that, I suddenly
remembered that I'd smashed the foot of one of the goons
last night. I shook my head. After farting around so much,
maybe things were finally starting to go right.

I waited until he'd gone downstairs and out the entrance
before I got up from my chair. He hadn't noticed me, and I
didn't want him to.

From behind some bushes at the entrance to the building, I watched him get in his car, a large, late-model piece
of Detroit shit. When he pulled out, I hurried to my car and
went after him.

One problem with the Checker was that it didn't look
like every other car on the road, which could be trouble
running a tail. Still, I kept enough distance that unless he
was specifically looking for a tail—which didn't seem to be
the case, since he didn't do any fancy moves and just went
in a nice straight line—I doubted he would spot me. He got
on the freeway and headed even further west, finally turning off at the canyon that went through the hills to Malibu.
There were few places to turn off here, and I was able to
drop even further back.

He went all the way to the end, then turned left onto the Coast Highway. After just a few minutes, he pulled into the driveway of one of those junky little beachfront bungalows. If it had been anywhere else the place would have rented for about $350 a month, but since this was Malibu, the tab was closer to ten grand. That included the mountain on the other side of the road that periodically fell down on top of you, and the winter storms that occasionally ripped off the front of the house. But you got to say you lived in Malibu, and everyone knew you must be real hot shit.

I pulled over and watched the thug get out of the car and go into the house without knocking or ringing the bell. I noted down the address, then moved close enough to get the license numbers of the guy's car and the new black Mercedes that he parked next to.

There was no place convenient for me to work a stake-out, either with or without the car, so I turned around and headed back.

I figured that whoever lived in that house wasn't likely to be going anywhere too fast.

Not unless I started chasing them.

SIXTEEN

It was about 7:30 by the time I made it back to my place. After checking that Tawny wasn't hiding someplace, ready to jump out and fasten her mouth on me, I stripped down and tied a towel around my waist. I put a couple of ice cubes in a large tumbler, poured a good dose of pale amber tequila over them, squeezed a quarter of a lime, and dropped it in. The stuff smelled like fermenting hay, and the first swallow had the jolt of lighter fluid. Then it got as mellow as a sunset off Puerto Escondido, way down on the Mexican coast.

I lit up a strong French cigarette, pulled the phone over to me by the cord, and called the service. Besides some marketing research outfit curious about which body odor I found most offensive, the only message was from Natalie Orlov, two hours earlier, saying she'd wait at the office until I called her.

She answered on the first ring.

"Oh, Sam! Good! I didn't think you'd call in time."

"Are you in *your* office now?"

"What? Of course . . . Oh! . . . No, it's okay. I'm on a different phone."

"Good. In time for what?"

"It's very interesting. Late this afternoon, I got a call—no, make it that *Mister* Orlov got the call. Like I usually do until I know what it's about, I acted like Mr. Orlov's most competent and protective executive assistant."

"Right. Who was it?"

"Someone calling himself Mr. Jones. Said he wanted to discuss the purchase of certain photographs, and that he was sure I—rather, Mr. Orlov—would find his proposal very attractive."

"Oh, really? What did you say?"

"I was noncommittal, but acted like I knew what it was all about."

"Good. And you arranged a meeting for tonight?"

"Right. Between nine and ten. Actually, he proposed it. I put him on hold for a while, then told him that Mr. Orlov wouldn't be able to make it, but would send a representative—a Mr. Smith—who'd have full authority to negotiate. Did I do all right?"

"Perfect. Where's the meeting?"

"The Golden Palms on Vermont."

"Yeah, I know it. What room?"

"206."

"Okay. I'll be there."

"Do you think this is going to be it?"

"We'll see. It looks like it's going to be something."

"Will you come and tell me about it afterwards?"

"Sure, if you want. You going to be at the office?"

"No, I'll be at home."

"Okay. I'll see you later."

"Did you have any luck this afternoon? Did you find out anything?"

"Bits and pieces. I'll fill you in after I see Mr. Jones."

"Okay. Sam—be careful."

"Sure."

I hung up and tried to think of the last time someone had told me to be careful. I couldn't remember, but I had the feeling it was a dirty cop whose toes I was stepping on. This time it sounded a lot better. Not that I was likely to pay any more attention to it.

I poured some more tequila into the glass and carried it into the bathroom, where I sipped from it as a steaming shower beat on me for ten minutes. My arm had started to ache where I was hit with the pipe, but the hot water and the drink seemed to pretty well take care of it. A couple of minutes of cold water ended my shower, and I felt up for the evening.

I didn't know if I was finally going to get to meet the elusive Mr. Joshua, but whoever it was, I didn't intend to breeze in with only a smile and some spiffy chatter. After I dressed, I got a nice, comforting Police Special out of my desk and put it into the holster at the back of my belt.

Scrubbed, armed, and with a mild tequila buzz that would be gone in half an hour, I was ready—if not for action— certainly for dinner.

I decided on the Lalibela, an Ethiopian place not too far from where the meeting was set. One of the most beautiful women I'd ever seen took my order. She was tall and slender, with a profile like Nefertiti and skin like aged honey. Her eyes were the darkest brown, and her shiny black hair hung in a hundred narrow braids, each ending in a tiny blue or red bead. With every movement they rattled softly, like wooden wind chimes in a gentle breeze. When an even prettier girl brought my food, I decided that it hardly mattered if it was any good. It was worth the price just to be able to watch them move around for forty-five minutes.

The girl put down a large round platter covered with a white, spongy, pancake-like bread called *injera*. Around the platter she put down several bowls and a basket with more *injera*, this time folded.

I spooned the contents of the bowls onto the flat *injera*, which took the place of a plate. There was a big mound of *kifto*—Ethiopian tartare, raw red beef, finely chopped and blended with *berbere*, a complex mixture of extra hot paprika, cardamom, fenugreek, and about a dozen other spices. There was a stew of chicken and hard-boiled eggs in a dark red sauce, again based on *berbere;* it smelled of exotic markets and tasted hot enough to char my tongue. The third bowl contained lentils and large green roasted chiles, and the fourth was a cooling salad of chopped tomatoes, cucumber, and still more chiles.

I tore off pieces of *injera* and used them to pick up bits of meat and vegetables, then popped the small packages into my mouth. The bland, doughy *injera* provided a nice contrast to the strong, rich stews, and a couple of light, fuzzy French beers washed it all down pretty nicely. By the time I'd put away enough protein for a hungry village, the round *injera* was stained dark with the juices and sauces, and I finished off by eating what had been my plate. I would have been content to sit there for the rest of the evening, watching those glorious Ethiopian ladies glide back and forth, but after a couple of small cups of thick, bitter coffee and a couple of cigarettes, it was getting close to ten, and time to go.

In keeping with the way things are named in L.A., the Golden Palms Motel was powder-blue, without a palm in sight. Lacking the character of the hot-sheet joints on Sunset, its main feature was that every room had a view of the West Coast headquarters of an outfit that promised to raise the intelligence of its members. Considering where most of them started, it wouldn't be a hell of an achievement, but there was evidently no shortage of takers. The building, a former hospital bizarrely repainted a bilious green, now hulked over its surrounding neighborhood like an enormous malignant toad.

I went up to 206 and knocked on the door. I wasn't going to be sucker-punched two nights running, so I was ready to have the gun in my hand in about a second. The door opened a crack and someone looked out. Then the door shut, I heard the chain taken off, and it opened wider.

"Mr. Jones, I presume," I said, laughing when I saw who was there.

"Mr. Smith?" the guy said, also laughing as he stepped back to let me go in.

It was Harry Demorest, a P.I. who had an office on Olympic. It wasn't such a swell address, but it was far enough over the line to put him into the Beverly Hills phone book. That gave him a lot of work from the same folks who shopped on Rodeo Drive, and a tax bracket I'd need a ladder to reach. I'd run into him a few times, and while I knew he wasn't worth anywhere near the fees he charged, I supposed he was okay.

He was in his late forties, with drooping eyelids and a permanent two-day growth of beard. He wore dark gray slacks, an old tweed jacket, and a shirt with a button-down collar. He always kept the top button of his shirt undone, and the knot on his dark knit tie was always pulled down. He wanted to seem casual, but I knew it was all carefully calculated, a cross between East Coast prep and old B movies, just the kind of look that would make his clients feel they were getting a genuine private eye. For really big cases, he probably put on a trench coat.

I sat in one of the two chairs. The room was Basic American Motel, color-coordinated, wood-grained, and one hundred percent synthetic. A skin flick was playing on the TV.

"Nice place you got here," I said.

"Lean times, Sam. Gotta watch the old expense sheet."

"Right. You'll probably put in that you stayed at the Hilton and pocket the difference."

Demorest shrugged. "Whatever." He moved to turn off the television, then paused as a corn-fed blonde with tits like a couple of weather balloons peeled off her dress. When it cut to a guy in a rubber suit outside her bedroom window, he grunted disgustedly and pushed the button.

"What are you doing here?" he said.

"The same thing you are, I suppose. What's the deal?"

"I'll give you twenty-five grand, and you'll give me the pictures, and a guarantee that if there are copies, they won't be used, sold, or in any way distributed."

I shook my head.

"Okay. Twenty-five over whatever was paid."

I shook my head again.

"Okay, okay. Forget that expense bullshit. An even fifty, but that's as high as I go."

"Maybe that's as high as you'll go, but I suspect your client'll go a lot higher. What are you trying to do—pocket the difference again?"

Demorest sighed. "Well, there goes the profit, but maybe we can go to a hundred."

I stood up and headed for the door.

"Oh, sit down! All right. One fifty, but that's it. Now, do we deal, or do we start court action, and give all the money to the fucking lawyers?"

"I don't think your client wants that. I think your client'll go a lot higher."

Demorest shook his head resignedly. "You may be right, but I've exhausted my authority. I'll have to get back to you."

Well, I'd smelled money, and there it was. Probably a quarter of a million, maybe more. Now I only had to find out what it was for.

"Do you have the material?" Demorest said. "Are you prepared to deliver if we come to terms?"

"Yeah, sure."

"Okay. I'll talk to my client tomorrow, and give you a call."

"Who's the client?"

"Just who you obviously think it is. Who else would have that kind of dough?"

Swell. I was really making a lot of progress. I tried to figure if there was any point in continuing to play it cute, and couldn't see it.

"Look, Harry—how about filling me in a little?"

"What do you mean?"

"There's a few things I'm not clear on."

"Like?"

"Like who you're working for and what they want to buy."

"You're shitting me."

I shook my head.

"Jesus Christ! You mean you bargained up to one hundred and fifty K plus, and you don't even know what the fuck this is about?"

"In a word, yeah."

"Shit, Hunter! No wonder everybody in this town thinks you're an asshole."

"Maybe. But what does that make you? You're the guy I bargained with. The big-deal Beverly Hills P.I."

Demorest looked real pissed off, then thought for a minute, and shrugged. "Good point. What do you want to know?"

"What the story is."

"You're really working for this Orlov guy at SLEAZE?"

"Yeah."

"And you don't know about this?"

"Do I have to keep saying it? No. I was hired for something else, but it seems to be running in a different direction. Right now, it looks like we may be working on the same thing, but from different sides. So tell me who you're working for."

"The network, of course."

"What network?"

Demorest shook his head, as if he still couldn't believe it. "The NTN—the National Television Network."

"And what are these pictures that they want? The First Lady in a compromising position?"

He laughed. "What a bloodcurdling thought. Makes you shrivel right up. No, it's much bigger than that. It's Alana Lanier."

"Who?"

"Jesus, Sam! Where you been? She's all set to be the hottest thing in town. 'The Girl Next Door'? That six-week trial series that hit the top ten and that everyone's picking for the number-one show in the fall? Hell, it seems like she's on the covers of half the magazines."

"You mean the blond bimbo with the tits and the sleepy eyes?"

"Yeah, that's the one. She's going to be the new Fantasy Queen of half the men and boys in North America. If you had a nickel for every guy that was going to jerk off thinking about her, you'd be a rich man."

"Oh, shit!"

"What?"

"I just remembered something I'd heard."

It was the little mobile hooker. She'd complained that she was turning tricks in a van, while—what was her name? Alice?—while Alice had gotten away and done okay. She even said she was called Alana now. And I hadn't paid any attention to it. Goddamn. And what else? That Alice was Joshua's private property. Obviously she hadn't gotten away. Another few pieces fell into place. Jesus, Hunter! You may be slow, but you sure are clumsy.

"And SLEAZE has pictures of her?"

"That's the word. Or at least that they were trying to get them. I thought that maybe that's what you were hired for—to track them down."

I shook my head.

"And you never heard this before?"

I shook my head again.

"You know, Hunter, I think your client may be jerking you around."

The same thought had occurred to me. No, she'd said, there was nothing special in the works, nothing out of the ordinary. Shit. Natalie Orlov had more than a few questions to answer. Suddenly I was no longer looking forward to seeing her. Shit.

"I still don't see what the big deal is," I said. "Half the women in Hollywood have posed for skin pictures. Hell, some of them even do it after they become stars. When the pictures surface, maybe it's a little embarrassing, but who really cares? A youthful indiscretion, they call it. It's news for a couple of days, and then it's forgotten."

"Yeah, you're right. Except this isn't a little bare tit for an auto parts calendar. What we're talking about is pictures—it's either stills or an eight-millimeter movie, I don't know which—of Hollywood's hottest new star sucking off what could be the entire Southern Cal defensive backfield."

"Oh."

" 'Oh' is right. Little bit hard to pass that off as a youthful indiscretion. Triple X doesn't quite fit with the image of wholesome innocent sexiness that they're selling."

"You know for sure that's what these pictures are?"

"That's what I hear. And let me tell you, it's got the brass at NTN shitting in their pants. It's been a long time since they've had a number-one show."

"Which would be killed if those pictures came out?"

"No question. They'd have no choice."

I nodded. With what thirty seconds of advertising on a top show went for, 250 grand was actually a small price to pay to protect a potential gold mine. In fact, there was so much at stake that some people might think it could be worth virtually anything—and not just money—to suppress those pictures. Yeah. This had to be what was making all those shadows dance.

"This help you?" Demorest asked.

"Oh, yeah. Lots."

"You think we can deal?"

"You go talk to your people, and I'll talk to mine, and we'll get back together."

"Okay. But let's take care of this fast, or it'll take care of itself. And that'd be too bad, because we can both do pretty good out of this if we play it right."

"Maybe. I've got a few things to get straight first. . . . You ever hear of someone named Edward Flight?"

He gave me a funny look. "From what I hear, he's the s.o.b. selling the pictures."

I nodded.

"You sure you don't know about this?"

"I didn't think so. How about a guy calling himself Joshua? The Sword of Truth?"

"No. No."

"You know who this Alana Lanier is involved with? Husband? Boyfriend? Manager?"

"No idea."

"You know where she lives?"

"I think I heard somewhere in Malibu."

I nodded again. That was the answer I was hoping for. "You know the address?"

"I can probably get it for you."

"Do. Call it in to my service." I stood up, then remembered something else. "You know anything about a lawyer named Philip Prince?"

Demorest shot me another look. "I thought all this stuff was supposed to be news."

"It is."

"Then for a guy who doesn't know what's going on, you seem to say all the right names."

"Why?"

"Philip Prince is another one who's been making noise about selling the pictures."

"Oh, yeah? To the network?"

"No, to private collectors."

"What's his connection?"

"Don't know. But he's the kind who gives shysters a bad name. He mostly acts as a middleman for people with dirty habits who want to keep their hands clean. Real high-class stuff."

"Yeah. It looked that way. . . . You didn't plant a bug in the SLEAZE office by any chance, did you?"

"You found one?"

"Yeah."

"Then it wasn't mine. What's going on with all this stuff?"

"I'll let you know when I find out."

I headed for the door. I was anxious to see Natalie Orlov, and I figured that if I stayed around much longer, I was liable to give away something that I didn't even know I had.

Demorest gave me a look that said I wasn't pulling anything on him, but he didn't push it. He turned the TV back on, and gave a satisfied grunt.

The blonde was spread-eagled on the bed, and Rubbersuit was snapping his latex.

SEVENTEEN

From the motel it wasn't very far to where Natalie Orlov lived. Her place was on one of those winding streets up in the hills above Hollywood, close to the famous sign. It was small, white stucco and bright orange tile, with irregular angles and miniature turrets that made it look like it came out of a Munchkin village.

Only I wasn't in much of a mood to appreciate its charm. I was feeling really stupid, and that made me really mad. It was hardly the first time that a client had tried to play a game with me, but I hadn't figured Natalie Orlov that way. And that made me even madder.

I parked the car, stormed up the front walk, and pounded on the door. Natalie Orlov opened it part way and looked out. Before she could open it further, I pushed past her, slamming the door behind me.

She was wearing a cream-colored, nubby cotton pullover shirt, open at the neck and hanging to just above her knees, like an old-fashioned nightshirt. From the way it draped, it didn't look like she had anything on under it, but I didn't much feel like appreciating those charms either.

"Okay, lady, just what kind of number are you running on me?"

She stepped back, putting her hand up to her throat and looking real worried. Which was fine with me.

"What's the matter? What happened?"

"Come on! Cut the shit, okay? It's not going to fly."

"What—"

"Save it. You do innocent bewilderment really well, but I've already seen it. If you want to play charades, get another boy."

112

"I don't know what you're talking about. Will you come in?"

She turned and moved from the small entry hall into the living room. I had the feeling she was buying time, but I followed.

The room was compact but nicely decorated, with a couple of dark red Berber carpets on the wood floor and some good abstract collages on the wall. Sliding glass doors opened onto a cedar deck circling a small pool that was intensely turquoise under the night sky.

She sat at one end of the couch and motioned that I should join her. I scowled down at her for a bit, then sat.

"Sam, I—"

"I don't think I'm really all that interested in anything you've got to say. I sure as hell don't care about an apology. I am kind of curious what the point was, but I'll live without knowing. If you wanted me to do something, why didn't you just tell me instead of having me stumble around like I was wearing a bag on my head?"

"I still don't understand. If you'll tell me what you're upset about, maybe I can explain."

I looked at her. It sounded genuine, I guessed, but I wasn't sure anymore about my instincts where she was concerned.

"What's to explain? I found out about Alana Lanier."

"What?"

"You're still doing it? I asked you if you had anything special in the works, and you said no. What was it? Did it slip your mind that you're running a spread on the big new TV star? 'The Girl Next Door'? Shit!"

She had been leaning forward tensely, but she suddenly sank back and her expression cleared, like a light had just been turned on. "Oh! So—"

" 'Oh, so,' " I mimicked. "Yeah, that's what I'm pissed off about. Surprise, surprise. How do you expect me to do anything if you don't give me the straight story? What do you think—I enjoy looking like a jerk? You may be paying the bills, but it doesn't include that. . . . And by the way, you can probably get a good quarter mill for *not* running the pictures."

Her eyes went round.

"You see," I said, "I'm pretty fucking good even if I don't know what's going on."

"I know you are. Can I say something now, or do you want to yell at me some more?"

"Go ahead. I'll yell later."

"Before you cut me off I was going to say, 'So that's what he was talking about.' "

"What's what who was talking about?"

"Do you know who Jason Pinkham is?"

"No."

"Well, if you look at the front of SLEAZE, you'll see that it's published by Hot Pink Communications."

"Which is this Jason Pinkham?"

"Right. He owns the whole thing, or just about. I'm just a hired hand—salary plus a tiny piece of the action, and the action hasn't been that great."

"I thought you were the one running it."

"I am. I make all the decisions, I take care of all the business. This magazine is just one of a lot of things that Jason's got going. He's kind of a personal conglomerate. He likes to come up with ideas and put them in motion, then turn them over to people he trusts while he moves on. He keeps track of things, but from a distance. Every once in a while, though, he exercises his publisher's prerogative and gets directly involved with what goes into the magazine."

I nodded. I was beginning to see where this was heading. "Go on."

"Well, a couple of hours ago I got a call from him. He told me to hold onto the issue we're just getting ready to send off and to clear half the space. Then he said I should get onto the printers and quadruple the run, and tell our ad agency to start getting print and radio space for a national campaign."

"Did you ask him what was up?"

"Of course, but he wouldn't tell me, just said it was going to be the biggest thing ever for the magazine."

"Where is he? In town?"

"No. I don't know where he is. He said he'd be back soon. He has a place in town. It was a really bad line, so I think he may have been out of the country. He travels a lot."

"Has he done this before—set up something without telling you?"

"A couple of times. That's the way he works. Keeps whatever it is to himself until it's all set."

"Doesn't it bother you?"

"Sure, but it's his magazine."

"What did he have the times before?"

"Celebrity skin," Natalie Orlov said, nodding. "Somehow he'd gotten a line on someone who had pictures that were taken before whoever it was became known."

"Does that kind of stuff make a difference?"

"With the right promotion, you betcha. And the girls before were strictly minor-league. If we had a real star bare-assed . . ."

"Like Alana Lanier?"

"Like Alana Lanier. If that's what Jason's got, quadrupling the press run might not be enough. What did you find out?"

I told her about my meeting with Harry Demorest, and she listened without saying anything. She frowned when I told her about the pictures, and shook her head when I explained how much NTN was willing to pay.

"So," I finished, "when Demorest told me that SLEAZE either had or was trying to get the pictures . . ."

". . . you assumed I must know about it?"

"Yeah."

"I can see why you were so hot. Are you still?"

I shook my head.

"I'm glad."

I realized that the knot around my diaphragm was no longer there, so I guessed maybe I was too, but I didn't say it. Instead, I asked what she thought it would do if the magazine ran those pictures.

"The Girl Next Door giving head? Shit! We probably couldn't print enough copies."

"Could you run something like that?"

"We could probably find a way. . . ." Natalie Orlov looked down at the floor and her voice trailed off, then she looked up at me. "The question is, should we? I mean, I've made a big deal of only using girls who are willing to pose. Alana Lanier sure as hell isn't, not at this time, no matter what she did before. . . . No, I think it stinks."

"But you've done it before."

"I wasn't happy about it then, but it really didn't make

that much difference. The pictures weren't all that serious. They didn't hurt anybody. But this . . . This is going
to ruin her, right when she's gotten a break. It's not worth
it, no matter how much is involved."

"That's what you say. What's Jason Pinkham liable to
say?"

"Don't know. If I had to guess, I'd say he'd go by the balance sheet and the bottom line, and the hell with anything
else. It's no secret the magazine's not doing that well."

"It's not?"

"Oh, we turn a profit, but just. Not nearly big enough for
Jason. My guess is he's looking for a big score and then
will get out—either sell it or fold up."

"Meanwhile, you're up front taking the heat."

"That was always part of the deal. Besides, I'm not
alone. I hired you." She gave me a smile, and I felt a
tingling at the base of my spine.

"Will Pinkham back off if he hears you're being hassled?"

"On a deal this big? Would you? I'm not sure I would if I
were in his position."

"What's the guy like?"

"A hustler. Oh, I don't mean like a con man. He's just
always moving, hooked on action. Loves making deals,
juggling things. I met him when we were both undergradu-
ates. He was supporting himself by showing stag films to
fraternities. That was in the days before neighborhood the-
aters went hard-core. He used some of the profits from that
and teamed up with an enterprising chemistry student to
manufacture LSD. Not only did he clean up, but he got out
clean, and as far as I know, he's been legit—more or less—
ever since. Not surprisingly, after that little adventure—
with a cool half million or so in a safety deposit
box—undergraduate life seemed a bit slow, and he went
out into the world. And prospered, by all accounts. He's
been into T-shirts, and sandwich shops, and real estate,
and video games, and who knows what else. Whatever he
does, he seems to have a good sense of when to get in and
when to get out. Unlike some of us."

"How'd you get with the magazine?"

"I ran into him soon after I'd gotten my Ph.D. When I
started grad school, everyone said to go into medieval lit,

because that was the one area where there was a real
shortage, and there'd be no problem getting a position afterwards. So I thought, why not be practical for once, and
took the advice. Except I wasn't the only one getting it,
and by the time I was through, there were six hundred ap-
plicants for every opening. That's what I meant about bad
timing."

"Another triumph," I said, "for the fucking system."

"Fucking system is right. It sure fucked me. When I realized what had happened, I was so goddamn frustrated
and angry and depressed, I didn't know whether to jump
off a bridge or blow it up."

I nodded. Unless you were on top of the system, you got
buried by it. The only other choice was to not give a shit
about the system, which moved you outside it. And once
outside, you became one tough son of a bitch for the assholes to contend with.

"It was about then," Natalie Orlov continued, "that I
saw Jason. He told me some of the things he'd done since
I'd known him, and some of the things he was working on.
One of them was this magazine. He had the idea that there
were a lot of guys who found all those gorgeous women
in the other skin mags kind of depressing, since they
wouldn't ever know anyone like that. He thought there'd
be a place in the market for a magazine in which most of
the girls spreading their legs were just like the wives and
girlfriends, something obtainable, a plausible fantasy. I
rolled my eyes or something, then he said why didn't I run
it. I thought he was joking, but he wasn't. At first I dis-
missed the idea, but he kept after me, and I decided, why
not. I'd played by the book and look at all the good it had
done me. I'd had it, so what the hell. Maybe this was my
chance to score, to find a way to get out."

"The hotel in the South Pacific?"

"Yeah, except I'm not going to get there. There haven't
been enough profits, and my piece of them is too small to
amount to much."

"Until now."

"This Alana Lanier thing—if that's what this is about—
could do it. Only I don't think I can be part of it. If Jason
goes through with it, I think I might have to quit." Natalie
Orlov shrugged, raising her eyebrows.

This was a complicated lady, and I wasn't at all sure I understood her. Oh, I understood what I saw—or what she let me see, or maybe wanted me to see—but I had the feeling there was more there, and that was what I didn't know about.

I also didn't know what I'd be able to do for her. The situation seemed to be growing increasingly convoluted, layers within layers, wheels interlocking with wheels, each moving independently but also setting other wheels in motion. An elaborate piece of machinery that was rapidly picking up speed. I guessed the first thing was to see that she didn't get caught in the clockwork. Then I'd see what else I could do.

I explained to her what I'd found out, how things now looked. The connection between Alana Lanier and Joshua and the Sword of Truth. How the Sword could either be a way to threaten or a way to stay hidden. How Joshua—or whoever—had made the same mistake I'd made a little while before, had heard that SLEAZE was after the pictures and had assumed that meant Natalie Orlov. How it now looked like the guy in Tijuana was involved with the pictures, and how Philip Prince apparently had something to do with both the pictures and the dead porn broker.

Natalie Orlov shook her head. "This is all very confusing."

"Yeah, hardly anything makes any sense, but at the same time it all feels like it hangs together. I don't know—I've got the idea we're still missing the center."

She leaned forward, wrinkling her forehead and looking at the floor. "What do you mean?"

"I'm not sure I know. I'll have to see if I can find out."

"What's next?"

"If Alana Lanier's address is the same as the one I followed the bruiser to, maybe I'll pay a visit."

"To do what?"

"I don't know yet."

"Well, be careful."

This was the second time she'd said that. I looked at her, then she stood up. "This has been a hell of a day. I'm going to have a Jacuzzi. Join me if you want."

On the way to the glass doors, she pulled off her shirt and dropped it on the floor. I'd been right, she wasn't wear-

ing anything under it, and I'd also been right that there
was a good body beneath her loose clothes. She had a fairly
broad back, a very narrow waist, curving hips, and a
round, tight ass over sleekly muscular legs.

I watched her settle herself in the pool, thought a moment, then stripped down and went in. She looked up, gave
me a leisurely examination, and smiled. "I'm glad you decided to come in."

I lowered myself into the deep, bubbling, tiled basin.
The water was about ten degrees over body temperature,
shooting out in hard jets that dug into the muscles, persistently probing, battering, until everything loosened up,
smoothed out, floated to the surface and away. I closed my
eyes and drifted with it.

After a while, Natalie Orlov stood up and gracefully
dove into the pool proper. When she surfaced, she motioned to me. I stood, then dove. The water was like a mild
electric shock, startling at first, then pleasantly tingling. I
felt good. Very good.

Natalie Orlov came toward me. Her short hair was plas-
tered to her head. Her green eyes seemed very large, and
the corners of her mouth were curled in a subtle, knowing
smile. The water came halfway up her breasts, making
them float slightly, brownish-pink nipples large and round
and hard.

One more step and they grazed my rib cage. I stepped
back and put my hands beneath her breasts, feeling their
solid weight as they bobbed above my open palms. My
thumbs grazed the tips of her nipples, barely touching her.
Her body seemed to stiffen and tense and finally started to
tremble. A low moan came from deep in her throat. She
put her strong hands on my shoulders, and let her hips
float up in the water. Softly, slowly, she lowered herself
onto me and sighed. My hands brushed her hips, the curve
of her ass. She took her hands from my shoulders and
floated free, connected to me at only one point. Almost im-
mediately, she tensed and spasmed, then again, and again,
and finally a long shudder that caused her back to arch,
forcing her head back into the water and pushing her
breasts up out of it.

She floated off me, eyes cloudy and glazed. Silently, with
only a light touch, she raised my legs and lowered my

shoulders until I was floating on my back. Her mouth started moving over me, slowly, lightly at first, then more insistently. Ears, neck, chest, belly. I was suspended, lost somewhere, hanging from a spider's thread, dangling from the night sky. I strained, and then her mouth closed over me. My head dipped back. Behind me, between the trees, was a chunk of dark mountain. High up, white, illuminated, I saw a piece of the damn sign. LYWOO.

EIGHTEEN

It was about four when I left Natalie Orlov curled up and sleeping contentedly. I hadn't much wanted to go, which was probably the reason I did. Somehow, I didn't want to wake up there. Maybe that would come eventually, but not yet. She was causing strings to vibrate that had been quiet for a long time, and I wasn't at all sure I wanted them to start humming again. Fuck it. I had a few things to take care of first, then I'd see.

By the time I got up in the morning there was a message with the service from Demorest. I was expecting it, but I still grinned when I heard that Alana Lanier's Malibu address was the same as the one I'd followed the goon to. He also told me the name of Alana's husband was Dirk Primo. That sounded like something a cheap gangster would use to pick his teeth. The other sound I heard was the click of pieces falling into place.

I put some coffee on to brew, then stepped into a hard, scalding shower for five minutes. Most of the damage from Tijuana was gone, but there was just enough residual soreness to heighten my anticipation. I dried off and pulled on an old pair of gym shorts.

I found some sourdough bread in the fridge and cut off a couple of slabs. I spread a tin of chopped jalapeños on the bread, added some onions, covered the mixture with some slices of Jack cheese, and stuck it all under the broiler. When the cheese was bubbling and starting to get crusty brown, I took the stuff out and ate it along with a big chunk of pineapple as I flipped through the paper.

Beyond the usual bunch of stories about politicians competing to be the world's biggest asshole, about the only thing interesting was that there was a medical alert in effect. With the third consecutive day of below-normal pollution, a lot of people were turning up at emergency wards complaining of chest pain and difficulty breathing. Seemed their systems could no longer deal with clean air. They were assured that it was nothing serious, that the wind would soon be shifting and things would be back to normal. They were sent home with a pack of unfiltered Mexican cigarettes to tide them over. I lit up another unfiltered French cigarette and sucked in a lot of it. Adapt or die.

I was about to push myself away from the kitchen table when the back door opened and Tawny wheeled in. Besides rollerskates she had on a bathing suit that wasn't much more than two dots and a dash. She must've been on her way to a job interview to be dressed so conservatively.

"Hi," she chirped.

"Hi. Don't you ever knock?"

She shook her mane of thick hair and looked puzzled, like she couldn't imagine that she wouldn't always be welcome. Actually, looking at that luscious body, glistening with baby oil and as juicy as a bursting plum, I figured she was probably right.

I stood up and tried to sound businesslike. "What can I do for you?"

It was the wrong question. With a quick motion, she pulled off the two small circles that made up the bikini top and dropped the shred of fabric to the floor, leaving me looking at two other circles, nice and brown and puckering.

I shook my head. "I've got to go out. I meant, are you here for a reason, or is it just social?"

"I've got a message for you."

"Oh? From who?"

"Some guy was here last night looking for you."

"What guy?"

She screwed up her face like she was thinking, then looked embarrassed. "I forget. I was just the tiniest bit spacey last night. I went to write it down, but by the time I found a pencil, I couldn't remember where I put the paper, and then when I found the paper, I didn't know why I wanted it. Sorry." She looked momentarily contrite, then brightened. "I do remember that he had a dog's name."

"Huh? You mean Spot? Fido?"

"No, silly. Not like that. You know—like King, but that's not it."

"How about Prince?"

Tawny smiled. "That's it."

"What did he look like?"

"Old. Gray hair. He was real nervous. He didn't hear me come up, and when I asked him if he was looking for you, he jumped in the air. I thought he was going to have a heart attack."

"Yeah, that's Prince. Do you remember the message?"

"Yeah, that he wanted to talk to you. Said it was real important."

"Did he say where I could find him?"

She shook her head. "No. He said he'd call you today."

"That's it? Nothing else?"

"That's all. He drove off right after."

"Okay. Thanks."

Tawny looked expectantly at me for a minute, then asked, "Don't messengers usually get a tip?" She put one hand on an outthrust hip, while the other cupped a bare breast, her fingers lightly stroking the nipple. The tip of her tongue came out and circled her smiling lips.

"Yeah," I said. "Keep your wheels oiled."

"Ooh, you're no fun!" She pouted, then with only a quick thrust of her hips, she caused herself to roll across the kitchen floor and up against me. "Everything is always oiled," she said.

In her skates she was almost as tall as I was, and her round full breasts pressed into my chest, leaving two shiny circles of baby oil on my skin. Her hands went under the waistband of my shorts, fingertips delicately probing. Images of last night jumped into my head.

The hell with that.

I pulled off the tiny patch that was the bikini bottom. Everything was always oiled.

More images. The turquoise pool. The cool air. The dark sky. A touch.

Fuck it, I thought.

And did.

NINETEEN

An hour later, after another shower had washed off the sweat and the oil and Tawny's young, healthy smell, I was on the freeway heading west. I had that nice empty feeling—clean and light and nasty—that meant I was ready for anything. I wasn't necessarily looking for trouble. I just wouldn't mind if it came along.

I cruised by the Malibu house and saw that both the Mercedes and Warthead's sedan were parked in front. I went down a ways, then parked off the road. I cut through the patio of a small apartment house to get to the beach and started walking back.

In the sand in front of each house there were signs announcing that the beach was private property and that there was no trespassing. Bunch of charmers. I wondered if they thought that included the ocean as well. Shit. Given some of the guys who lived there, they probably figured they had an option on the sunset and had it contractually tied up for the next twenty years.

An overweight clown in a designer sweat suit jogged by, gasping and wheezing. The network of broken veins across his cheeks and nose glowed like something in an infrared aerial photograph. He gave me a dirty look for being on *his* sand. What a swell neighborhood.

I found the house and stood on the beach in front of it looking up. It was two-story, pale stucco with weathered wood trim. There were sliding glass doors and a small balcony on the upper floor, another set of glass doors opening onto a wooden deck on the lower. After a couple of minutes, I saw a figure looking out from an upstairs window. I couldn't see much except the general shape, which looked

to be short and slight. I waved in a friendly, familiar kind
of way, then started walking toward the deck.

By the time I reached it, the figure was downstairs behind the glass door. He was all in black, not more than
five-six and very lean, with narrow bony shoulders and
slim hips. His shirt was unbuttoned to his belly, displaying
a hairless, sunken chest and the usual Hollywood gold
chains. His pants were sharply creased and tapered down
to shiny black boots with pointy toes. His dark hair was
slicked straight back from a high forehead, and a fair-sized
gold ring dangled from one ear. His skin was so white it
had a bluish tinge, and was stretched tightly across his
cheeks and jaws, like there was no flesh between the skin
and bone. A spiffy pencil-line mustache outlined his upper
lip. I couldn't see his eyes behind the large, impenetrable
sunglasses, but I had little doubt that this was the skeleton that had scared the shit out of Hugo Depina.

He slid the glass door open about six inches, and I said,
"Hey, Josh! I hardly know you without your beard."

He stood very still for a minute, then said, "I don't know
what you're talking about." His voice was somewhere between a whisper and a hiss.

"Come on, Josh! The old sword's not that rusty, is it? It
must still have a few good cuts left in it, even though it
looks like you have reached the Promised Land."

"You've made a mistake."

"I don't think so, Josh. I mean, I can see a lot has happened, but it hasn't been that long since you were providing the cheapest blowjobs this side of Bangkok. What did
you call it? Sucking for God? Well, shit!" I gestured to the
house and the beach. "It sure looks like God started sucking for you."

With his dark glasses, I couldn't tell how he was reacting. I had the sense that his wiry body had tensed and
stiffened, but all he said was, "Who are you?"

"Come on, Josh. You can do better than that. The
name's Hunter. I ran an errand for you. I came by to give
you a receipt."

"I told you—you're making a mistake. You better get out
before you make any more."

I stared at him, then shook my head and sat in a canvas
deck chair and stretched out. "We got some stuff to talk

about. Tijuana. A guy named Flight. Another guy named Prince. Threatening letters. How you might get booted out of the Promised Land. Stuff like that."

His thin lips pulled back, revealing crooked, yellowed teeth. "It's your funeral, asshole."

He snapped his fingers and Warthead, the Human Refrigerator, came up the steps to the deck and stood over me. He was about a yard across and more than two yards high, as solid-looking as a brick wall. And probably just about as bright, judging from his face, which was kind of flattened and blurred, like he was wearing a stocking over his head. He had a long, black police billy club in his right hand, which he slapped rhythmically against his thick leg.

I started to smile. So much for not looking for trouble. I'd have to work on my technique.

Yeah. In about five minutes.

"How's the foot?" I said. "I guess the ribs must be pretty sore too."

Reflexively, Warthead touched his right side and winced. He was a real swifty, all right.

"You're pretty tough, aren't you?" I went on. "Especially when you got help. And it's dark. And you can sucker-punch someone and then chloroform him. Yeah, quite the hero."

He started breathing through his mouth, heavily, wetly, a sound like a clogged filter in a swimming pool. I glanced over at Joshua. "How do you keep the brute from drooling on the furniture?"

The small man flicked his head. "Dump this garbage."

I smiled up at Warthead. I felt very loose, but at the same time completely taut, and I had the taste of expectation in my mouth.

He moved forward, lifting the club high, then bringing it down toward my head with all his force. But he was slow and awkward, and I rolled out of the chair as he started his downward swing. I rose to my feet while he was still stumbling around from the momentum of the missed blow.

"Nice shot," I said. "If I'd been asleep, I'd be dead now."

He turned toward me, dull little eyes narrowed, mouth open, his flattened, lumpy face turning red. He took two quick steps and again tried to smash the club down on my head, but I caught his wrist in my left hand.

"No, that's not the way you do an overhead smash."

He tried to hit me with his free hand, but I caught that wrist as well.

"No, that's not any better."

His features distorted even further with anger and effort. We hung motionless for a moment, frozen, as he tried to force me down and I pushed back. He was a lot bigger and stronger than me. My hands stretched barely halfway around his enormous wrists. I knew I couldn't hold him off much longer, and I couldn't let him get the advantage.

"Which foot was it?" I said, then suddenly stopped resisting and let him push me down with all his straining power. I dropped to my left knee, which landed squarely on top of his canvas-covered foot. I heard him scream like a wounded moose, and I felt the foot flatten and spread and ooze like a broken egg as a dozen tiny bones shattered and were ground to dust. Frantically, he tried to pull back, but I continued to hold his wrists and kept my knee in place, and every attempt to escape caused more crunching sounds in his foot.

"Or was it the other one?" I said.

I released his wrists and brought my elbow down hard on his left foot, on the toes, and I heard them smash. Then quickly again, higher up on his foot, and I felt the tendons pop and tear. Then one more time, and the shoe started to turn red.

I stood up, feeling a lot better than I had for a couple of days. Things were evening up.

Warthead staggered around moaning and growling, his eyes glaring red with pain and hate and frustration.

"You see," I said pleasantly, "it's not quite so easy if you've got someone who sees you coming."

"You're dead," the big man croaked.

Somehow he threw himself at me, howling, furiously swinging the club. There was still enough force there to take my head off, but he was wild, and I was able to duck and weave out of the way. Finally, one backhanded swing left him wide open, and I came in low and threw an uppercut that just about ripped his fucking jaw off and sent blood and a mouthful of teeth spraying across the deck. He crashed through the railing, landing spread-eagled with a thud that shook the house, then lay motionless, face buried in the sand next to a No Trespassing sign.

"Don't worry about cleaning up," I said, turning back to Joshua. "High tide'll wash him away, along with all the other shit on the beach."

"And maybe you'll go with him." A large blue-black automatic was pointing at the base of my sternum. The dark glasses were pushed up to the top of his head, and for the first time I got a look at his eyes. They were closely set and just the way they'd been described, a weird color, almost yellow, and slightly crossed. I knew he must be looking at me, but it seemed like he was looking to one side or the other. It was disconcerting, and coupled with that strange color, more than a little eerie. The worst, though, was that the eyes were as cold and hard as a pair of cat's-eye marbles. No wonder he scared everybody; the eyes said that you didn't exist for him, or that you were of no more consequence than a bug walking across his table. I felt a drop of sweat run between my shoulder blades and down my spine.

"I don't think that would be a swell idea," I said.

He laughed briefly, with about as much warmth as his eyes displayed. "No, I guess you wouldn't. It looks okay from my side, though. You're in my house. I'm just defending my property against an intruder who's already shown how violent and dangerous he is. I think it'll play."

I shrugged. "Maybe. But do you want that kind of attention? Especially now. I know this is a town that thinks there's no such thing as bad publicity, but unless you're a rock 'n' roller who self-destructs, death usually isn't regarded as prime PR material."

"I can handle it." He laughed again. "Better than you. How does it feel, asshole? To know that I hold your life in my hands?" His finger pulled the trigger back a ways, and he gave me a twisted smile.

"Maybe it's mutual. You don't know who I've told what about you."

"You don't know shit."

"Then pull the fucking trigger and get it over with!"

Still smiling, he took two steps forward. The gun was steady, and his eyes seemed to be on my face. "So long, sucker."

I forced myself not to look at the gun. Since I couldn't hold his eyes, I focused on a spot between them. I don't think I even flinched when the hammer clicked on an empty chamber.

I doubt that I would have been so cool if I hadn't heard about the little power games he'd liked to play with his followers in the Sword. I figured that was what he was doing this time, and acted accordingly. Besides, if he'd really planned to shoot me, there wasn't much I could've done anyway.

"Most people scream or faint or drop a load in their pants when I do that."

With his controlled, whispered voice, I couldn't tell if he was disappointed. I didn't answer, though, just kept staring between his eyes.

"Most people would be used for bait on the pier after Ernie got through with them."

"He was slow and clumsy. Maybe he could muscle little girls or old people, but that's about it."

He looked at me some more, but I still couldn't read what he was thinking. "You said you wanted to talk," he finally said.

"Yeah."

He pushed the sunglasses back down to his nose. I heard the safety on the gun click. "Come on," he said, and went into the house.

The living room was small and not very well furnished, filled with the kind of mismatched, slightly worn stuff that you find in rented places. Old newspapers and magazines were scattered around, some dirty plates and glasses, beer cans and bags from fast-food joints, overflowing ashtrays. It didn't look like the kind of place Hollywood's newest star would have, but maybe they wanted to feel like they were holed up in a fleabag motel. About the only things that didn't fit with this were the expensive portable video recorder and camera that were on the floor in the corner, but video junk had become as much a Hollywood essential as the vial of coke on the mantel or the box of poppers in the fridge.

Joshua sat down on a bamboo-frame couch, crossing his skinny legs and stretching his arms across the back. I sat in a small, uncomfortable armchair, the cheap kind that you find in insurance-company waiting rooms. The gun sat on the coffee table between us, hardly seeming out of place.

"So? Talk," he said.

"Okay. I know you're the guy who used to dress up like an extra in a bad epic and call himself Joshua."

"The name's Primo. Dirk Primo. Never heard of Joshua."

"You were the leader of a ragged bunch of losers that was called the Sword of Truth. You liked to make like it was a religion, but it was really an excuse to peddle the services of a lot of pathetic little runaways who were either too stupid or too doped or too scared to get out."

"Never heard of it."

"Before becoming a prophet-slash-pimp, you were a two-bit hustler, a bullshit preacher, a scuffler after an easy buck. You ran small-time cons, and maybe did some hard-core skin."

"Quite a colorful bio. Too bad it's not mine."

"Look, pal, why don't I just take your denials as given? Save us both some time."

He tilted his head back and yawned, like he was real bored with all of this, and I stared into his dark sunglasses. Usually I'd want to see the eyes to find out how I was doing, but this was one guy I was just as glad not to.

"Okay," I went on, "you or one or your buddies have been sending cheerful little notes to Natalie Orlov, promising all kinds of ugly things'd happen to her unless she changed her ways. I don't know what the point is, unless it's to provide you with a cover. Which—as you see—it's not doing very well. Then you had a bug put in her office. Then—"

"You're crazy!"

"Then you hired a turkey named Hugo Depina to pose as another turkey named Philip Prince, and you got me down to Tijuana. Where I arrived just in time to get set up for the murder of a piece of scum named Edward Flight. Who has something to do with the pictures of Alana or Alice or whatever it is you call her. Everything seems to have something to do with those pictures, and it's starting to look like half the guys in this town are trying to either buy or sell them."

"Is that it?"

"Just about. The real Philip Prince—one of the guys trying to sell the stuff—is running scared. Probably with good reason, since I saw your boy coming out of his apartment yesterday. My guess is he was waiting for him, but Prince never showed. I know a lot's at stake, but you're getting awfully sloppy."

"You through?"

"Yeah, for now."

"Interesting story," he said in his low voice, his lips forming a sneer. "Too bad it's all bullshit. Too bad you can't prove it."

"Oh, I can prove some of it. Enough to get people asking questions, looking around real hard. Enough to generate noise and heat, and I don't think you need either of them right now. The big boys at the network like things quiet and cool. If things don't get that way pretty fast, they may just decide the hell with it, even if the pictures never turn up."

Joshua nodded, sneering again. "Okay, so that's it. What do you want? A grand? Two? All this shit ain't worth much more."

I shook my head. "The guys at NTN don't quite agree, but I'm not here for money. I'm here to give you a message. Lay off of Natalie Orlov. She's got nothing to do with this. She doesn't have the pictures, she's not trying to get the pictures, she wants nothing to do with the pictures. Until last night, she'd never heard of them. You're putting pressure on the wrong person, and I'm here to see that you stop. I don't give a shit about Flight or Prince or anything else you might do. I don't care about your problems, or how you deal with them. Ice as much of that slime as you want. But if you make them Natalie Orlov's problems, then they become my problems, and then *you'll* really have problems. Understand?"

He sat motionless on the couch, dark glasses pointing toward me like the bulging blank eyes of some predatory insect. Then he turned his head slightly, gestured with a hand, and said, "Come here, honey."

I turned around. On the stairs behind me was the object of all the frantic activity. Alana Lanier wore a short silk Japanese robe, tied around the waist and barely reaching the middle of her thighs. Her body, revealed by the cling-

ing fabric, was soft and firm and full, lusher than the or-
chids painted on the silk. She had thick, touseled blond
hair, creamy pale skin, and turquoise eyes beneath sleepy-
looking lids. Even at a distance you know she smelled
warm, like she'd just gotten out of a sun-soaked bed, and
she exuded an unconscious sensuality that said she was
ready to get back in it at a second's notice. If even a frac-
tion of that got captured by the camera, it was no wonder
everyone was so hot and bothered.

She came down the stairs and stood next to Primo. He
pulled on her arm and she sat on the arm of the couch. She
seemed to be staring over my shoulder, her expression
blank and unchanging, and I thought that maybe she was
tranked up to her softly curving eyebrows.

"She's really something, isn't she?" Primo said. The
back of his hand brushed her smooth cheek, then continued down to her graceful neck and across her collarbone.
Slowly his hand moved lower and pushed aside the robe,
revealing a heavy, milky breast with a large pale pink nipple. Alana didn't react, just continued to stare off into
space.

"Look at that," he said, lifting her breast in his palm.
"Before much longer, every guy in the country is going to
cream thinking about these tits. And they're mine." He
squeezed her breast hard, pinching the tip of the nipple between his thumb and forefinger, but still she didn't react.

Primo removed his hand, then leaned forward, lifting
his glasses. "This is your lucky day, pal. Not only did I decide not to waste you, but I'm going to give you what every
other guy can only dream about. You're right—I want to
keep things cool. I think this'll make us square." He put a
hand on her back and pushed, and she stood up. "Go on.
Show him where your real talent lies."

Alana looked down at him, then started for the stairs.

Primo looked at me with a cold smile and those dead yellow eyes. "Go on. Don't be a jerk. Get lucky." He leaned
forward, took the gun from the table, laid it on his lap, and
continued to stare.

I had to deal pretty regularly with a lot of creeps and assholes, but that guy was a whole new species. I didn't figure
there was blood inside him, just some green viscous slime.
My inclination was to rip his fucking head off and watch it

ooze out, but I stood and followed Alana Lanier up the
stairs. I figured I should see how this thing played out.

We went into a bedroom that was about as messy as the
downstairs part of the house. She went over and shut the
door, then stood in front of me. She pulled the sash around
her waist and the robe fell open. She let it slide from her
shoulders and down her arms to the floor.

Her body was just on the edge of ripeness, almost too
heavy, too bountiful, like grapevines at the end of summer,
threatening to sag with the delicious weight of the fruit.
The breasts demanded to be squeezed, the belly stroked,
the hips caressed, the soft inner thighs gently bitten. It
was the kind of body that in a few years would cross the
edge, would thicken and spread and yield too easily, but
right now it was a fantasy, a promise of impossible pleasure. Except that her expression—dull, resigned, indiffer-
ent—showed no animation, no sense of pleasure, no more
presence than a rubber doll.

She knelt before me. Her eyes looked straight ahead as her
fingers went to my waistband, working to open my belt.

I caught her wrists in my hands and pulled her hands off
of me. I lifted up and raised her to her feet. For an instant,
puzzlement or confusion replaced the vacant expression in
her eyes. She tried to drop to her knees again, but I held
her wrists and squeezed hard enough to make her wince
and struggle to get free.

"You don't want me?" she said.

"Sorry. Not like this."

"But I have to."

"Why?"

"Because he told me to."

"You do everything he says?"

She looked at me, then turned her head away and
nodded once.

"Why?"

She continued to look away. I put my hand around her
jaw and turned her head back until she was again looking
at me. "Why?"

She smiled sadly and shook her head, as though it was a
real dumb question.

"You don't have to anymore," I said. "Don't you know—

you're a real hot property now. You can do what you want, not what he tells you to do."

She gave me that same smile. "You don't understand."

"Sure I do. You're scared. Well, you don't have to be. Put your clothes on, and I'll take you out of here. You can go for good. You can do what you want. You're a goddamn star."

For a second, there was life in her eyes, and I thought she was going to do it. Then it faded, and she shook her head. "I can't leave."

"You like being humiliated? You get off on being treated worse than a five-dollar whore? Shit! Your picture is on magazine covers, for chrissake!"

"I can't. I can't."

"So you say. Why not?"

Her eyes held mine, then she said, very matter-of-factly, "He'll kill me."

I started to tell her she was being stupid, then decided that maybe I wasn't so sure. I got a card out of my wallet and put it in her hand.

"Keep this someplace. If you decide you want to walk, give me a call and I'll get you out of here. Then we'll decide how to keep you safe. Think about it. You don't need to take this shit anymore."

Her eyes were no longer lifeless. They were just impossibly sad. I watched as a tear formed and rolled down her cheek. So much for my pep talk. I caught the tear with my thumb. Her skin was very smooth.

When I went out the door, she was still standing—naked, shoulders slumped—in the center of the room. The latest goddess in a town that only worshiped the bottom line.

Primo was at the foot of the stairs, holding his pistol against his chest like a security blanket. He gave me an ugly, leering smile. "How about that, huh? She really plays that old instrument, don't she? Bet you never felt anything like that. I guess that makes us even. Right, pal?" He waved the gun at me.

I grabbed the hand that held the gun and shoved the end of the barrel hard into his throat. I raised his sunglasses and put my face close to his.

"Just remember what I said, asshole. Any more trouble from you and I'll be back and make you eat your own fucking liver, piece by piece. In fact, I hope you give me a reason to come back."

I yanked the gun from his fingers and hurled it toward the opening in the glass doors. I missed, and a four-by-seven sheet of glass shattered, sending shards dropping to the outside deck with a nice tinkling sound.

"That's better," I said. "We needed some air in here."

TWENTY

Despite the sign that clearly stated that there was no trespassing, flies were starting to settle on Warthead's bloody skull. I looked back at the beach house, expecting to see that it too was black with flies or crawling with pasty maggots. But I guessed that was just the way it smelled.

I took off my shoes and socks, rolled up my pants, and started to run on the firm sand just above the waterline. I ran for about half a mile, pulling in salt air in an attempt to clear my mouth of a foul taste, trying to loosen the tight muscles that had wanted to twist Primo's scrawny neck until it snapped, cracking it like the carapace of a giant roach under my heel.

Goddamn! I routinely saw a lot of shit, but the setup I'd just left was something else. There were so many assholes in this town throwing their weight around, playing power games, that usually it barely registered, but that son of a bitch . . .

Finally I stopped running and bent over, putting my hands on my knees, taking in slow, deep breaths until my heart stopped pounding.

I walked back to my car and got in. I found a pay phone and called the service. Harry Demorest wanted me to call him at his office. Natalie Orlov had called and left a message that the operator was too embarrassed to repeat, but that she said she intended to try out with her boyfriend that night. I wished her luck.

I looked up Demorest's number in the Yellow Pages. His ad promised prompt reliable results, and assured his fancy clients that "Discretion is our middle name." Funny, I'd had the idea it was Franklin.

"Okay, Sam," he said. "I had a talk with Ogden Winters

136

this morning. That's the V.P. that I deal with at the network. You were right. They're prepared to go higher, but they want the principals to negotiate. So why don't you have this guy Orlov give him a call."

"I'll pass the message along, but you should know that Orlov doesn't have anything to do with it."

"What? I thought you said—"

"There was some confusion last night. It seems to be getting clearer." I explained what Natalie Orlov had told me.

"So it's Pinkham who's got the pictures?"

"Right. You know him?"

"I know of him. A real speedster. But it sounds like he hasn't gotten the merchandise yet."

"Maybe not, but from what he said, it seems like he's close."

"Close is no cigar, Sam. I think maybe I should give the man a call."

"He might be out of the country."

"The network can find him."

"Let me know if you come up with anything. Pinkham's the mover, but Orlov's taking the heat, and my job's to make sure it doesn't get too hot."

"What's up? You sound like you actually care."

I sneered at the receiver, then said, "Keep me posted, huh?" and hung up.

I called SLEAZE. It took Natalie Orlov about a minute to get to the next office, where there was a clean phone.

"Look, lady, you've got to stop leaving messages like that," I said. "It makes the operators crazy. Not to mention that it'll ruin my reputation."

She laughed. "Are you kidding? I think I just made your reputation."

"Thanks a whole lot."

She laughed again. "Don't mention it. . . . You know, I was sorry to find you'd gone this morning."

"Yeah, well, I had to get an early start. Don't take it personally."

There was a long pause. "Okay, I won't." Another pause. "Sorry. That came out all wrong. It sounded clingy and whining and self-pitying and guilt-inspiring—all the things I never want to be. I *was* sorry you weren't there

this morning, but I think it was mainly selfish. It's okay
. . . really."

I had the feeling that it was okay, that she understood,
even if I wasn't quite sure that I did. Or maybe *that* was
what she understood. Oh, shit. Who cared? Fuck introspec-
tion.

"Did you go to Malibu?"

"Yeah. Still there," I said, and gave her a very brief account of my visit. I told her there was no doubt that Dirk
Primo and Joshua were the same person. I said that while
he didn't admit anything, I was equally sure that he was
the two-bit Machiavelli behind all the confusion.

"I explained to him that you don't have anything to do
with his problems, and told him that we'd both appreciate
it if he stopped bothering you."

"Is that what you said?"

"Maybe I phrased it differently."

"I can imagine. What did he say?"

"Not much, but I think he got the message."

"Was there trouble?"

"No, it was easy. The hardest thing was not tearing his
fucking head off. Which I still want to do, by the way."

"So that's that?"

"I guess. We'll see. This guy is really a weasel—vicious,
but I don't think very bright. He's so used to having people
lie down in front of him I don't know how he'll take someone calling him on it. Even if it's in his own interest to let
it slide. At least he now knows you're not involved. And so
does Demorest, by the way. I just talked to him. Seems the
network will go higher than one fifty, but they want to negotiate direct. So I told him it was Pinkham they want to
talk to, and Demorest said he would try to get in touch."

There was a long delay before Natalie Orlov said, "Are
you sure that was a good idea?"

"What can it hurt? This whole situation came about because everyone thought you were the one after the pictures. I figure the more people who know you're not, the
better."

Another delay. "Maybe . . ."

"What's the problem?"

"Oh, nothing, I suppose. It's just that part of the deal is

that I'm the one in front. Jason's strictly behind the scenes."

"Except that this time he's hardly staying in the background, so that should cancel your responsibility. I always figure that Rule One is to not be more concerned about someone than they are about you. Besides, maybe this whole thing can get taken care of without your having to have a confrontation. Principles are fine, I guess, but they can fuck you up. Or so I've heard. Personally, I wouldn't know."

She laughed. "I'm not so sure about that." I didn't say anything, and she laughed again, a really nice sound. "Okay, have it your way. . . . Is it over now? Are we at the end?"

"It looks like it should be . . ."

"But?"

"But I'm not quite convinced. There are a hell of a lot of loose ends still dragging around. And . . ."

"What?"

"I don't know. Like I said last night, somehow I have the feeling I'm still missing the center, that I'm still just seeing the shadows. But my instincts haven't exactly been in sync so far, so it's probably all bullshit. It'll pass."

"Would a Jacuzzi help?" I could almost hear the smile, half a deliberate leer, the other half a genuine grin brought about by the leer. "Tonight?"

Yes? No? Maybe?

Fuck it.

"Sure," I said.

TWENTY-ONE

I gave a call to one of the loose ends. There was no answer at Prince's office. I put the dime back in and tried his apartment. It hadn't even finished the first ring when it was picked up and a voice said, "Yeah?"

"Prince?"

"Who's this?"

"Who's this?"

Neither of us said anything for a minute, then I hung up.

Prince was getting so many visitors these days, he should start to charge rent.

At least I knew it wasn't Warthead. And since I couldn't think of anything better to do, I decided to see if I could find out who it was.

About a block away from his apartment building I began to get a pretty good idea. There was an ambulance, four or five black-and-whites, and what I took to be two detective's unmarked cars. It didn't take a hell of a big leap to figure that Philip Prince was the center of attention . . . and probably not the picture of health.

I cruised slowly by, but didn't see anything except the usual clusters of yokels who gather at things like this, exchanging lies and meaningless speculation. There was nothing like a little police action to make a neighborhood come together. And nothing like the cops starting to ask the spectators questions to send them all scurrying back indoors again to peek out from behind their curtains.

I went down about a block and parked in front of a fire hydrant. There were so many cops around, there was no way I was ever going to get a ticket. No one wanted to do stuff like that, and each would leave it for someone else to

take care of. There are few things more reliable than the
fundamental laziness of the police.

I strolled back through the milling crowd, but didn't
pick up anything worth hearing. At the front of the building the two ambulance attendants were leaning against
their vehicle, smoking cigarettes and looking at the latest
issue of SLEAZE. They bent close to examine the pictures,
poking each other in the ribs and making sounds like agi-
tated chimpanzees. Two more loyal readers.

The tiny courtyard of the apartment house was filled
with more people, all looking up at the second floor. The
door to Prince's apartment was open, and lots of uniformed
cops were standing outside on the balcony, trying hard to
look like they had something to do. They didn't make it.

I waited a couple of minutes, but nothing happened.
What the hell? I went up the stairs to the second floor.

Just as two of the cops moved to block my path, a guy
came out of Prince's door. He wore a wrinkled brown suit
whose lapels were more than a few years out of style, and a
wide, stained tie of the same vintage. He was short and
sort of square, with the thick shoulders and chest of a
boxer, the kind who's willing to take a little punishment in
order to get inside and dish out even more. His lip was
curled in a permanent expression of bored disgust, but his
eyes made it clear that this was not a guy you'd want to
pull a fast one on. You might think you could waltz by him,
but he'd stay after you, nipping at your heels until you
pulled you down. Then he'd get your throat.

He looked up, spotted me, and winced. "Oh, shit!" he
said, and came over. "I got about four hours too little sleep
last night, my wife's giving me grief this morning about I
don't know what, my car had a fucking flat tire, and I'm
constipated like I been eating cement. And now you show
up, Hunter. This really must be my day."

"Nice to see you too, Burroughs." I'd been involved with
him once before. He was tough and nasty and a son of a
bitch. I didn't like him, but he was straight, very straight,
very out front. He didn't exactly care for me either, but he
didn't push it, and in the past he'd been willing to give me
some room. I'd also had the feeling he hoped I'd screw up so
he could come down hard.

"What are you doing out here?" I said. "This isn't your division."

"I got tired of dealing with guys like you, so when a Homicide opening came up in West Valley, I transferred." He scowled at me. "Fuck of a lot of good it did. You know, my horoscope said I'd run into someone from the past. I was kind of hoping for someone I liked, like the Sunset Strangler, or maybe that junior sadist who got off on running down old ladies with his motorcycle."

"Sorry to disappoint you."

"Hunter, you'll never disappoint me." He gave me a nasty little smile. "Now it's my turn. What are *you* doing out here? I don't suppose you felt compelled to return to the scene of the crime, did you? Want to confess?"

I shook my head. "Prince owed me money for a job I did for him. He's been putting me off for a long time. I came by to see if I could collect."

Burroughs nodded, and gave me a look that made it clear that he'd buy that line right after he saw a flock of winged pigs flying overhead. But he didn't say anything.

"You said you were now in Homicide. Does that mean I'm not likely to be collecting from Prince?"

Burroughs shrugged. "Come on."

I followed him into the apartment. A couple of guys were looking for fingerprints in the living room. We went through to the small bedroom just as a flash went off.

"All through," the cameraman said, and went out.

The double bed took up most of the room. In the center of the bed, stretched out and tied around the wrists and ankles to the bedposts, was the body of a thin young man. He was naked, his chest, belly, and thighs covered with dozens of short, shallow cuts. The streaks of dried blood looked very dark against skin that was the kind of phosphorescent white that corpses get after they've been sitting for a fair amount of time. The smell in the room was already pretty strong, and Burroughs went over to open the window.

I walked to the head of the bed. The guy had long, dirty blond hair. With his face swollen, blue-black and sickly pink from a severe beating, it was difficult to know what he'd looked like in life, but I was pretty sure I'd never seen him. He had a skull and crossbones tattooed on his left forearm. There was a small oval of crusted blood, nearly

black against the pale skin, around the carving knife that
had been buried in his chest up to the handle.

"Well?" Burroughs said.

I shook my head. "Never seen him. Who is he?"

Burroughs looked hard at me. "You really don't know,
do you?"

"Should I?"

He shook his head, then pointed to a pair of faded jeans
on the floor in the corner. There was a wallet sitting on top.
"The I.D. says his name's Victor James."

"Means nothing."

"He wasn't much. Beach bum. Hung around the piers—
Santa Monica, Malibu. Was picked up a couple of times.
Vag, trespassing. Breaking and entering once, possession
once. We think he probably dealt a little."

"Doesn't sound like he'll be missed."

"Probably not."

"Who tipped you?"

"We got a call. Anonymous. Said there were sounds of a
fight, screams."

"You guys didn't break any records responding."

Burroughs gave me a disgusted look. "Very funny. The
call came in"—he looked at his watch—"about ninety minutes ago."

I nodded.

"Yeah," Burroughs said. "Someone gave us a hand. The
estimate is that he was killed yesterday, probably late afternoon, early evening."

I nodded again, keeping my face blank. That didn't come
as a big surprise. Warthead's handiwork was starting to
look familiar, as was the delicate touch of his boss. It was
the Tijuana setup all over again, only this time with
Prince as the stooge.

Burroughs looked at me, then at the body, then back at
me. He didn't look happy, but I doubted that the son of a
bitch ever did. I followed him out of the room, out of the
apartment, and down the stairs. He told the ambulance attendants that they could pick up the meat and continued
on to his car.

"I don't suppose you have anything to tell me?" he said.

"What could I know?"

"Like where Prince is? Like why the guy was in the

apartment? Like why the guy was killed? You know, stuff like that—the kind of stuff that can help the police in their investigation."

"Sorry."

"Right. But you will tell us if you happen to hear of anything?"

"Oh, sure."

" 'Oh, sure.' Why don't I believe you, Hunter?"

I shrugged. "I don't know, Burroughs. Maybe you just don't have a trusting nature."

"Maybe not. Or maybe I just don't like it when you show up around dead bodies."

I looked at him, then gave him a nice friendly smile.

He gave me a disgusted look. "You just better watch your ass," he warned.

I shrugged. So much for friendly.

TWENTY-TWO

The San Diego Freeway had its usual midday traffic jam, cars bumper-to-bumper for no particular reason. Shit. This was a city built for the automobile, but it seemed that traffic jams were now perpetual, unending. Another triumph for the goddamn planners, success to the point of failure. There was no longer a rush hour here, only times when the traffic moved and times when it didn't. At least this was one of the first kind, and I was going along at a nice steady fifteen miles an hour up the hill.

I had plenty of time to examine the RV in the lane next to me. It was longer than a school bus, a double-decker with probably more floor space than my entire house. It had Nebraska plates and was covered with decals from every roadside tourist trap west of the Mississippi. Three kids were hanging out the upper windows, shrieking their heads off, wired to the gills on Cokes and Twinkies. The little woman, a honey in a pink housecoat and turquoise hair curlers, was hanging laundry out on the back porch. I pulled ahead and saw that the guy driving was hunched over the wheel, bug-eyed and completely tense. Ah, that was freedom, all right—dragging a whole fucking motel around on your back.

At the top of the hill, traffic thinned and I coasted down to Sunset. Ten minutes later I went through the gates of the elegant old hotel where, from the line of sleek black cars stretching far down the curving road, it looked like they were having a convention of limo drivers. I pulled into a space between two of the boats. All down the line, guys in neat little mustaches and nifty pearl-gray uniforms gave me dirty looks, like they thought rust was contagious.

145

The hotel gardens were being tended by a multinational force of illegal aliens—Asians, Latinos, and West Indians from at least six different countries. I started across a carpet of lawn and they all froze, studying me with some concern. When they decided I was not Immigration, they went back to work. Since they were the ones who kept the place running, they probably didn't have much to worry about. On the other hand, fear kept them cheap and docile, so maybe they did. But they were happy, because they'd escaped from being exploited.

I reached the large pink stucco bungalow that for thirty years had been the nerve center of Cora Cardiff's empire of gossip and innuendo. She was the last of the great Hollywood columnists. Maybe she was no longer able to make or break a career, but there was very little that went on that she didn't know about, so she still had a fair amount of power. And a lot of readers.

She was a leathery old lizard, as juicy as a piece of beef jerky and just about as tough. She only left her room—known as the Lavender Lair—twice a year for plastic surgery. She'd long ago run out of parts to be pulled or scraped or inflated, and she was now on her second or third total overhaul. Except when dealing with muscular young women, she displayed all the warmth and friendliness of an ice pick in the eye. I'd known her for a long time, and she seemed to like me. Which was probably not a hell of a character reference.

I went in the front door into the living room, where half a dozen hard-looking young women were sitting at desks talking on telephones and taking notes in steno books.

"Okay, let me get this straight," I heard one of them say. "Hot coffee was poured on her head. Then she kicked the guy who did it in the balls. . . . Oh, she kicked somebody else and it was in the face. Why?. . . I see. Now who had the gun?. . . Right. So she wasn't threatened directly, was she?. . . Look—I don't care if she and her hairstylist are suing for two million. If we can't put some sex in it, the story won't fly. . . . Okay. If you can get confirmation that she likes to have that done to her, then maybe we can do business. . . . Right. You too. Have a nice day."

I went on through to Cora Cardiff's bedroom, then stopped in my tracks. Everything was different. Or rather everything was a different color. Where there had been various shades of purple, the quilted satin walls, the plush carpet, the silk hangings were now a bright, iridescent green. Neon lime.

But the occupant had not changed. There was a rasping laugh, followed by a shout of "Dear boy!"

Cora Cardiff gestured that I should come over to the enormous bed in which she was sitting, wearing an emerald negligee that hung loosely on her scrawny body, and propped up among grass-colored cushions.

"You redecorated," I said.

"Yes. I was feeling the need of a change. Purple seemed—I don't know—awfully last year, don't you think? I wanted something more *courant*. So the last time I went down to Antigua to have my tits tightened, I told them 'kiwi fruit.' What do you think?"

"Are you talking about your tits or the room?"

"Dear boy!" she croaked, then laughed again. "You really know how to charm a girl. That's probably why I'm so fond of you." She patted the bed with a scaly brown claw. "Sit down."

I sat, but far enough away that she couldn't conveniently make a grab for my kiwi fruit.

"One day, dear boy!" she said, smiling and nodding. "One day we will have our moment." Then briskly, "In the meantime, I assume you want information. Go ahead. What can old Cora tell you?"

"I'm not exactly sure what I want. What do you know about Alana Lanier?"

"Ah, The Girl Next Door. I know a little. Though I guess I should find out more, since that's the name on everyone's lips these days." She paused. "And, from what I've heard, nearly everyone has been on her lips at one time or another."

"Go on."

Cora shrugged her bony shoulders. "I'm certainly not judging the girl. This town has never treated attractive young women very well. There are far too many of them, so their price is very cheap. It doesn't even take hope to buy them anymore, just the possibility of hope. 'You come to the party and maybe you'll meet someone who can do you some good.' So they go to the party, and they spend most of

the time on their knees in a cabana providing the one service the caterer doesn't take care of. There's no question
they do some good, but aside from small protein supple-
ments to their diets, I'm not sure what good they get. Still,
the next night there's another invitation, and so on and so
on. In case you hadn't noticed, dear boy, sometimes this is
not a very nice town."

"And that's what Alana Lanier did?"

"Actually, I gather it wasn't even that nice."

"What do you mean?"

"I mean that most of the girls are at least semi-willing
participants in the game. They buy the line, or they kid
themselves into believing it. But apparently Alana was
only there because her boyfriend or husband—what does
he call himself?"

"Dirk Primo."

"Right. Can you believe it? Honestly, some people! Anyway, she was there because dear Dirk made her. She was
his ticket into the parties, the way he got close to all the
fancy people who otherwise wouldn't have let him park
their cars. There used to be a word for people who did
that."

"You mean pimp?"

"That's the one. Now they're called executive assis-
tants." Cora gave a rasping laugh. "I must remember that
for my column."

"So what happened? Someone liked her technique and
put her into prime-time? Come on. The most the casting
couch ever got anyone was a bit part, not her own show."

"Don't be too sure. You'd be surprised at the number of
decisions that are made because of what goes on beneath
the boardroom table. Did I ever tell you about the five-
million-dollar fuck? But no, you'll have to wait for my book
for that one. . . . Anyway, you're probably right. What I
suspect happened was that someone finally looked under
the table to see who was there, and that was all it took. But
you should go talk to Abel Youngman. I hear he's behind
'The Girl Next Door.' You know him?"

"I know of him."

The name probably wouldn't mean very much outside of
this town, but he was quickly becoming one of the big pow-
ers in the business, a deal-maker. He rarely got listed on

the credits, but he was the man who got things going, and who always got himself a nice chunk of the action in return.

"As I said," Cora Cardiff went on, "that could've been enough. Alana Lanier's not my type—a bit too soft—but I can still see that she is extraordinary. The camera doesn't just love her, as they say, it adores her, it caresses her, it positively drools over her. Whatever it was that poor Marilyn conveyed, Alana conveys. In spades. At some point I suppose she may have to act, but for now she just has to *be.*"

I shook my head. "Maybe, but I would have thought that her . . . uh . . . previous career would've made people at NTN awfully nervous."

"Oh, they're cautious people, all right, but these days the hint of a scandalous past doesn't necessarily do any harm. It could even help."

"What if it's more than a hint?"

"You mean a tabloid running an article like 'My Three-Minute Romance with Alana Lanier?' It'll boost ratings by five points."

"No. I mean proof. Pictures. Movies. Real hard-core."

Cora Cardiff looked surprised, a very rare reaction for her. "Surely not."

"There are a lot of people running around right now who think so."

"Tell me."

I gave her a very brief, very edited version, telling her about Demorest, the network, and Pinkham, but omitting Natalie Orlov and the bodies.

She shook her head. "Interesting. I would've thought the network would have been more careful. Maybe not." She paused, then shook her head. "No. I still think that it'll turn out that everyone's chasing a shadow, that it'll just be a nasty rumor. Even so, it is something I should look into. Thank you, dear boy." She made a halfhearted grab at my crotch, but I moved out of the way.

"You going to use it?"

Cora Cardiff thought a minute, pursing her thin lips and looking more than ever like a dried fig. "I doubt it. Alana would be the only real victim, and I think she'd been through enough, don't you? I do like her story, though.

Dirk Primo runs her like a cheap whore, thinking that he's going to hustle up some big-time action for himself in Glitter Gulch, and then she's the one who scores. It's nice—a Hollywood version of virtue rewarded."

"Yeah, right. Except that asshole still treats her like a piece of meat. And who the hell do you think is raking it in?"

Cora gave me a dry smile. "First, there isn't that much to it right now. There's the prospect of a great deal, but that's only *if* things work out. So far it's just a little bit of gold dust, not the mother lode. Second, there may in fact be justice after all."

"What do you mean?"

"You don't know? Well, it seems—and I just love this— that the network wouldn't deal with good old Dirk. I mean, would you negotiate with someone calling himself Dirk Primo, for chrissake? It seems fairly obvious that he's a . . . a . . ."

"A low-life piece of shit."

Cora barked a laugh. "I suspect you flatter him, dear boy. Anyway, they recognized that he was not a person they wanted to have anything to do with. So they arranged for Alana to have lawyers and agents and managers looking after her interests."

"But he controls her, completely controls her. Why would he agree to let other people in?"

"Because otherwise there's no deal. Even if this Dirk person is not the swiftest thing on two feet—as I gather he's not—it was obvious he had no choice."

"And he was right," I said. "He'll still end up with everything."

Cora smiled again. "Not necessarily. All these new people are looking out for Alana's interests, not his. If they're doing their jobs, they've probably set up something like a trust account to make sure Dirk doesn't get too close. Oh, he'll get some of the gravy, but he may not get the main course, and maybe eventually he won't get anything."

"I wouldn't bet on it. Like I said, he's got her sewed up."

"But let's hope. Wouldn't it be nice to have a happy ending for once?"

I looked at her and shook my head. "And I thought you

only went all squishy over female body builders. Hell!
You're not so tough."

"Who is, dear boy? Who is?" She looked almost wistful,
then an inner door opened and she smiled.

A woman entered, wearing high heels and fishnet tights
and nothing else. She was tall and tan, with close-cropped
hair like a boy's crew cut and dark, hungry eyes. She had
muscular shoulders and arms, breasts like a pair of giant
plump grapefruits, and she moved with the slow, sure
stride of a stalking cat.

"This is Monika, my new protégée," Cora said proudly.
"She's the Mud Wrestling Champion of the Southwest."

"Yeah, right," I said. "I didn't recognize her clean."

Cora smiled. "She's not, dear boy. Believe me, she's
not."

TWENTY-THREE

I was beginning to get a feeling about what might be going on. But it didn't make much sense, and I couldn't see what I could do about it anyway. Maybe there was no reason to do anything, but somehow I didn't think I was at the end yet. So, without any better ideas, I told my service to let Philip Prince know he could reach me at the Dragon's Gate, and I headed downtown.

The restaurant was on the edge of Chinatown. It took up the second floor of a large, nondescript warehouse, but to get to it, I had to go under an ornate ceremonial gateway and through what looked like a Hollywood set designer's opium-smoked fantasy of the Summer Palace. Everything was red lacquer and gold trim, turquoise tile and curling pagoda roofs; just to liven things up, there was about eight miles of sizzling neon. The court of an electric Kublai Khan.

The Dragon's Gate was known locally as the Dragon's Breath, because of the guy who owned the place. He was Hong Kong Chinese, short and Buddha-fat, moistly gleaming, like he's been carved out of melting butter. He had a mouthful of gold teeth, an abacus for a brain, and a finger in everything that went on in Chinatown, clean and dirty. Thanks to a fondness for fish sauce, he also smelled like something that had been buried for a couple of centuries in a Ming tomb. It was enough to water your eyes, but since he ran the best dim sum in town, the place was always busy.

The owner took me to a small table on one side, and after the air cleared, I looked around. As usual, all of the large round tables in the center were filled, mostly with Chinese eating, drinking, and talking at a furious pace. A dozen

large trolleys were being pushed through the narrow
aisles, each piled high with bamboo steamers or covered
with layers of small plates and bowls. I took a pull on my
Tsingtao beer and settled back for a pleasant few hours.

It was a good thing Prince called me about ninety minutes later, or else I might never have left, just continued to
sit there, sampling each new treat that was wheeled by. As
it was, my table looked like I had tried to barricade myself
behind stacks of empty dishes and steamers. Each had contained a taste of something—stewed chicken feet, curried
snails, octopus with black beans, shrimp toast, sui mai,
har gow, spring rolls, steamed buns, fried dumplings, and
lots more, probably enough for a table of eight, but who
was counting. The small Chinese girls who pushed the
trolleys looked disappointed when I finished my last beer
and stood to go.

"Twenty minute more," one of them said as I went out,
"you would have been champion."

When I finally ran down Prince, he didn't exactly look
like he was up for an award. Not unless they were giving a
prize for the guy who most resembled warmed-up puke.
His shirt was dingy and his suit was rumpled. His hair was
messed and dotted with greasy specks of dandruff. He
hadn't shaved, and his skin was a pasty gray, with darker
gray smudges under his eyes. About the only place he had
good color was his bloodshot eyeballs.

I found him at the back of a parking lot for a takeout
chicken joint in Hollywood. The rear door of a beat-up old
Dodge was open, and he was sitting sideways on the back
seat, feet on the asphalt, looking at one of the sex tabloids
that are sold on every street corner. The rag was open to
the full-page ad of an outfit called Boobs Unlimited, who
claimed they had the biggest tits in town in their service.
Judging from Prince's blank stare, though, it didn't look
like he was savoring the close-up pictures of the merchandise.

"Kind of makes you hungry for fried eggs, doesn't it?" I
said.

Prince made a sound like "Yiiii!" and jumped up,
smashing his forehead against the door frame. Then he
hopped around for a while, groaning and holding his head.

"Funny—you don't look like Mr. Popularity," I said when he stopped hopping.

"Huh?"

"That's what you seem to be right now, wouldn't you say? I mean, you've got people posing as you. And you've got NTN's private eye interested in what you're doing. And you've got hired thugs staking out your apartment. And you're on the shit list of one of the town's leading psychopaths. And now you got the boys at Homicide looking for you. Like I said—Mr. Popularity."

"What! What? Wha—" Prince turned even grayer, and I wondered if he was going to collapse. I wondered if I cared. "Homicide?" he said weakly, leaning against the car.

"Yeah. Have you been home since I saw you?"

He shook his head. "I spent the night in the car parked behind a gas station."

"You know a kid named Victor James? Early twenties, skinny, dirty blond hair, tattoo of a skull on his arm?"

"No, who is he?"

"He's the one the cops found naked tied to your bed. One of your kitchen knives was planted in his chest."

He started sputtering, then coughing, and finally dropped back down to the car seat. And I thought I'd broken the news pretty gently. Oh, well.

"Is this for real?" he asked after he caught his breath.

"It was made to look like a sex crime. You know, a little B & D that got out of hand. I wouldn't have thought that was your style, that, if anything, you liked to be on the receiving end. But it hardly matters. As far as the cops are concerned, you're suspect number one. In fact, unless you've got a really solid alibi for late yesterday afternoon, the cops probably won't bother looking any further."

"Oh, shit."

"I guess that means you didn't see anybody yesterday."

He shook his head, staring at his feet. "I didn't do it."

"Oh, I know that. So what?"

Prince looked up. "You said somebody was staking out my apartment. Maybe . . ."

"Yeah. I saw him yesterday coming out of your place. At just about the right time. His name's Ernie. That's the same guy who aced your buddy Flight."

"Then you'll tell the police—"

I shook my head. "Even if I wanted to get involved—which I don't—it wouldn't do any good. Just my word, no proof. And besides, a couple hours ago I ripped the guy's face off. He'll be long gone, either out of town or halfway to Catalina feeding the fish."

"But you said you could help me."

"When did you see my card?"

"Last night. I didn't know where to go, so I went back to my office. But I got scared to stay there, and I went to your house."

"Then you slept in the car?"

"Yes. Can you do anything?"

"Maybe if you'd been straight with me yesterday, and told me some things that I needed, I might've been able to do something. But now you're a little late, and I've got a pretty good idea about what's been going on. Somehow, Flight got hold of some pictures—probably a nice, explicit film—of Alana Lanier, made before she became The Girl Next Door. Even a scumbag like Flight could tell that that was much hotter stuff than he ever dealt with. But that was right up your alley—wasn't it?—since most of your business is acting as the agent for people with nasty tastes. So I figure he got you to try and flog the stuff. Only it was a lot hotter than anybody figured, and some people didn't much want the goods to get on the market. Therefore, exit Edward Flight. Except maybe it turned out that he no longer had it. Therefore, exit Philip Prince. If you still have the shit, maybe you can save your skin. Then you'll only have to worry about the cops."

"But I don't have the film. I never did."

"You mean you weren't trying to find a buyer?"

"I didn't say that. You got things mostly right, except for that." Prince was very pale, and his forehead glistened with sweat. "Look—about two weeks ago Eddie Flight calls me up. I'd done business with him before. Like you said, I have clients who collect . . . uh . . . exotica, and in the past, I'd been able to do some good for both of us. Anyway, he tells me he's got this film of Alana Lanier sucking off all these guys, and did I think I could move it. Did I ever! There're collectors in town who specialize in just that kind of thing. Celeb porn. And it always goes for top dollar because it's hard to come by. I figured we could maybe get ten Gs for it."

"That much?" I said, sounding impressed.

"Oh, yeah, if it was the real thing. That's very big-time."

I looked at Prince, wrinkled and gray and dripping sweat. Very big-time. Shit. He wasn't just a slug, he was a stupid slug. "Go on."

"Anyway, I say sure, and ask him to send it up. He says he doesn't think that's a good idea. Then I say, okay, I'll go down and take a look at it. But he says I can't do that, 'cause he's got it in a safe place. So I say, okay, send me a couple of stills so I'll have something to show. And he says that it's too hot, and he doesn't even want to let stills out. Well, I know that Eddie knows that you have to have something to show, and I get the idea that maybe he doesn't really have anything. So I ask him."

"And what does he say?"

"He assured me that he did, and would give me a description of it. I said that wasn't enough, and he said it had to be, that he had his reasons. Maybe he did, but I told him he'd have to get somebody else. After all, I've got a certain reputation in this town."

I stared at the oozing glob of gray slime and thought he was probably right about that. "So what happened?"

"So the next day Eddie calls me back and says he'll give me a thousand bucks against my cut if I'll feel out the market and see what it looks like. Under the circumstances, I agreed to go ahead. I thought, what did I have to lose?"

I smiled at Prince. "Surprise, surprise . . . So who'd you talk to?"

"The people who I thought might be interested, who could afford it."

"*Who?*"

Prince started to squirm. "That's confidential."

"Shit, Prince. You peddle fuck films. That's not exactly part of the lawyer-client relationship. Is Jason Pinkham one of your clients?"

"Who?"

I thought the reaction was genuine, that he didn't know him. "Never mind," I said. "You go to any magazines? Maybe go to the network?"

SLEAZE 157

"Of course not."

Of course he didn't. That would involve climbing out from under his rock.

"So what did your clients say?"

"There was interest, naturally, but without seeing the merchandise, no one was willing to commit. Then I discovered that maybe I'd been right all along."

"About what?"

"That Eddie didn't have the film."

"Why? What'd you hear?"

"Well, a few days ago, I got a call from Abel Youngman. He said he heard I had a film to sell, and he was interested. I thought I was really going to score. Youngman's big, you know. So I went to see him, and I described the product. He listens real carefully, only he's got this funny look on his face. When I finished, he asks if he can see it. I say yes, but I don't have it. Then he asks if I've seen it, and I have to tell him no. Then he says someone's playing a game with me, and I ask him what he means." Prince paused, then shook his head. "Now get this. He says that he knows all about the picture I described, because it's his. And he says there was only one print, so what was I selling? But I don't have an answer. Then he tells me I better get one, because this is a pretty sensitive issue, and he says I also better be careful, because I might upset some people that I didn't want to upset."

"So what did you do after that?"

"What do you think? I called that bastard Flight to find out what's going on. Only I didn't get him. I kept trying for a couple of days, but no good. Then the next thing I know, you come in and tell me he's been killed. Now you tell me there's a body in my apartment and the cops are looking for me. Holy shit! What's going on?"

I shrugged. "Like Youngman said, it looks like you upset some people."

"But I didn't do anything."

Prince was starting to whine, and I was getting tired of him. As far as I was concerned, he was a fucking leech, and I didn't give a shit about what happened to him. But he had a point—he hadn't done very much. At least not enough to account for what was going on. Not that old Dirk seemed to need much of a reason for anything, but still . . .

Something, though, sounded vaguely familiar, and I asked if he at least got his thousand bucks.

He nodded, looking down at the ground, obviously feeling very sorry for himself. "The next day. Somebody brought it to me. Cash."

"Who?"

"Don't know. I'd never seen him before. Big guy."

"Describe him."

Prince lifted his head, shrugging listlessly. "Big—bigger than you. Real short hair. No neck. His face looked kind of flat, like it'd been pressed in."

I stared at Prince, but he was too busy examining his dusty shoes to notice. Suddenly, some very interesting possibilities opened up. I wasn't about to share them with Prince, but I thought I might give him something. Maybe it would help to stir things up.

"Sounds to me like that was Ernie."

He looked up. "You mean—?"

"Yeah, the guy I was telling you about."

Prince looked scared and confused.

"He works—or worked—for Dirk Primo."

"Who?"

"Maybe you know him as Joshua, the last of the great prophet/pimps."

"What?"

"Dirk Primo lives with Alana Lanier."

Prince blinked several times, dazed, like he'd been in a dark room and suddenly was hit with a five-hundred-watt spot. There was a lot of light, but he didn't know what the hell it was all about. Wincing, he pressed his temples with his fingers. "What should I do?"

I looked down at him. There was the smell of old grease from the back of the chicken joint. Or maybe that was his cologne. I was ready to leave.

"You've dug yourself a big hole," I said. "Maybe you should get in."

As it turned out, he did.

TWENTY-FOUR

Abel Youngman lived in the hills above Sunset. His house dated from the twenties, when taxes were low, and the ruling kings and queens of Hollywood had seriously considered building a wall around Beverly Hills in order to keep out the rabble. It was appropriately feudal: forty-something rooms, towers, terraces, and massive gateways, all constructed out of foot-thick blocks of sand-colored granite. Considering the neighborhood, it was a mere bungalow.

I'd called ahead. Guys like Youngman are tougher to get to than most heads of state, but I made a few cryptic references to Alana Lanier and home movies, and he agreed to see me. I was kept waiting for about fifteen minutes before someone who looked like an apprentice mortician showed me into the office.

Youngman was sitting behind a desk that was long enough for small aircraft to land on. He had dark permed hair and a closely cropped beard, both of which showed a little gray. He wore a designer cowboy shirt, an Indian turquoise necklace, and tinted aviator glasses. A large diamond stud sparkled in an earlobe. He was my kind of guy, all right.

Just to show what an important fella he was, he didn't bother looking up. "What do you have, and how much do you want?"

I didn't say anything, just sat down and stared at him. After a couple of minutes, Youngman was having a hard time not looking up, but he must've thought his dignity was somehow on the line, so he kept flipping through the papers in front of him. Christ! Another Hollywood asshole. I lit up a cigarette and waited. Finally, he raised his head and glared at me.

"I want about five minutes," I said, smiling. "Maybe ten."

"Huh?"

I had the feeling I was the first guy he'd seen in weeks who wasn't hoping he'd write a check. I told him who I was. I explained that I was working on a job, and that every time I turned around I ran into people who seemed to have something to do with some hard-core footage of Alana Lanier.

"Aw, shit! I'm out of town for a couple of weeks, and when I come back everybody's talking about Alana and that goddamn movie. What a fucking mess. And now you. What's your interest? You buying or selling?"

I shook my head. "Neither. And I've got no interest one way or another. It's just that this deal is making waves, and people who have nothing to do with it are getting splashed. So far, all I've picked up is a lot of background noise. From what I hear, you may be the one person who actually knows something."

I waited for Youngman to say something, but he just looked at me suspiciously while he ruffled the edges of the papers with his thumb.

"Look," I said, "as far as I know we're not in conflict. I know this movie is causing problems. If you've got anything to do with that TV show, it's got to be causing problems for you."

"Oh, I got something to do with it, all right—a nice piece of the action."

I didn't say anything. Youngman looked at me some more, then sighed, and nodded his curly head.

"Okay. I don't see what good it's going to do you, but this is the story. . . . About a year ago, a friend comes over with something he wants to show me. Says it'll really crack me up. This is a guy that thinks plastic turds are high comedy, but I say okay. What it turns out to be is your basic home-movie orgy, and not even very well done. Only one of the featured players is Louis Spore, and that's what was supposed to be so funny."

"Who's Spore?"

"A studio V.P. with a shitload of clout. A real prick— very stiff, very formal. So, actually, it was kind of funny to see him dancing around, waving his little piece of meat and shaking his flabby white ass. So we watch it for a few minutes, then there's a cut to a naked girl going down on somebody, and my friend starts to turn off the projector. Only I stop him because I can't believe what I'm seeing. Even with shitty light and worse camera work, and even though it wasn't your most flattering pose, the girl was something else. Goddamn! It just jumped off the screen. There was sex and sensuality and great looks, all right, but that wasn't all. What really got me was the sense of availability combined with a kind of sadness, resignation. Vulnerability, maybe you'd call it. Whatever it was, it was just there—naturally—and it was devastating. It fucking blew me away."

Youngman stood up and walked to the window. He looked out for a minute, probably checking that no rebellious peasants were storming the parapet, then turned back.

"I held onto the film, and for the next couple of weeks I kept going back to it. It was mostly that girl doing a bunch of guys, but even so, every time I saw it I was more convinced that she really had something."

"This is Alana Lanier, right?"

"Right. Only I didn't know who she was then, and nobody knew who'd made the film or where it came from. For all I knew, the girl was long gone. Finally, I called up Spore." He laughed. "I think he wet his pants when I complimented him on his film debut and said I hadn't realized he had such a short subject." Youngman laughed again. "Anyway, I found out the movie was made about two years before—that'd be three years ago now—and that I should see a guy named Dirk Primo about the girl."

"Did Spore say what his connection with Primo was?"

"Not then. He wasn't anxious to talk. But later, after I'd done some checking, Spore told me that the guy had stayed for a while at a ranch he has out in the hills near the county line. That's where the movie was made. At the time the guy called himself something else."

"Joshua?"

"That's it. He had all these girls with him. It was supposed to be some kind of religious group, but I never got that angle. It just sounded like a lot of fucking and sucking to me."

"Yeah. Not quite mainstream theology."

Youngman laughed. "Not quite. But it made a believer out of Spore for a while."

"Then what happened?"

Youngman shrugged. "It's kind of fuzzy, but this is what I put together. Apparently, Spore started getting scared of this guy—which after I saw him, I could understand—and tried to get rid of him. Only Joshua isn't going anywhere. So Spore has the gang arrested and thrown off his property. But then they come back, and Spore's even more scared. Seems the guy wanted Spore to get him into the business. As what, I don't know. Probably the head of fucking MGM. Well, Spore says there's not that much he can do, but maybe he can make some intros, open a few doors. Spore tells him that for a guy of his ability, that should be enough."

I nodded. That fit with the little pieces I'd picked up, and filled in some of the spaces. Once he saw a way into the big time, he knew he had to make a complete break. "So," I said, "exit Joshua, enter Dirk Primo, Hollywood sharpie."

"You got it. And Spore suddenly decides there's a lot of business in Europe that needs his attention, and he's hardly in town for six months. When I called him, he hadn't seen or talked to Primo for almost a year, and that was just fine, he said, because the guy still scared the shit out of him. He said if I were smart, I'd keep my distance too, or I'd be buying myself a lot of trouble. I'm beginning to think maybe I should've listened."

"Instead, what'd you do? Check out Dirk?"

Youngman nodded, then walked back behind his desk and sat. "He was easy to find—real high-profile—out there hustling the hustlers."

"Using the girl as bait."

"Yeah. A real pretty picture. I could see that the guy was poison—psycho city—and nobody needs that kind of grief. But there was also the girl. I couldn't stop thinking about her. It got so I felt I didn't have any choice. So I finally bit the bullet and called Primo." Youngman gave a terse laugh. "The son of a bitch thought I was calling to make him a producer or something, for chrissake! Couldn't believe that I was interested in Alana, not him. . . ." He shook his head. "Anyway, I set up a screen test. I had to find out if there was really anything there or not."

Youngman paused, again shaking his head. "Was there ever! It was better than I'd even hoped. And it wasn't just me. Everyone who saw the test agreed. She was dynamite, absolute one-hundred-proof dynamite. And I even had a project in development that was perfect for her."

"'The Girl Next Door'?"

"Right. It would show her off, without asking her to do something she couldn't do yet. It would establish her, and at the same time give her a chance to learn. Like I said— perfect. But first, there were some things we had to know about. Like, if we put in all the time and money to launch, were we going to get an unpleasant surprise somewhere down the line? I mean, besides what we knew about, was there anything else? Other movies, as bad or maybe worse? While we were working to make her a hit, were we liable to find her featured at some Times Square S & M parlor? Questions like that."

"So you did check?"

"Of course."

"And?"

"And Primo swore there wasn't anything to worry about."

"That was it?"

"Shit, Hunter! What kind of stupid schmuck do you think I am? Of course that wasn't it. Believe me, I had a lot of checking done. Found out who made the movie."

"Let me guess. An insect operating out of TJ named Eddie Flight."

Youngman looked surprised. "How'd you know that?"

I shrugged. "Go on. You send somebody down there?"

"I went myself, only I didn't let on what it was about. Acted like I was a client. I had the film with me, and I asked him if there was any more material with those girls. Made like I really liked it. As it turned out, there were a couple shorts using some of the other girls, but nothing with Alana. Then I asked about her specifically, said she really turned me on. But Flight had nothing, and he said he didn't think there was anything. He really wanted to make a sale. If there had been anything, I was pretty certain he would've gotten it for me. So it looked good. And all

the other checks came up empty. No film, no stills, no tape.
Nothing. Alana was clean."

"Except for her personal appearances."

Youngman waved that off. "We figured that was man-
ageable, finesseable. So that left only one problem."

"Dirk Primo."

"Right again. No way were we going to get involved in a
project where we had to deal with that wacko." He shook
his head. "Actually, after seeing the test, some of the boys
at NTN probably would have stretched out their necks to
Dracula in order to sign Alana, but I got them to go along
with me."

"So he was eased out. That must've pleased the shit out
of him."

"I can imagine. Fortunately, the network took care of it,
which was fine with me, because that's one guy I wouldn't
want to have pissed at me. What I did was to arrange for
the people who would look after her business."

"And are they?"

"I think they're doing a good job."

"Yeah, real good. The bastard still treats her like she
was his property, a goddamn two-bit whore."

Youngman flinched. "What do you want? I can only do
so much, you know. She's been treated like dirt for so long,
that's what she thinks she is. Maybe it'll take a while before she realizes that she's not. But until she does . . ." He
shrugged. "Look—I like the girl. I feel sorry for her, for the
way she's treated. Believe me, one of the things I want out
of all of this is to do her some good."

I gave Youngman a look that let him know he'd be
getting my vote for Humanitarian of the Year.

"Yeah, sure," he said. "I'll do myself some good, too. So
what? That's the way things work here."

I looked at him. I wondered if he realized he wasn't that
different from Dirk Primo. He just paid better wages. But
it hardly mattered. Like he said, that's the way things
worked here. It was all buyers and sellers, so you might as
well get the best price, and the hell with it.

"Okay," I said. "So it all checked out all right, you took
care of your problems, everything goes ahead, and it looks
like it's going to pay off big. Then what? You got one of
those unpleasant surprises?"

"Yeah. I go away for a while, and when I come back I hear people are talking about this home movie of The Girl Next Door. At first, I'm not concerned. You know how things go—some guy in a bar brags that he made it with her, and somebody else says, 'Oh, yeah? Well, I made a movie of her,' and before you know it, it gets a mention in the *Reporter*. This is a fuck of a small town, and the drums are always beating. Especially if it's bad news. So I figure it's just bullshit and will go away quick enough. But it doesn't, and I keep getting phone calls. Finally I hear that some goddamn ambulance chaser named Prince is the one going around on this, so I get in touch. I ask him what he's got, and he describes the movie that I had, the thing that got me going. So I think, what the fuck is going on here? On the one hand, I think that I was right, that it is just bullshit, since I *know* that nobody's got that movie. On the other hand, I think that maybe there is something here that I should know about."

"So what'd you do?"

"So I scared off Prince and got onto my good pal Dirk, and asked him what he knows." Youngman grimaced and said, "Aw, shit!"

"What'd he say?"

"He said he doesn't know anything about that, but it's funny I should call him, because he's been trying to get hold of me about something else. Right away I know it's something I don't want to hear. And I was right. He says he doesn't know about what Prince is doing, but he had just picked up some chat that Eddie Flight is trying to set up a deal with some skin mag."

"SLEAZE."

"Shit. Is there anybody that doesn't know about this?"

"You said it—drumbeats. That news must've made your day. When was this?"

"Three days ago. And you're right, it fucking delighted me. Goddamn! We're all set to grab the number-one spot, and at the exact same time our star is going to appear in full color performing who knows what sexual acts. I could already hear the sponsors running for the exit. What a nightmare!"

"Did you tell that to Primo?"

"Damn right I did. I suggested that he have a little talk

with his former associate. Find out what he was up to, and see what he could do to stop it. I told him that if we didn't head this off at the pass, we were all going to be hung out on the line, and it would be a long time before any of us got pulled back in."

"That it?"

"I also called the network. Those guys hate to get bad news, but it was their problem too. I thought a whole floor of V.P.'s were going to drop with coronaries at one time. 'What should we do? What should we do?' Bunch of old ladies. Sounded like a coyote had gotten into the hen house. Chickenshit jerks. So I told them to get in touch with the magazine and see if they could work a deal. I haven't heard yet how it's going." Youngman leaned back in his chair, pulling at the diamond stud in his earlobe. "That's it. Now what can you tell me?"

The idea I had gotten after I'd seen Cora Cardiff was looking better. Maybe it wasn't as fancy as a theory yet, but it did account for a lot of stuff. I figured I was maybe about three-quarters there. All things considered, that wasn't too bad, but I still wanted to think it through. Until I did, I didn't feel any more inclined to share with Youngman than I had with Prince.

"I can give you a couple of things," I said, "but first— what happened to the original movie? You still have it?"

"Hell, no! I burned it as soon as the deal started to come together. . . ." He stopped for a moment, then smiled. "Actually, I only burned the part with Alana. I kept Spore's footage. I send him a still every once in a while."

"I gather it was the original. Could it have been copied?"

Youngman gave it some thought. "I've been wondering that myself. A year ago I was pretty sure it hadn't been. Even with what's been going on, I still feel about the same. After all, nothing has turned up yet. Besides, the quality of the original was so bad that a dupe would probably be worthless. . . . But I could be wrong about both."

I nodded. "My guess is that you're not. Also that you don't have much to worry about in terms of the pictures turning up. I think your first reaction was right—it's all smoke and bullshit."

"Well, that's the best thing I've heard in days. . . . Wait

a second. There is something I should worry about, though.
Is that what you mean?"

"Maybe. I guess you don't know that Eddie Flight had
his brains blown out in Tijuana two days ago."

"Oh, shit."

"Or that the police are looking for Prince. A body was
found in his bedroom."

Youngman grimaced. "Primo?" he asked, his voice
barely audible.

I shrugged. "Don't worry. I don't think it can be
proven."

As I went to the door, I saw that Youngman had turned a
color that didn't go very well with his turquoise necklace.

First Prince, now Youngman. There must be something
wrong with the way I broke bad news.

I'd really have to work on it.

TWENTY-FIVE

Harry Demorest had left a message with the service that I should call him. Said it was important, but there was no answer when I tried back. A store in Hollywood had also called, telling me that they were having a two-for-one sale on leather briefs, and if I ordered right away, they'd throw in studs for free. It was hard to pass up that deal, but I headed back to my place.

I spent the rest of the afternoon sitting in my backyard going over things. Some pieces still didn't seem to fit, but even more did, and the more I thought about it all, the more certain I was that I'd finally gotten a handle on what had been going down. Goddamnit! No wonder it'd felt like I was chasing shadows.

At one point, I called Natalie Orlov. She sounded happy to hear from me, and full of questions. I told her that I was thinking of grabbing dinner at an Italian joint in Hollywood and that she could meet me there if she wanted. To discuss the case, I said.

"Right," she said. "The case."

Yeah, right. Shit.

When I got to the restaurant, though, there was a message from her saying that something had come up and she couldn't make it, but that she was still expecting me later back at her place. I didn't have anything better to do until then, so I let a Sicilian beanpole with a knife scar on his cheek show me to a table.

Inside, it looked like a second-rate pizza parlor—Formica tables and a bad painting of Mount Etna covering one wall—but the owner was said to be well-connected with some heavy East Coast types, the kind who were in linen supply or who claimed to be olive oil importers. They swore

it was the only decent place west of Mulberry Street, and
they spent a lot of time there when they came to the coast.

I ordered some mussels, some squid, some pasta, and
half a barbecued sheep's head, and settled back to enjoy
myself, pulling on a bottle of icy Amstel. Then, from two
tables away, a woman's voice cut through the background
noise like fingernails on a blackboard. It was British, high-
pitched and nasal, and she didn't so much talk as whinny.
When she wasn't complaining about the food and the service, she was complaining about how the world seemed un-
willing to recognize her evident superiority.

I turned and glared at her. She looked about the way I'd
expected, squarish and tweedy, with a long upper lip, enormous teeth, and the horsey look common to the British.
Judging from the size of her haunches, I thought there
might have been a Clydesdale among her ancestors. Or
maybe a member of the royal family.

After another couple minutes of listening to her drone
on, I was quickly going off my feed. I took the plastic rose
out of the Chianti bottle on my table. I stood, went over to
her table, and laid the thing in front of her.

"A token of recognition," I said.

She batted her bleary little eyes at me and whinnied in
pleasure. "Of what?"

"Of the fact that you're the loudest and most offensive
person in this room."

She flushed, then paled, then snorted angrily at the man
across the table from her. "Are you just going to sit there
and let him insult me?"

The man was small and gray, with little twitchy rabbity
features. He looked at the woman, then at me. I was probably twice his size, and I hoped he didn't think he had to do
something.

He stood, looking up at me, then he took my hand and
shook it. He turned to the woman. "He's right, Eunice.
You are loud, and obnoxious, and an absolute embarrass-
ment." He picked up a large platter of fettuccine with clam
sauce and dumped it on her head. "I'll be outside when
you've finished your meal," he said and strode out, seeming a good foot taller.

Eunice sat there for a minute, then ran after him, leaving a trail of limp noodles and a vacuum of silence. This

was broken by a dark, beefy guy in the corner raising his glass of wine to me and saying in a husky voice, "Hey, pal! Have some scungilli on me."

He wore a white-on-white silk shirt and a large diamond on his little finger. Like Fettuccine Eunice, I thought that was exactly where I'd like to have the scungilli, but I just gave him a wave in acknowledgment and went back to my table. I shook my head. I was really getting mild-mannered.

At least the food was all right. The mussels, steamed in their own juice with garlic, green onions, and a splash of dry vermouth, were sweet and fragrant. The squid were deep-fried little rings, crispy golden on the outside, chewy within. There was a big pile of spaghetti, glistening with oil, dotted with chunks of fried garlic, sticky with tangy Parmesan. And the sheep's head, looking like something in a biology book, provided a variety of tastes and textures—tongue, brains, flesh—in one bony package. When I was through, some strong, slightly gritty coffee nicely settled everything.

I left the restaurant puffing on a cigarette and feeling pretty good. I was in a commercial district, and the streets were dark and empty as I walked the few blocks back to my car. It was so quiet I could hear burglar alarms going off around the city. And then I noticed the footsteps behind me.

I stopped to look into a shop window. Not a very original move, but the footsteps stopped. Turning my head slightly, I caught sight of two figures about half a block back. I continued on, keeping my stride easy, hoping I still looked unaware. I turned the corner to the street where my car was parked, and saw two more figures leaning against a wall. As I appeared, they moved into the sidewalk. I felt my fingers twitching, and a smile began to form. Maybe it wasn't my first choice for after-dinner exercise, but it'd do.

The guys blocking the way were big, dressed in torn, dirty jeans and heavy, scuffed leather jackets. One of them had an elongated shaved skull that made his head look like the end of a giant prick. The other's head was too small for his body, and he had a face like a bat. A dead cigarette dangled from his lips.

"Got a light?"

The footsteps behind were close, and I heard a half-stifled chuckle. They were all set to have a good time, and I sure didn't want to be the one to spoil their fun.

"Yeah, sure," I said to Batface.

I put my hand in my jacket pocket and wrapped it around my wad of keys, letting one stick out between my first two fingers. Still trying to look casual and unconcerned, I took a step forward as I withdrew my hand, like I was going to hold up a lighter. Instead, as my hand cleared the pocket, I surged forward in one smooth, fast motion, driving my fist into the side of Batface's head. I felt the key pierce his cheek, then I pulled it toward me and there was a squishy, ripping sound. As I whirled to face the guys behind me, I heard Batface scream in agony, and saw his hands go up to his shredded face as blood poured onto the sidewalk.

A guy with long red hair and a wispy beard over pimply, scabby skin was coming on fast. A bit too fast, because I caught him square on the nose with my elbow as I turned. I heard the bone in the bridge shatter and felt the cartilage tear. He dropped to his knees. His eyes crossed, and as his hands went up to his face, I saw he had a tattoo on the back of one of them. It was a sword, the bloody tip pointing toward the knuckles. I realized that this was not just your random street crime, but a search-and-destroy mission sent out by my favorite prophet-pimp. I also realized that they didn't have to do a hell of a lot of searching, since I'd made the date with Natalie Orlov on the bugged phone. For the first time, I was glad that she'd stood me up.

I turned slightly and faced the fourth member of the party, a tall wiry kid with the eyes of a ferret and no front teeth. He was wearing a T-shirt that said "Eat Shit and Die" on the front, and he had a long blade in his hand. I had a hunch he knew how to use it.

"Didn't your mother teach you not to play with strangers?" I said.

"Who's playing, fuckhead?"

He started to circle and move in, poised on the balls of his feet, knife ready to jab like a snake. I stood still, ready but unsure whether I wanted to make the move or wait until he made his. Then I felt something come over my head from behind me, and I got my left hand up just in time to grab a heavy chain and keep it from garroting me. It was Baldy, moved in close and pulling hard. I heard his breathing, and when I got a strong whiff of lime after-shave, I recognized Warthead's partner from Tijuana.

"What's the matter?" I said. "You forget your chloroform? You're going to wish you hadn't."

"So are you. This time you're dead."

He yanked hard, and it took all my strength to keep from having my windpipe chrushed by my own hand being forced back.

Eat Shit moved forward, in a hurry now, and no longer cautious. I roared as loud as I could, startling both of them for an instant, and that split second was all I needed. Dragging Baldy with me, I took two quick steps and threw a kick with all my force at the kid with the knife. I caught him where I'd intended, right in the crotch, and I felt his testicles turn to jelly beneath my toe. Eat Shit hung in midair, like a cartoon character who'd just discovered he'd run over the edge of a cliff. With my free hand I grabbed a lot of hair and pulled him down. His knees hit the pavement with enough force to shatter.

"Nobody fucking comes at me with a knife and walks away after!" I yelled, and kicked him again, this time right under the word "Shit." I felt his ribs tear away from his sternum like a cracking wishbone. As he fell back, I pulled Baldy forward again, and gave the kid a new face with the bottom of my heel.

With my left hand I pushed the chain away from my throat, and felt Baldy press against my back. His fear started to smell stronger than his cheap after-shave.

"You know what they say about riding the tiger?" I said. "It's easy to get on. The problem's getting off the fucker. Right, asshole?"

With my right hand I reached back, trying to grab his head, but I couldn't get a grip on his smooth, sweat-slick, shaved head, and he kept slipping free. Finally, I caught an ear and pulled forward until his chin was resting on my shoulder.

"Right, asshole?"

He was trying to get away, but I had him. I turned my head, and said, "Right?" one more time, then took his nose between my teeth and bit hard.

He started to whimper and tried to twist his head loose, but I was tasting his blood and he got nowhere. The chain came loose in my left hand and he was pushing on my back now, sobbing, frantically trying to get away, but I didn't let go. At last, pain and terror gave him the strength he needed, and he broke free.

I turned and saw that he was standing five feet away, staring at me in disbelief, blood gushing out of his head. I put my hand up to my mouth and took out the thing between my teeth. I looked at the nose, then at the piece of cartilage and skin in my other hand that had been his ear.

"These are yours, I think," I said, and tossed the two things to the ground at his feet.

He turned and ran, and I heard glass breaking to my left. The guy with the red beard and broken nose was coming toward me, waving a broken beer bottle and growling like a cornered grizzly. He probably expected me to wait for him, but I crossed him up. I moved to him without any hesitation and grabbed his arm while he was still making threatening gestures. I caught his wrist and looked at the back of his hand.

"Nice tatoo," I said.

Then I covered the hand that held the bottle and slowly forced his arm around until the jagged edge was pointing at his midsection. He wasn't very aggressive anymore. In fact, he was trying his hardest to get away, but he wasn't going anywhere just yet, and I stared at him and shook my head.

"What's the rush? Don't you have time for a beer?"

Slowly, I pushed his hand toward him. His eyes were round and his mouth was opening and closing soundlessly as he shook his head from side to side and tried to suck in his gut. He couldn't suck far enough. When the bottle touched his shirt, a high, thin, keening sound escaped from somewhere inside him. The pitch rose as the bottle cut into the skin and a red circle spread on his shirt. He struggled to get away, but I grabbed his chin whiskers and pulled, and that kind of quieted him down. I took the bottle out of his hand and held it up to his face.

"You know, you ought to be more careful. You could hurt somebody with this." I looked at him, smelling the

stink of panic. "You look like you could use a shave," I
said.

That did it. He ran, leaving me holding a handful of
beard with pieces of bloody flesh attached to the roots. I
dropped the stuff on the ground with the other bits.

I looked down. If there'd been more of them, I might've
ended up with enough parts to assemble a thug of my own.

Maybe next time.

I reached my car.

I was kind of in the mood for dessert.

TWENTY-SIX

As I went up Natalie Orlov's walk, I noticed a curtain in a front window pull aside for a second. The door opened before I got to it and Natalie Orlov stepped out and stood on the porch. She was wearing a pair of baggy dark green coveralls, like a garage mechanic, but they weren't quite baggy enough to disguise the fact that she didn't have much on under them. I began to think that my transmission might need some work.

Then I noticed that she was looking at me with a funny expression—surprise, or maybe concern.

"Don't worry, it's not mine," I said, motioning to the blood that covered a large part of my shoulder and chest.

"What happened?"

I shrugged. "I guess our friend decided he wasn't going to let things lie. A few of his boys were waiting for me when I got out of the restaurant."

With her fingertips, she touched the stains on my shirt. They were still damp.

I shrugged again. "His boys'll need a little more than dry cleaning to get back to normal."

Her eyes went round, then she shook her head. "You've had a busy day with them."

"Hell, it's been a pleasure."

"You're sure you're all right?"

"Sure." I looked at her. There seemed to be a tightness to her mouth, something in her eyes. "What's the matter? What happened?"

She hesitated, then turned and went inside. I followed, closing the door. In the living room, she finally turned back to me.

"Jason called this afternoon."

175

"Oh? What did he say?"

"I didn't speak to him. He left a message that he was coming in tonight." She sighed, frowning.

"And you think there's going to be some sort of show-down?"

She nodded.

"I kind of doubt it," I said, sitting on the couch.

Natalie Orlov raised her eyebrows, then sat in an arm-chair facing me. "What do you mean?"

"I mean, I don't think Jason Pinkham's going to have any pictures. I don't think there are any pictures. I think this whole thing is a scam."

"What? I don't understand."

"There are still a few things *I* don't understand, but everything that I do understand points in that direction. Our friend Joshua, now known as Dirk, is running a con. One hell of a con."

Natalie Orlov didn't say anything, just looked at me with considerable interest. I started to explain it to her, telling her what I'd found out—not in the order that I'd picked up the bits and pieces, but in the way that seemed to make sense of them. It took about twenty minutes to run through it. Along the way, she asked a few questions to get things straight, but mostly she just listened. The phone rang a couple of times. She said she thought it was Jason, but she ignored it, wanting to hear me out before she talked to him.

I started with how people seemed to regard the guy as a con artist, and how, before his most recent incarnations, old J-D might have practiced that trade at a low level. Except for a real fondness for violence, I hadn't come across anything that contradicted the possibility, and having to be heavy-handed only meant that he wasn't very good. Or he might have been that dangerous creature, the con man who goes around the bend and starts to believe his own lines, in which case almost anything was possible. In any event, it was clear that the guy was a manipulator.

Then I told Natalie Orlov about Dirk's adventures in Tinseltown. How he pimped the girl in order to get close to the big movers and set himself up in business. How the break came, only it wasn't for him but for the girl. And if that wasn't bad enough, the final insult came when the network did everything they could to maneuver him out of the picture.

"That must have really pissed him off," I said, "a guy who always wanted to be in control, who always came down hard on anyone who got in his way. My guess is he spent a lot of angry time trying to figure how he could even things up. Then, when Alana hit big, he saw his chance."

He knew, I went on, how concerned everyone had been about Alana's piece of eight-millimeter hard-core that had been made during the Sword of Truth days, and how carefully they had checked that there wasn't any more footage around. But after all that, suppose something turned up, at just about the worst possible time? It would scare the shit out of the guys at the network. Even more, if Dirk was the one behind it, it would give him the chance to make a big score. Alana hadn't started to hit the big bucks yet, and the way things were set up, Dirk would have a tough time getting his hands on much of it. This scheme would get Dirk something for himself, something he didn't have to squeeze out of Alana's managers and accountants.

Best of all, the sharpie must've realized that he didn't need anything concrete to pull it off—just create the illusion that the pictures existed. I explained that nobody had ever seen anything, but if you got enough people talking and acting as if something was real, it was real. Or as good as, which was the way you set up a big con.

So, I told Natalie Orlov, Dirk started making it real. He could do a lot himself, but he couldn't do everything, because he had to keep some distance, couldn't let it get back to him. Who better to go to than Eddie Flight, the same low-life creep who had made the original movie? Dirk obviously knew the guy, and Flight's previous involvement gave the whole thing added credibility. While it was possible he had conned Flight as well, I guessed the porn dealer was in on the setup from the beginning.

Natalie Orlov didn't understand why I thought there was a connection between Dirk and Flight. I jumped a little ahead of myself and explained that the money Flight gave to Philip Prince as an advance was delivered by one of Dirk's goons. *That* was the piece that brought a lot of the others into place for me.

Once Flight was involved, everything could go ahead.

Flight got Prince, who he had worked with before, to peddle the film—or more to the point, the idea of the film. The
fact that Prince was describing something that had once
existed was a nice touch, one more piece of misdirection.
Prince thought something was fishy, but he was being
paid, so he didn't look too closely. Obviously, the plan
wasn't to make a sale, but to get people talking. In the
same way, I figured that Flight himself probably approached Pinkham, got him interested, adding another
layer of so-called reality. They didn't approach the network directly because in a con, it's always better to make
the mark come to you. And while all this was going on, or
maybe even before he started it, Dirk was sending letters
to the magazine.

"As far as I can tell," I said, "my first reaction was right.
It was just wind."

"Then why send them?" Natalie Orlov asked.

"Two reasons, I think. The first is just more of the same,
another element—another angle—of the illusion. He
wanted to make you a believer. There was so much heat,
we figured there must be a fire, which was exactly what we
were supposed to think. The other is that they provided a
kind of cover for Dirk. If it ever came down to it, if he was
ever questioned, he could always point to the letters and
say, 'What do you mean? I was trying to scare them off.' He
didn't plan to do more than threaten, any more than
Prince was supposed to make a sale."

"But why SLEAZE?"

"Why not? He needed something, something big enough
so that the network saw there was real danger. Maybe he
knew about your arrangement—you and Pinkham—and
figured he could exploit it. It's not common knowledge, but
it's also not a complete secret. He found out enough to
know who N.E. Orlov is, so he could probably get the rest.
Most of all, though, I think he needed something local for
this to work, and most of the other mags are put out back
East."

Natalie Orlov was slowly nodding her head. I thought
maybe a smile was starting to show around the corners of
her mouth. "Go on."

There wasn't that much more. Once Dirk got things
going, he had to keep track of what was happening. Flight

could do a lot of that, but not everything. So Dirk put a bug
in the office. Some night when the building was deserted,
five minutes in and out—no big deal—and he's got ears.
And what does he hear? That Natalie Orlov is bringing in
a detective.

Maybe that's a complication he didn't count on, I said,
but then he sees that maybe he can use it. He's getting
close to payoff time, but there are a couple of problems.
Like the one guy who knows it's a scam, and the other guy
who suspects it. So he hires somebody to pose as Philip
Prince, and I go down to Mexico. With one move, he can get
rid of Flight, get rid of the detective by making him the
stooge, and send a loud message to Prince. Pretty nice. If I
manage to get myself out of the jam—one way or another—it doesn't even matter that much. Dirk feels pretty
well insulated, and I just become one more player contrib-
uting to the plausibility of the setup. Except maybe I was
no longer an asset, so he decided to take me out tonight.

"It's funny," I said after I gave Natalie Orlov a chance to
consider it all. "If I'm right, Flight wasn't killed because
he had something, but because he knew there wasn't anything. But who the hell would look in that direction? So his
death added one more confirmation to the whole charade."
I shook my head. "You know, I kept saying that I thought I
was missing something, that I wasn't at the center. Maybe
this is what I was feeling—there is no center. There's only
smoke where the center should be."

"But if you're right, how's he going to get anything out
of this?"

"He's obviously figured out something . . . or thinks he
has. If I had to guess, I'd say he'll go to the network and
tell them that he can get the pictures, but they have to give
him the money. Whatever he decided he can get, which
will probably be less that the network is willing to pay."

"They wouldn't go along with that, would they? Not
knowing what they do about him?"

"Hell, I don't know. Whatever they pay won't be that
much to them, not compared to what's at stake. And they
could cover themselves a little if they think he's trying a
fast one. Give Dirk the money, but tell him that this had
better end it forever, that if there's ever anything else,

that's it. They pull the plug no matter what. No more gravy train. They might figure it'd be worth the risk."

Natalie Orlov was rocking a little in her chair, and smiling broadly. "Jesus! Did I ever get the right detective."

"Maybe."

"What do you mean, maybe? You figured it out, and I'm sure you're right."

"Maybe. There's still a few things . . ."

"Like what?"

I told her about the dead kid in Prince's bedroom. It didn't seem to fit with anything I'd come up with, and it didn't seem to have much point.

"Of course," I said, "maybe that is the point—that there's none. From everything I've seen and heard, Dirk is capable of doing just about anything. Like tonight, for instance. When it comes down to it, I'm not at all sure how his mind works. . . . Which is another problem."

"What?"

"Everyone says the guy is not very smart. Cruel but stupid. And as far as I'm concerned, they're right. Terrifying little girls, inflicting pain, that's his line. So how did he come up with this?"

"Who else could it be?"

I shrugged.

"Who knows?" she said. "Maybe for once he got smart."

"Maybe. After all, look at me."

Natalie Orlov smiled. "I am." She stood, then came over and knelt on the couch beside me. "What are you going to do?"

"I don't know. You're paying the bills. What do you want me to do?"

She gave me a slow, mischievous grin. She leaned forward, giving me a nice look down the front of the coveralls, and started batting her eyes at me. "Golly, Mr. Hunter," she said, making her voice high and squeaky, "I'm not sure. I think this zipper might be stuck. Maybe you could start with that."

"This zipper?"

She looked at me, lips slightly parted, breathing shallowly through her mouth. Then she nodded.

The zipper came down with a long hiss, a sound echoed by Natalie Orlov slowly exhaling. A shrug of her shoulders, and the coveralls slipped from her arms and bunched around her waist. A gleam of sweat appeared on her upper lip, and another between her breasts. Her nipples looked hard and dark and seemed to vibrate slightly to an inner tremor.

She stood, and the coveralls dropped to the floor. She stepped out of them, then came over to me. Her scent was strong and seemed to come off her like waves of heat. She buried her face in my shoulder, still damp with blood, and breathed in deeply.

She leaned back, and I saw that her face was flushed and her eyes were hot. Her fingers tore at my shirt, and when it was open, she pressed against me and held herself there for a long moment, then slowly slid down until she was on her knees, undoing my belt, opening my pants. As she exposed me, her breath started coming in long deep, gasps.

I stood, lifting her to her feet. With her arms around my neck, she stepped up onto the couch, then slowly bent her knees, lowering herself down to me. At the first touch, she started to tremble, tremble, holding there, right on the edge, holding, waiting, on the edge. Then with a sudden movement, she dropped her body, plunging me deep inside her. Wrapping her strong legs around my hips, digging her fingers into my shoulders, she pressed tight against me as the spasms shook her.

Later, much later, we were in the pool, silently floating in the warm water of the Jacuzzi. The air was thickening, and the night sky was a white-gray; the clear weather was over. I felt fine, as light and empty as the bubbles that frothed briefly on the water's surface, then vanished with a pop.

The phone rang again. Reluctantly, Natalie Orlov rose out of the water and went inside.

In a few minutes she came back, clutching a fluffy white terry-cloth robe around herself. Her expression was puzzled and strained.

"That was Jason," she said, frowning and wrinkling her forehead. "He's in town. He says he's got the pictures."

TWENTY-SEVEN

"I'm going to go see him in an hour," Natalie Orlov said.

"You want me to come with you?"

"I'd like that." She sighed, then turned and went into the house.

So much for feeling fine. I got out of the pool, dried off, and pulled on my pants. I kept a gym bag with a change of clean clothes in the trunk of the car. I went out and got it, and put them on. I also put on the gun that was in the bag. I didn't know why, but I had the feeling things might start to get hot.

I called the service to see if there was anything I should know about. The guy with the moving van had called to say he was prepared to give me a really good deal on a load of coffins he'd picked up. That should have been funny. Instead, it just seemed appropriate.

Harry Demorest had called again a couple of hours before. He said I should call him. He said I was making a mistake. Thanks, Harry. I wouldn't have guessed.

I tried him, but the line was busy.

Natalie Orlov seemed nervous and distracted, and took a long time getting ready. I figured she was thinking about what she would do if Pinkham intended to go ahead and use the pictures. I let her know that I'd listen, but she didn't want to talk.

I didn't much feel like it myself. Shit! The only problem with my theory was that it was wrong. Goddamnit!

I tried to wrap my brain around this latest development, but it wouldn't go. About all I managed to come up with was that maybe everything was in fact the way it had originally looked. Maybe I'd made a mistake identifying Dirk's goon with the guy who'd brought Prince the money, and it was somebody else. Or maybe it was the same guy, and he was playing a double game. He'd seemed about as bright as a boiled potato, but like Natalie Orlov had said, you never knew. Maybe he wanted to break with Dirk and went to Flight, or maybe Flight had come to him.

Or maybe it was Prince. He was the type who only used the truth as a last resort, so maybe he hadn't been straight with me. Maybe this was something he'd cooked up with Flight, and now that things has gotten a little too hot, he was desperately trying to cover his ass.

Or maybe . . .

The hell with it. I was tired of thinking. And it sure didn't seem to do much good. What I wanted was to tear some more bodies apart—one in particular—then ask my questions. Maybe with my thumbs digging into a throat I'd start to get some answers.

When we got out to the Checker, Natalie Orlov forced out a tense laugh. "It feels like I should get in the back," she said. She got in the front, but she didn't have much more to say on the ride out to Pinkham's place.

He lived in Brentwood, land of the two-million-buck ranch house. People in Brentwood liked to think they were rustic and countrified. Right. And Marie Antoinette liked to dress up as a shepherdess.

We got there shortly before eleven. It was a low, sprawling redwood house, nearly hidden behind jade plants the size of trees.

The lights were on, but nobody answered the doorbell. Natalie Orlov said he liked to do laps in the pool, so we went around to the side and through the gate next to the garage.

The backyard was brightly lit. We followed a brick path through some fragrant lemon trees, stepped onto the concrete deck that surrounded the large rectangular swimming pool, and froze. Natalie Orlov's eyes went round and her hands went up to her mouth. She started to make frantic panting sounds, like an asthmatic struggling for air.

I stepped in front of her and put my hands on her upper arms, gripping hard. "Is that him?" I had to repeat the question twice before she silently nodded her head.

"Go out to the car and wait for me," I said, but she didn't move. I turned her around and, half pushing, half carrying her, quick-marched her down the path and out the gate. "Go to the car and get in."

She took two steps, then stopped and looked at me over her shoulder. "Go!" I said. "Fast!" And finally she went.

I went back to the pool. Jason Pinkham was in it, but he wasn't doing laps. He was floating face down, dressed in sneakers, jeans, and a light-colored, long-sleeved shirt. There was a dark, ragged hole between his shoulder blades. The water was murky green-brown, the color of runoff in a gutter, and I was pretty sure there was a much bigger hole in his front. I didn't see any reason to get a confirmation.

I went up to the house. The glass door was open, and I stepped through. Inside it was very neat and straight—ashtrays empty, cushions fluffed, magazines in tidy piles—as if the house had been cleaned and then not occupied for a while. I quickly walked through the large rooms. There was no sign of a struggle or chase, no indication that there had been a search.

In the bedroom there was a canvas carryon suitcase and a leather briefcase lying on the bed. Both were closed. Using a handkerchief, I opened the zipper on the suitcase. There was a pair of cords, a pair of loafers, a couple of shirts, a sweater, a toilet kit. Everything was neatly folded and packed, and I couldn't tell if there had been anything else in the bag. If anyone had gone through it, they'd been careful.

The briefcase wasn't locked, but again I had no idea whether or not something had been taken from it. There were no pictures or film or anything like that, only a few files relating to other activities, and a couple of business magazines. In a leather pocket secretary, there was the passenger copy of a first-class ticket for the one o'clock flight out of New York. A one-way ticket. There were several credit card receipts from New York restaurants for earlier in the week, and a little notepad with a phone number written on one of the pages. Harry Demorest's number.

I put everything back the way I'd found it and closed both the cases. I checked the closets and the dresser drawers, but saw nothing except what you'd expect.

Next to the bedroom was a small office, but it didn't look like anyone had been in it. The top of the desk was clear, and the thin film of dust covering it was smooth and undisturbed. In one of the drawers there was a loose-leaf binder that served as an address book, and I flipped through it. I saw Natalie Orlov's numbers, I recognized the names of a few celebrities and Hollywood types, but I didn't see any entries for Flight or Prince or Primo or Alana or anyone else I'd heard of.

I didn't want to hang around any longer than necessary, so I hurried through the rest of the house. I didn't know what I was looking for, but I didn't come across anything. I left the way I came in, made a check around the pool, then went back to the car.

Natalie Orlov looked grim, but more composed. She turned to me as I got behind the wheel.

I shook my head. "Nothing."

I started the car and got the hell out of there. I headed back toward Hollywood, but after about ten minutes, I turned onto a side street and pulled over.

"Why?" Natalie Orlov said very quietly. "Why?"

"I don't know. To get the film? Shit. I can't figure this. All I'm sure about is that he's made a big mistake. This isn't some piece of scum in Tijuana, or a beach punk that nobody gives a shit about. If his idea was to cool things out, he's just thrown gasoline on the forest fire. . . . At least he's acting more in character now, being stupid." I tried a smile, but Natalie Orlov didn't seem to notice. "You said Pinkham left a message. Was it taken on your phone?"

"Oh, Christ! I didn't . . . I didn't . . ."

"Don't start thinking you're responsible, 'cause you're not."

"But I—"

"You didn't do anything."

But she wasn't listening, just staring down and shaking her head, talking more to herself than to me. "I thought we were at an end, but it keeps getting worse and worse. . . . I don't know . . . I don't know . . ."

I raised her head, and held her eyes with mine. "Believe me," I said, "it is nearly over. Just hold on."

After a minute, she gave me a weak little smile and nodded her head once. "What can we do?"

"The first thing, we'll go back to your place, and you'll get some things, and we'll check you into a motel."

"Why? What for?"

"I don't know if Dirk got what he wanted. If not, he may come looking for you. I don't think you should be any place he can find you. I also don't think you want to deal with the cops just yet, do you? If Dirk can't find you, neither will they."

"Are you going to call them?"

"In a while, I guess. I don't see much rush. If I can, I'd like to give them something more than the location of a body."

"But suppose somebody else reports it, and they come looking for me?"

"Simple. You got a threatening phone call, and you got out of the house. You can show 'em the letters if they don't believe you. . . . All right?"

"All right."

Half an hour later, I'd gotten a room in one of those places on Sunset where they don't pay much attention to who checks in. A spectacular six-foot-tall black woman wearing a clear plastic jumpsuit was loitering near the stairs. "How 'bout a threesome, sport?" she called as we went up.

Natalie Orlov looked around the room. About the best that could be said for it was that it smelled like a bottle of disinfectant had been spilled on the ratty carpet.

"Hunter, you really know how to show a girl a good time," she said, and worked hard to give me a smile.

I looked at her.

Didn't I just.

TWENTY-EIGHT

Shit! What a fucking mess!

I'd tried to act cool and businesslike to keep Natalie Orlov from getting crazy, but once I left her, I didn't feel very businesslike. I just felt pissed off.

At myself for getting things wrong. At the son of a bitch who was doing it. I could almost see him smiling, that goddamn snake's grin. I wished there were a couple of his boys making a move on me right then. Had there been, there wouldn't have been enough left of them to go into a doggie bag.

But that was only a wish. Things were getting ugly, which didn't particularly bother me, except I wasn't sure what the hell to do about it. I had a couple of ideas, but rubbing them together wasn't likely to generate enough friction to make a spark, much less incinerate the asshole. Still . . .

I called the guy who'd checked out the bug at SLEAZE. He didn't sound exactly pleased to hear from me, said he was in the middle of something. I assumed he meant someone, but at that point, I wasn't too concerned about spoiling his social life. I said I wanted to hire him. See if he could trace whoever had made the bug, and find out who it was sold to.

"There probably won't be a name, but get a description."

"Now?" he said, getting ready to protest.

"Yeah. Get on it right away."

"Aw, Sam, give me a break. You won't believe what I've got here. She's got this tattoo—"

"You mean the butterfly or the goldfish?"

"Oh, shit."

"Right away, huh? It's important."

"Right," he sighed.

I didn't know what good it would do, but it couldn't hurt. Before, it had been enough for me to know that Dirk was behind everything, but with Pinkham's murder, I needed more. I had to be able to prove it, demonstrate connections. Without that, it was only a story, and not one that was likely to thrill the cops. But with a couple of tangibles, everything would hold together.

I put another dime in the phone and tried Harry Demorest again. As I listened to the busy signal, it started to sound like it was mocking me, and I began to get a gut feeling that I didn't like a whole lot.

His office was on Olympic, west of the monument that celebrated the successful campaign of some film stars in the twenties to keep Beverly Hills from becoming part of L.A. The victory meant that their taxes stayed low and that they got to keep their own police department, which functioned—and still does—like a private militia, not so much concerned with enforcing the law as maintaining their bosses' privileges. It was a swell setup. An outsider could get busted for not being color-coordinated, but a resident could get anything short of an ax murder overlooked as a minor indiscretion.

The front entrance to Demorest's building was locked, but one of the skeleton keys I carried got me in the service door at the rear. I went up the back stairs to the second floor. A light showed at the bottom of the door, but I heard nothing coming from inside.

The door was unlocked, and I went in. The reception area was empty, but the door to Demorest's office was half open, and the lights were on. I called his name. Nothing. I went across and looked in.

Harry Demorest wasn't doing laps either. He was slumped in a chair. In a pattern I was starting to get tired of, his feet were tied to the chair legs and his wrists to the arms. His shirt was open, and his chest had been pretty badly sliced. Circular burns covered the backs of his hands and the skin around his eyes. After he'd been tortured, somebody had fed him the barrel of a gun and blown the back of his head off, spraying blood and bone and brains across the framed photographs of his celebrity clients that hung on the wall.

My stomach knotted, but I wasn't exactly surprised. It seemed that I'd been running a little behind for this whole thing, and still was. I was beginning to feel like the guy who followed the parade, cleaning up after the horses. It wasn't a feeling I enjoyed, but I couldn't see how to catch up.

I was obviously missing something—something pretty big. If there was a set of circumstances that made sense of Pinkham's murder, I couldn't see how it could also apply to Demorest's. If it was connected with the pictures, they were on opposite sides of the issue. So maybe there was a reason to remove one or the other, but why both? And unless it had been just for fun, Harry had been tortured to reveal something. He'd obviously found out something—I knew that from his messages—but what? And what had he told them? And which, of all the mistakes that I'd made, had he referred to? Shit. Things were picking up speed, and I was falling further behind.

From the condition of the office, it looked like Demorest had put up a fight. A lamp was on its side, a chair was overturned, the telephone was off the hook on the floor, along with everything else that had been on the desk. From the appearance of the wounds, it looked like it had happened some time ago, and I wondered if he'd been taken by the same guys who'd come after me. I didn't owe Harry anything, but I kind of hoped so.

I quickly looked at the stuff on the floor. About the only thing that I thought might relate to this was the top sheet of a pad of lined yellow paper. Near the top of the page were two New York phone numbers. The lower half was covered with the kind of geometric patterns that a lot of people make while talking on the phone. In the middle of the doodles, with a box around it, was the word "NO," underlined three times. An arrow ran from that box to another holding the words "What then?" Down at the bottom of the page, Demorest had written "LAX 3:00."

I copied down the phone numbers, and left the office without looking back at what once had been Harry Demorest. I didn't figure I had anything to say to him.

Outside the air seemed heavy, and my chest felt tight . . . though it might not have been the humidity.

I drove a few blocks away, then pulled up at a phone

booth. There was no answer at the first number. At the second, I got an answering machine: "Hi. This is Jason Pinkham. I've had to go to the coast for a couple of days. If it's really important, you can reach me there. If not, I'll talk to you when I get back."

I'm afraid you won't, Jason, I said to myself as I hung up. I shook my head. He'd sounded awfully alive.

I got back in the car and headed toward Malibu. The way things were going, I didn't really expect to find anybody, but I had to make sure.

There were no lights on, and no cars in front. I went around to the beach and up onto the deck. The broken window hadn't been covered, and I walked in.

I looked around, but didn't get anything except the impression that there'd been a hasty departure. Swell.

Was I chasing him? Or was he chasing me?

Or was I chasing my tail?

TWENTY-NINE

I thought about going to the motel where I'd stuck Natalie Orlov, but decided instead to go back to my place. Just as well.

I turned onto my street, then hit the brakes. Halfway down the block, I could see that the lights were on in my house. I could also see that there was a black-and-white parked in front, and another car that I thought might be Burroughs's. Apparently the evening wasn't quite over yet.

I quickly shoved the car into reverse and went back around the corner. About a mile away, I stopped at a pay phone and called my own number.

"Yeah?" a voice answered.

"Is Burroughs there?"

"Hold on."

There was a delay, then another voice also said, "Yeah?"

"There's a beer in the fridge and a can of peanuts in the cupboard," I said. "Make yourself at home, Burroughs."

"Hunter! Where the fuck are you?"

"Someplace else. Which is where I'd like you to be. What are you doing?"

"I want to have a little talk. Why don't you come home?"

"You want to talk? Talk."

There was a long pause, then Burroughs said, "Philip Prince."

"What about him? I told you everything I know."

"That's right. Something about his owing you money, wasn't it?"

"Something like that. What's going on?"

"We found him tonight. He was in his car. Parked in the hills not too far from where he lived."

"Yeah?"

"He was in the front seat. Most of his brains were in the back seat."

I hardly reacted. I was getting used to this. "Suicide? I guess that wraps up your case."

"It would. Except for two things. There wasn't a gun . . ."

"Oh? What's the other thing?"

"He had your card in a pocket. On the back it said, 'If you've got trouble, maybe I can help.' Did you?"

Good question. Maybe I did. Did I care? Not a whole lot.

"Look, Burroughs," I said, "I'm in business. That's a business card. I give 'em to lots of people. I don't keep track." I shook my head. That was what Prince had said to me the first time I saw him. I should have been able to do better than that.

Burroughs must've thought so too. After another long pause, he said, "Like I told you this morning, I get kind of twitchy when you—or your name—turn up around dead bodies."

"Come on, Burroughs. What's the big deal? For all I know—or you know—somebody might be trying to make things hot for me."

"I didn't think you needed any help for that."

I didn't say anything.

"You know, Hunter, I might even buy your lame line. Except there's this other thing."

"What other thing?"

"When we got to your place—just to have a friendly chat, you understand—there was a note stuck in your door."

"So?"

"So it was from Philip Prince. You want to hear it?"

"You want to read it to me?"

"Why not? It says, 'I got the item we were talking about, but I don't want anything to do with it. If you want it, I'll find someplace to hide it where we met. Then I'm gone.' I don't suppose you know what he's talking about, do you?"

"Not a clue, Burroughs. If I find out, though, I'll let you know."

"Cute. But that's not the right answer. Once, maybe. Not twice. I've got two bodies now, which means I got no time for cute. So I want to start hearing something from you. Fast."

I thought about it. He was right. I should probably give

him something. Besides, I figured it might help to liven things up.

"Actually, Burroughs," I said, "you've got more than two bodies."

"What?"

"There's a guy named Jason Pinkham out in Brent-wood. Blasted in the back."

"What?"

"And there's a P.I. called Demorest in his office on Olympic. He must look a lot like Prince."

"What?"

"Are you taking this down? I don't think they've been called in yet."

"What?"

"And a couple of days ago—you might have gotten a sheet on it—there was a guy named Flight in Tijuana who bought it."

"What?"

"You're repeating yourself, Burroughs. The guy who's responsible is Dirk Primo. He lives in Malibu, but he's not there anymore. I checked."

"What?"

"There may be another body or two washing ashore, but they're just hired hands. Nothing to worry about."

"Wha—Hunter!"

"Now, it's been real nice talking to you, Burroughs, but I've got some stuff to see to. I think you do, too. Turn out the lights when you leave, would you?"

As I hung up, I heard my name. I grinned. It was loud enough to make the receiver vibrate in my hand.

Burroughs was pissed, all right, and I was sure he wanted more than ever to get hold of me. But I was also sure I'd given him enough to keep him busy for a while, and I hoped a while was all I needed. When I did finally see him, I wanted to be able to give him a wrapped package, not some fantasy out of *Weird Tales.*

I got on the freeway and headed into Hollywood. It seemed like I'd been doing nothing but traveling back and forth across the city. For the first time, though, maybe I was going to get somewhere.

I cruised by the fried chicken joint where I'd met Prince that afternoon. It was closed and dark. There was a chain across the entrance to the parking lot, and it was deserted. I knew this could be just one more setup, but I checked the cars parked on the street and the nearby doorways, and didn't spot anyone. I thought about staking it out for a while, then decided the hell with it. I was armed, alert, and fed up. If someone wanted to pull something—fine. I'd pull something back. And rip it out by the fucking roots.

But nothing happened. I drove back, parked in front, and walked into the lot. I looked around. There was just empty blacktop with parking spaces marked off on it. About the only place something could be hidden was the large trash container behind the chicken stand. It sat on rollers, so the bottom of the bin was about six inches off the ground. I got on my knees, looked under it, and saw a flat shape pushed in about a foot. I got it out. It was one of those book-sized vinyl-covered boxes holding a videocassette.

And that was that.

I stood and listened and waited. Nothing. I went back to my car and got in. Nothing. I moved to the corner, stopped, and checked the rearview mirror. Still nothing. I drove off.

It seemed too easy.

It was.

THIRTY

I found a twenty-four-hour video store and rented a re-corder. The clerk, a puffy character with yellow skin and Coke-bottle glasses, said they were having a special that week on the Slut Series—*The Sluts Go to Washington, The Sluts Join the Circus, The Sluts Enter College.* I told him I'd seen them, and that while the characterization and di-rection were pretty good, I'd found the story lines a bit thin.

"How about *Teenage Sluts Meet the Wolfman?*" he called out, but I was already through the door.

I took the equipment over to Natalie Orlov's house in the hills. It was close and I was tired. Also, maybe I'd get lucky and be paid a visit by some of my new friends.

I hooked up the machine to her TV and loaded the cassette.

It was homemade, a silent job, but it was still pretty easy to follow the plot.

It opened in a bedroom, small and functional—bed, table, lamp. Alana Lanier was sitting at a dressing table, looking in the mirror and brushing her hair. She was wearing a clinging slip and nothing else. Everytime she moved her arms, her breasts shifted beneath the shiny fabric.

I could see what everyone was talking about. The camera held her like a lover, enveloping her, caressing her, lingering, exploring. There were no bad angles, only impossibly luscious curves, and she seemed to exude heat like a shimmering desert highway. Her eyes were heavy-lidded and dull, and I again had the idea that she was sedated halfway to oblivion, tranquilized to passivity. But even that seemed to work before the camera, creating a blurred combination of

195

sensuality and docility that—even knowing what I did and
not liking it—was difficult not to respond to. She had been
made into a sexual *thing,* beautiful and yielding and avail-
able, and the camera recorded it, and the images reached
deep, striking chords that were ordinarily still, touching
urges for power and dominance that were usually buried.
It was not nice, the idea of sexual master and slave, but it
was potent, very potent.

Every once in a while, she blinked and momentarily
tensed, as though someone off-camera was talking to her,
giving instructions. After one of these moments, she set
down the brush and, eyes closed, began to fondle her heavy
breasts, cupping them up and out, touching the nipples
that were straining against the glistening slip.

The camera zoomed back, giving a wider angle of the
room. It revealed a man looking in the window. His mouth
and chin were exposed, but the rest of his head was covered
with a tight-fitting leather mask, giving him the look of
some feral nocturnal creature. His tongue circled his loose
lips as he watched Alana caress herself.

A quick cut, and he was standing next to her. He
grabbed the top of the slip and ripped it off her. Alana shiv-
ered, not with pleasure, as he put his hands on her, press-
ing, rubbing, pinching, like he was kneading dough or
squeezing inflated rubber.

Alana turned her head and looked off to the side. She
paused, then sighed, looking sad and resigned. Her hands
went up to the man's belt, and she opened his jeans,
exposing him. Another glance to the side, and then she began to practice the trade Dirk had taught her, the way to
heaven according to Joshua. The camera lingered in close.

Later, they were on the bed in various positions, an illus-
trated manual of the way two bodies could combine, all
shot close and bright, The Girl Next Door having it off
with the Masked Asshole. There was easily enough stuff to
fill a dozen magazines, each more explicit than the preced-
ing ones, each giving form and shape and color to shadow
fantasies, to wet-dream visions. The Girl Next Door . . .
like you always imagined her. Shit.

I was about to turn it off when something at the back of
my brain started to itch. Something that my eyes had
taken in, but that I hadn't seen. I started to run the tape

back—fast search—not sure what I was looking for. And then I got it. Another few seconds, and I froze the frame. It was a close-up of Alana, with the Masked Asshole holding her head, guiding her as her mouth moved over him.

Goddamnit!

On his left forearm there was a tattoo of a skull and crossbones.

He never took off his mask, but it was the dead kid in Prince's apartment. The punk who hung around Malibu doing petty crime.

What did that give me? Maybe a new handle on this thing.

I gave it some thought. Maybe I wasn't so far wrong after all. As I'd originally figured, it was a hustle by Dirk. He could have gotten together with Flight . . . who set up Prince . . . who got people talking . . . who got the network panicked. But instead of trying to juggle smoke when it came to the payoff, as I'd guessed, he decided he'd better have something to deliver.

And since he didn't have anything, he would make something. No problem. I'd seen an example of the way he controlled the girl, and I'd noticed the video camera and recorder in the Malibu house. All he needed was another body, and Central Casting was just outside his door on the beach.

The big thing he had to watch out for was to keep the scam from getting out. The network would pay to suppress an old movie, but even they would probably draw the line if they knew it was recent, very recent. It was one thing for your hot new star to have once made a fuck film; it was something else if she was still doing it. Even the balance-sheet bastards at NTN would realize they couldn't have that kind of sword hanging over them, and they'd run like hell. No payoff now, no gravy train later. So Dirk eliminated his potential problem by eliminating Alana's co-star.

That explained one body, and the same reasoning could account for some of the others. If Demorest somehow found out what was going on, he'd blow the whistle to the network, maybe even figure he could make a criminal case, so he had to be taken out. Flight? It still looked like he was in on it from the beginning; taking care of him would remove

another liability, as well as a partner to share with. Or
maybe Dirk had planned to use Flight when it came to the
payoff, but Flight had decided he'd do better on his own
and tried a double-cross. That could account for Pinkham.
And since the tape was a very hot potato, it wasn't that
healthy to hold onto it. It could have gotten loose, and that
could account for Prince. Hell, for all I knew, Flight had
put it in the mail and it had taken a week to surface.

There were lots of possibilities. I didn't think I'd really
get to the bottom of it—too many people were dead—but
the outlines were clear enough. If I could connect another
couple of dots, I'd have a nice picture to present to Burroughs.

I remembered the files I'd taken out of Flight's office.
That could do it, I thought. I was optimistic as I went to dig
them out of the car, but again I came up empty—no names,
numbers, or subjects that seemed to relate.

I looked at my watch. It was nine a.m. back East, and I
tried the second New York number that I'd taken from Demorest. This time it was answered—Jason Pinkham's office. His secretary told me he'd gone to L.A. I didn't tell her
he wouldn't be coming back. Instead I asked a few questions. No, she said, she'd never heard of anyone named
Flight or Prince or Primo, and she didn't know anything
about pictures for SLEAZE.

So much for that.

At least I had the tape. And that meant it was Dirk's
move.

I stepped out into Natalie Orlov's backyard. Already a
warm and sticky day, the sky was a gray sulphur color, the
pollution so thick I could feel the grit on my skin, like
being downwind from a steel mill. The sun, as it rose above
the mountains, was a glowing red oval.

It looked like it was going to be a fucking lousy day.

THIRTY-ONE

I got a couple of hours of restless sleep. Distant voices spoke to me monotonously, repetitiously, like a record with a stuck needle, only I couldn't make out what they were saying, couldn't get them to move on so I could understand the message. More shadows danced, smoke figures swirling around me. They seemed to be trying to coalesce, form a new pattern, but every time I came close to seeing it, they dissipated once again, leaving me looking at random, meaningless forms.

I woke up feeling like my eyelids were sandpaper scraping my eyeballs every time I blinked, and with the sense that I was missing something. My brain tried to put it together while I slept, but it didn't succeed, and I was left with a tightness in my gut and a pressure on my diaphragm that told me something was wrong.

After a few minutes in the swimming pool and a long hot shower, I started to feel vaguely human, but I still had a sense of lurking trouble. I thought about it through a couple of cups of strong coffee, but still couldn't figure out what was bothering me. The hell with it. Time to get moving.

I took the videotape and drove to the motel, stopping on the way to get Natalie Orlov a big Styrofoam container of coffee. Except for a couple of girls in satin shorts and see-through blouses discussing their investment portfolios, the motel parking lot was empty.

I went up the stairs and knocked on the door. No answer. I tried the doorknob; it opened. The room was empty. The bed had been slept in, but nothing else seemed disarranged. There was no note.

I went back downstairs. I asked the girls in the parking

lot if they'd seen anything. They hadn't, but they said they
were having an early bird special—two for the price of one,
and they'd throw in a complimentary croissant. I gave
them the Styrofoam cup of coffee and told them I'd already
eaten.

The guy in the motel office didn't know anything either,
not that I'd expected him to. When you worked in a place
like that you counted the cash, kept your eyes on the floor,
and if you heard screams, you turned up the TV.

Fifteen minutes later I got to the SLEAZE office. The
butterflied receptionist had her hand under her tight
sweater and seemed to be having some trouble getting her
tits organized. Without looking up from her efforts, she
told me she hadn't seen Natalie Orlov since yesterday afternoon.

I went through to the office. A file folder lying on the
floor next to the desk was the only thing that seemed to be
out of place. I picked it up. It was labeled "Sword of
Truth," and it was what Natalie Orlov had kept the letters
in. It was empty.

I took the phone and opened up the receiver. The bug
was gone.

Goddamnit. My splendid timing continued. The lines
had been laid down, and now they were being pulled in. I
wanted to get tangibles, but I was left grabbing air.

The bad feeling I had was growing stronger. It was clear
that things were coming to a conclusion. But what? And
where was Natalie Orlov?

I checked in with the service. There was a message from
Natalie Orlov asking me to go to her house and saying she
would call me there. That should have been encouraging,
but somehow it didn't make me feel any better.

There was a mailman in the reception area. His bag was
on the floor, and he was trying to help the girl with her
problem.

"Is this any better?" he said.

"Oooh," she said.

Neither of them noticed as I went by.

Back at Natalie Orlov's place, I couldn't sit still. As I
roamed around, I again tried to come up with what was
bothering me. Beyond all the obvious things that were
fucked up, I still had the sense that I was overlooking

something, something central. But I couldn't get any closer than I had when I was asleep.

When the call finally came, I picked up the phone before the first ring had ended. It was Natalie Orlov. I asked her where she was, if she was all right.

"Sam, I—" she started to say, then she was cut off and a low voice, almost a whisper, said, "That's up to you, asshole."

It was Dirk Primo, and I knew then what the conclusion was.

"What do you want?" I said.

"I want a quarter of a million dollars in cash. Or else I let my boys have some fun. They're not feeling very good right now, and they need to have some fun."

"How am I supposed to come up with that kind of money?"

"You sell the tape to the network."

"What tape?"

"What a fucking clown. But you don't have to act any dumber than you already are, asshole."

"This isn't going to work, you know."

"It better, or your pretty friend here'll look like something that was run over by a truck." In the background, I heard Natalie Orlov cry out. "Understand? Nothing fancy, or bye-bye."

Primo's voice was a moist hiss. I could hear he was getting off on this, and I could picture his smile. I wanted to scream at him, tell him what I was going to do to him, but instead I only said, "Okay. What do I do once I get the money?"

"Be at this number at six. I'll tell you where to go."

I started to tell him that he'd better be sure she was all right, but the line went dead. I hung up and stared at the phone.

So I was going to be the way Dirk got the dough *and* stayed hidden. Prince must've gone to him, hoping to straighten things out, and he'd decided to use the lawyer as the way to get the tape to me. If Prince hadn't been there, he would've found something else. And Natalie Orlov was the way he made sure of my cooperation. He must've staked out her place, and I'd failed to pick up the tail when we went to the motel.

Was that what had been gnawing at me? It seemed like I finally should have all the answers, but something still kept nagging at me. Something didn't fit, and I couldn't get at it. Shit.

No time now. I had other things to worry about.

I called Ogden Winters, the V.P. at the network who'd hired Demorest. Fortunately, he knew who I was. Even more fortunately, the news of Pinkham and Demorest and Prince hadn't broken yet, so maybe I could negotiate.

I explained that I was representing SLEAZE, that I had the material under discussion, and that I wanted $250,000 in cash.

Winters went into this panicked whine about how it was too much, how he didn't have the authority, how he had to check first, how it would take time, how, how, how . . .

I cut him off. "We either deal right now, or it turns up on cable TV tonight and next month on every newsstand. Your choice."

I heard stuttering sounds in my ear. Winters obviously had become a V.P. because of his ability to make decisions. "How do I know . . ." he finally managed to get out.

"The only thing that matters is that I have the material. I'm selling it today. Are you buying? Gulp once for yes, twice for no."

After a long pause, I heard one gulp.

"Fine. When shall we make the exchange?"

"Tomorrow."

"No good. I'll be there in two hours."

"Bu . . . bu . . . bu . . ."

"Two hours. Have the money in a briefcase or something. Okay?" I hung up.

No way was I going to let Dirk Primo pull this off, but until I got Natalie Orlov out, I had to keep control. Which meant nobody could know what was really going on.

I didn't feel like hanging around the house any longer. I went back to the store where I'd gotten the video machine, then I decided to head toward West L.A. where the network office building was located. I figured I'd kill some time at a nearby Japanese fast-food stand whose sign said it was called The Led Rantern. An hour spent sucking in noodles and gobbling down smoky-flavored gyoza wouldn't

solve any problems, but it would at least keep me from
clawing at the walls.

When I'd finished with a birdbath-sized bowl of soup and
the platter of fried dumplings, I got another Sapporo beer,
lit up a cigarette, and swiveled on the stool to face the
street. Across from me, at a bus stop, a girl was sitting on a
bench painted with an advertisement for Ersatz, a new
perfume that said it was "For the real you."

She was sleek and slender and seventeen, golden blond
and golden tan, dressed in a skimpy halter top and cutoffs
that were about four sizes too small. Her legs were open
and stretched out as she ate a candy bar. She was totally
self-absorbed, moving the bar slowly in and out of her
mouth, tongue occasionally darting out to catch a drop of
the melting chocolate coating. She noticed me watching
her, and she gave me a sly smile as she opened her mouth
wider around the glistening candy.

I nodded to her. This was a town in a constant state of
arousal: perpetual estrus, thighs spread, membranes slick,
erectile tissue engorged, always ready, always willing. Always waiting for the next tingle, the next hit, the next
sensation, no matter what kind, what source, as polymor-
phously perverse as an infant, always wanting more,
something new, pleasure from any origin. And Alana Lanier was just the next jolt, the latest attempt to make the
sated, electro-shocked body twitch one more time. No, Natalie Orlov's speck of clean sand in the middle of an ocean
didn't look all that bad today.

But she was about as far away from it as she could get,
and I got off my stool and into my car.

The NTN building was one of those enormous concrete
boxes that looked like it could have been either a correc-
tional facility or a gigantic public lavatory. A plaque next
to the front entrance announced that the building had won
an award for architectural excellence. Something about
the harmony of form and function.

Two uniformed security men were waiting for me in the
lobby, and I was silently escorted to a top-floor conference
room. Seated around the large table were a bunch of guys
who were dressed like professional mourners, and who
looked at me as though I were bringing word that the

Fountain of Youth had been discovered and they were now out of work.

One of them came forward and said he was Ogden Winters. He had bleary, bulging eyes, a wide mouth, and resembled an albino frog. Shaking his hand was like grabbing a dead squid.

I held out the cassette. "You got the money?"

Winters led me to a briefcase sitting on the table. He opened it, and I saw it was filled with packets of new twenties and fifties. I handed Winters the tape, and he hopped down to the other end of the table where a VCR and a monitor were set up. I counted the money while the executives watched the tape. At what I figured was the moment Alana opened the Masked Asshole's zipper, they all groaned in unison, then each of them reached into a vest pocket, took out a pillbox, and popped a couple of tiny tablets.

By the time they finished viewing the tape, the V.P.s looked like they were ready to lose their collective lunches. They trooped down to my end of the conference table.

I gave them a big grin. "I think it'll pull about an eighty share, don't you?"

I heard gagging sounds from someone in the back. So much for easing tension.

They had a lot of questions. I was reassuring but not exactly responsive. Finally, they decided they had no choice but to make the deal. They gave me a stack of papers to sign—receipts, letters of agreement, deal memos, guarantees of exclusivity, anything their legal department could come up with. After the first inch of documents, I stopped looking at what I was signing. It was all bullshit anyway.

I picked up the briefcase and headed for the door. "Have a nice day," I said.

As one, fifteen guys reached for their pill boxes.

Back on the street, I looked up at the sun, a shimmering white smudge behind a canopy of gray shit, and wondered what the fuck I was going to do now. Getting the money was the easy part. Getting Natalie Orlov and myself out of this in one piece would be a whole lot tougher. No way was Dirk going to let us walk once he got the dough. We were the last connections back to him, and that meant we had to be taken out. But even realizing that didn't help. As long as he set the arrangements for the exchange, he could set the trap. All I could do was try to get an opening to break out. Unless I could come up with a way to change the plans.

I called the service. The electronics whiz had left a message saying he'd traced the bug. Twelve hours ago that would've been good news. Now I wasn't sure what difference it made.

There was, however, a call that made a difference. The operator said she didn't understand the message, but that a woman named Alana had called and said she was ready to get out.

I noticed that my hand had closed tightly on the receiver. "Did she say where she was?" I asked.

"She said they'd gone back to Jericho. Does that mean anything to you?"

"It means you just got a bonus, honey," I said and hung up.

They were back at the ranch in Jericho Canyon, the last home of Joshua and the Sword of Truth. It was a good choice—close to Malibu, yet remote enough to be hidden. And that suited me just fine.

I was smiling as I called the guy about the bug. As I listened to his report, the smile faded, and I felt my jaw muscles tense and my back teeth begin to grind together.

I suddenly knew what had been bothering me. The tightness in my gut was gone.

It had been replaced with a lump of black fury.

THIRTY-TWO

My mouth tasted of bile, and images of explosions with flying bloody limbs danced in my brain. I decided to screw finesse.

I went to a library and photocopied a large-scale survey map of Jericho Canyon. A couple of phone calls, and I found out which property belonged to the movie guy that Abel Youngman had told me about. According to the map, there was just one dirt access road up to the house. Better and better.

I went back to the Valley, to a twenty-four-hour bowling alley where I kept some stuff in a locker. At one time, I'd had a secretary and an office. Now I had an answering service and six cubic feet of locker space. Not exactly upward mobility. The next step was probably a TV tray set up on the sidewalk. But at that moment, I didn't give much of a shit about my business, or myself, or about anything except causing the maximum amount of damage in the shortest possible time.

I took another revolver out of a canvas gym bag in the locker and tucked it into my pants. Then I found a box of hollow-point cartridges and dropped it in my jacket pocket. The thought of football-sized exit wounds caused my lips to pull back. A guy coming into the locker room took one look at my grin and dropped a bowling bag on his foot.

With the accelerator pressed to the floor, it took me about forty-five minutes to get to the freeway exit for Jericho Canyon. It was an old road, narrow, twisting, and in need of resurfacing. Less than a mile into the canyon, and it was as if the city didn't exist. The hills were still green from the winter rain, though starting to get dusty and brown. Deer and coyotes and rattlesnakes and the oc-

casional mountain lion lived in the stunted forest of the
chaparral. For all of the cancerous sprawl of the city, you
still didn't have to go very far to find out what it had been
like before there was an L.A., before they got the taps
turned on and made the desert flourish with hot tubs and
drive-in dominance parlors.

A scouting vulture made a slow circle overhead. I took it
as a good omen.

After another couple of miles, I found the road to the
ranch and turned in. I rolled down the windows, turned on
the radio full-blast, and went fast enough up the bumpy,
rutted track to make a lot of noise. When I figured I was
about halfway up, I turned off the radio and the engine and
got out. I took the briefcase with the money and went into
the scrub. I wasn't planning to bargain, but I also thought
I should keep some options open. I hid it well, then I went
back and squatted down behind some thick, thorny bushes
next to the road.

In a few minutes, two figures came into view. One was a
short kid that I'd never seen. He had a narrow head and a
large pointy nose, giving him the look of a giant pale pink
rodent. He carried a shotgun. Slightly in front of him was
the red-bearded guy from the night before. His broken nose
was bandaged, and his chin was covered with a thick, dark
scab where I'd ripped out his whiskers. He was holding
something in his left hand, but I couldn't see what it was.

As they cautiously approached the Checker, I stood up.
"You the guys that ordered the pizza?" I said.

The short kid let out a cry of surprise. Red Beard turned
toward me. As he raised his left hand, I saw the rectangular metal box that was an Ingram submachine gun. It
started its stutter as he swept it toward me, but he was
still pretty wide when I fired once. The hollow point caught
him in the center of his chest and sent him flying backwards into the air.

The kid shrieked again as he was splattered with the
bloody, glistening fragments of Red Beard's lungs. Involuntarily, he pulled the trigger, but the shotgun was
pointed in the air and exploded harmlessly. The kid took
off. I threw a couple shots after him, but I missed, then he
disappeared around a bend. That was okay, I figured; let
'em know I was coming.

I went over and looked down at the body. Beneath it, the dry ground had already turned dark and moist. I picked up the Ingram and started up the road.

After a couple hundred yards, the road opened onto a large clear area. An old, weathered barn stood on the far side. Behind it, another hundred yards up the hill, was a rambling redwood and stucco house. Everything was quiet, like the pause that comes after a bomb stops ticking. They were there, somewhere, waiting. I would have to bring them out.

Sticking close to the edge of the clearing, I began circling around to the barn. When I got to about twenty feet from the open double doors, there was still nothing, but I knew it would begin as soon as I tried to cross to the building. I crouched low and started to run across the open ground. Halfway to the barn, things started moving pretty fast.

The bat-faced guy whose cheek I'd shredded jumped out from behind the barn, blasting away with an automatic. I hit the ground, went into a roll, and came up onto my feet pulling back on the trigger of the Ingram. The gun fires 1,200 rounds a minute, and they say it can cut a man in half. They're right. The magazine was empty in less than a second, but the son of a bitch was still in the air, twitching like a spastic puppet. Then he fell to the ground in three separate pieces.

At that instant, from the other side, a bullet hit next to my feet. As I turned to face it, I dropped the Ingram, brought my gun up, and, using the approved police academy stance—two-handed, knees bent—I emptied it in the direction of the fire. I didn't get a good look at the guy. Three of my shots caught him in the face, and his head exploded like a watermelon dropped from ten thousand feet.

As I pulled the second gun from my waistband, there was a sound behind me, from the barn. Before I could turn and set myself, I was sent sprawling to the ground. The gun went flying, and it felt like I'd been clipped by a truck.

My side burst into pain as something heavy hit me in the ribs. I rolled onto my back, blinked to clear my vision, and saw a heavy studded boot coming at my head. I rolled away and kept rolling, scrambling madly in the dust.

I managed to get to my knees. Coming toward me, stiff-

legged, was the bald guy from last night. He looked like
something Dr. Frankenstein had discarded. The skin
around his eyes was purple and puffy. He had a ball of
bandage, stained red, where his nose used to be, and another on the side of his head where his ear had been. He
was breathing heavily through his mouth.

"I'm going to tear you apart, motherfucker," he said.

His arm whipped around, and a six-foot length of heavy
chain came toward my head. I ducked out of the way, but it
still hit me across the back with enough force to knock me
face down again.

I saw his leg pull back, ready to smash my ribs again. Instead of trying to roll away, I rolled toward him, taking the
blow on my arm, but at the same time catching him off balance. I clawed at his jeans, pulling him to the ground, and
before he had a chance to recover I was on top of him, dropping a knee into his crotch as hard as I could. He grunted
in pain, and I slammed the palm of my hand into the center
of his face. He howled as the bandage came away and the
stitches tore, and thick blood gushed from his nose hole.

As I staggered to my feet, he lashed out; the chain
rasped across my neck and shoulders. He was roaring now
in pain and fury as he struggled to rise. He was almost on
me as I bent to get the gun from the ground. The chain
struck me again across the back, and I was knocked away
from the gun. I rolled again to escape the next blow, got to
my feet, and stumbled into the barn.

Before my eyes had a chance to adjust to the dimness,
someone came at me from out of the shadows. It was the
kid with the rat snout. More reflex than anything else, I
flinched out of the way, slipping to one knee as I heard
something whoosh by my head. I turned and looked up and
saw him descending on me. The sickle in his hand caught a
ray of light coming through a gap in the roof, and it glim-
mered like the sliver of a lethal new moon. He swung for
my neck, but I ducked, lunging forward, then rising to my
feet. I closed with him, getting my shoulder beneath his rib
cage and picking him up. As I started to move, carrying
him over my shoulder, I felt him trying to jab me in the
back with the point of the blade, but he had no leverage,
and my jacket was thick enough to cushion the blows.

Off to one side, I saw a large roll of barbed wire five feet high, and I ran for it. We hit hard, and the kid screamed as dozens of metal hooks went through his thin shirt and tore into his back. I bounced my body into his four, five, six times, lifting each time, then I heard the sickle drop from his hand as he wailed insanely. I grabbed him by his scrawny neck—my hand went three-quarters of the way around—and yanked him forward. His scream rose higher as bits of his flesh were torn out, stuck to the barbs. I turned him around, then, separating some of the strands, jammed his head deep into the bale. The guy whimpered twice, then his body slumped.

Suddenly, I was clubbed at the base of my skull with what felt like a double thickness of chain, and my entire body went momentarily numb. As my legs started to give way, I was seized from behind in a tremendous full nelson. My arms stuck straight out to the sides, useless, and the pressure that Noseless applied to the back of my neck was so great it felt like my head would be pushed off.

There was a whispered hiss. "Swing him around."

Half dragged, half carried, I was pulled back a few feet and turned toward the middle of the barn. The barrel of a big automatic was about two inches from my left eye. From what seemed far in the background, I saw Dirk Primo's crazy yellow eyes, saw his lips twisted into a cold smile.

"What's it feel like to be dead?" he said.

"What's it feel like not to have the money?"

"Oh, I'll get the money."

He took the gun away from my head, stuck it in his pants, and bent down. When he stood up, I was looking at the needle-sharp point of a six-inch-long stiletto.

"You'll talk." He smiled. "They always tell me what I want to know, sooner or later. I hope you'll be later, asshole."

The blade flicked out two, three, four times, each time causing an instant of pain, each time making a dot-sized break in the skin beneath my eye socket.

"Cut the fucker to pieces," Noseless growled.

The blade darted again, closer to my eye. I tried to move out of the way, but it was like my head was in a vise. I tried to squirm my upper body loose, but the goon's hold was unbreakable, and I knew he'd be able to maintain it a long time.

Primo drew the tip of the knife down my cheek. It was the lightest possible touch, but still it broke the skin like a razor blade. In a very little while, I would look like Demorest and the kid in Prince's apartment, and I'd tell him anything he wanted to know. I knew I couldn't wait much longer, couldn't wait until he started poking at my eyeballs. But I was held tightly, a constant downward pressure on my neck that even pain and fear and hatred would not give me the strength to break. I only had one choice.

The knife struck again, this time close to the other eye. I kicked out at Noseless's leg, and he responded by spreading his legs a little wider and pushing down even harder. That was what I wanted. I kicked at the other leg, then pushed up from my partially bent legs, offering as much resistance as I could. I heard a laugh like bubbling mucus next to my ear, and he pushed down still harder on my neck, letting his force tell me there was no escape. Suddenly I let my legs go completely slack and let my feet slide backwards on the dirt floor. He was pushing down, and the instant that my feet slid back between his legs, he lost his balance and staggered forward. I raised my arms and slipped out of his grasp.

I knew I had only a split second before he recovered and regained the advantage, and I used the time to drive my fist into his groin with as much force as my aching body could manage. I felt his balls squish, and he pitched forward, knocking Primo down and falling on top of the smaller man.

Dirk was hissing and spitting at the guy to get up, to get off him, to get me. By the time Noseless did get to his feet, I'd scrambled back and picked up the sickle. As Dirk pulled his gun out of his waistband, I charged him. I was on him as he got it clear, and swung the blade as hard as I could. His hand flew twenty feet through the air, still holding the gun.

For an instant he stared at his wrist, unable to believe what had just happened. Then, as the blood started spurting out in pulses, he clamped his other hand over the stump and began yelling wildly. His yellow eyes rolled and foam flecked his lips and he cried for Noseless to kill me, crush me, gut me.

I motioned with the sickle, and the monster looked at me

warily. His bald head was slick with sweat, and a trickle of
blood oozed from the hole in his face. It ran across his lips
down to his chin, and then dripped to the dirt floor, each
drop causing a tiny explosion in the dust.

He moved back a few steps and picked up the chain from
the ground.

"Kill him, kill him, kill him," Dirk cried, his voice no
longer a whisper but a shriek of total madness.

Noseless began moving forward, swinging the chain. I
backed up, and he continued to advance. Then I made my
move, jumping inside the orbit of the chain, and letting its
momentum pull me into him. As I closed, I brought the sickle down. The point hit the top of his forehead, and the
blade curved into his skull like a giant fang. I stepped
back. He toppled straight forward like a falling tree, dead
before he even hit the ground.

I turned to Dirk, smiling. "You were saying?"

He hesitated an instant, then turned and ran toward the
opposite end of the barn in the direction of the house. I hurried over and picked up the severed hand, now constricted
like a dead crab. I pried the gun loose, and dropped the
claw. I took a careful sighting and fired.

Dirk's right leg collapsed beneath him. He staggered a
couple of steps, hopping on the left, then fell to the ground.
He clutched at his thigh, tried to rise to his feet again, but
couldn't. He started to slither on his belly on the ground.
Appropriate, I thought.

In no hurry now, I went back out of the barn and re-
trieved my gun with the hollow points. I went back
through the barn, stepped outside, and looked around.
Everything was quiet again.

I strolled after Dirk, who was still trying to pull himself
along on the ground. I stood in front of him, and he stopped
crawling. Using my foot, I roughly rolled him over onto his
back, then stood over him, feet on either side of his body.
He was covered in sweat and dirt and blood. A froth of sa-
liva spilled out of his mouth, and his mad yellow eyes were
surrounded by red. He stunk of fear and evil, and I thought
of all the pain he'd fed upon.

I knelt down, laying a knee heavily across his chest. I
brought my gun up to his mouth, let it graze his lips. I tried
to push it into his mouth, but he clamped his jaw shut. I

pulled the gun back a few inches, then jammed it forward hard, shattering his crooked, discolored teeth. He gasped, and I shoved three inches of barrel inside his mouth, pushing, digging the end up into his palate.

"How does it feel," I said, "to know I hold your life in my hands?"

For the first time, I had the sense that his weird crossed eyes were in fact focusing on me, that maybe for once someone or something outside him actually had some reality.

"I should blow your fucking head off," I said. Then I pulled the gun out and stood up. "But I won't. That'd be too easy."

A look of relief washed over his pale skull-like face.

"Instead," I said, "I'm going to gut-shoot you. You'll die just the same, only it'll take longer . . . and hurt a whole lot more."

His eyes opened wide, a siren kind of moan came out of his throat, then it was drowned out by the sound of my gun exploding twice. His body jumped into the air, buckled, spasmed, then lay still.

I knelt down close to his head. His eyes were still open. He was still conscious. I took his remaining hand and shoved it into the gaping, oozing belly wound.

"You feel that? Those are your guts."

The look in his eyes told me that he could feel them.

"Looks like Joshua finally got the walls to tumble down, doesn't it? Too bad they fell on you."

I stood up. I didn't feel anything—not anger, or hatred, or satisfaction, or even the detachment of someone who kills a viper or a rabid dog—I was just empty.

I went back down the road and got the briefcase of money from where I'd stashed it. I got into my car and drove up to the house. By the time I got there, Natalie Orlov was standing outside. I took the briefcase and got out of the car. Natalie Orlov started to walk toward me. When she was about ten feet away, I tossed the briefcase down at her feet.

"There," I said. "That's what you wanted."

"What?"

"Your quarter million. Your ticket out."

"What? I don't—"

"Save it," I said. "It won't play anymore. Besides, what's the point now?"

She nodded once. "How'd you find out?"

I shook my head. "I probably could've figured it a long time ago if I hadn't been such a jerk. Maybe, maybe not, I don't know. But there sure were enough things that didn't quite fit. . . . That Hugo Depina was hired before I was. That the Sword of Truth never wrote letters. That I was always one step behind things. That Demorest told me I'd gotten things wrong. That Pinkham's name never turned up anywhere except from you. Most of all, that I didn't think Primo was smart enough to set this up. I kept saying that I didn't think I had the center. But even so, you almost made it. If I hadn't found out that you were the one who bought the phone bug, I never would've put it together. Or not for a long time."

"You traced it?"

"Yeah. I decided I needed something solid to give the police, not just some wild story. So I got the electronics guy on it."

"I didn't know."

"I know. It was after I left you at the motel last night. It was one of the few things you didn't know about. No wonder I was always behind. I was giving progress reports to the person who was organizing everything. Shit, lady! You really suckered me. I knew you were smart, but you sure figured the right way to play me. . . . Goddamnit! I cared."

She nodded. "I know. And it wasn't all an act for me. I want you to know that. You got to me . . . really. You still do."

"Swell."

"I knew you were the right man for this." She gave me a sad little smile. "You just turned out to be a bit too good."

"What was I supposed to be? Your insurance?"

"In part."

"How'd you sell Dirk on that?"

"The other part. I told him we needed somebody else to help make it all real, and to help me keep my distance. Which we did. He was easy to convince. Like you said, he's not very bright. And there's no one easier to hustle than a dumb hustler."

"I guess I proved that. Whose idea was all this? Yours?"

Natalie Orlov nodded again. "Dirk came to me a couple of years ago, wanting me to do a spread on Alana. He said he could make her do anything, just name it. He was a serpent, nothing but a pimp. I turned him down, and that was that. What I told you about the way I work is true."

"Admirable. Then?"

"Then, when Alana hit big, I remembered him. I asked around and found out how he was still with her, still in control, and how he was being cut out of the action. I got an idea that we could do each other some good."

"So much for principles."

She shrugged. "The magazine was going nowhere. I was going nowhere. Every day I wanted to get out more, and every day it was getting more remote. I saw a chance and grabbed it. A really raunchy spread on The Girl Next Door would blow the magazine through the roof. That was the only way I was going to score enough to get out."

"So extortion wasn't your first idea?"

"No. I wanted to put it in the magazine. Only, Jason wouldn't touch it. He thought it would be a rotten thing to do to the girl."

I laughed, not very pleasantly.

"You mean that everything that you told me—your noble stand, your statement of principles—was in fact what *he* told you. And *you* were the one who looked only at the bottom line, and the hell with anything else."

She shrugged.

"So that's what Demorest meant about my making a mistake. I sure did—a hundred and eighty degrees wrong. Shit. What then? You realized that you didn't need to run the pictures after all? Just con the network into thinking you were going to, and get them to pay off?"

"That's right."

"And in order to get somebody who'd both cover your ass and make it look real, you needed some reason for that person to get involved. Dirk told you—or you found out—about Joshua and the Sword of Truth, so you got the idea of the letters. You conned Dirk into thinking that was a way he could cover himself, but all along, it was supposed to backfire on him."

"Right again."

"Were you the one who wrote the letters?"

"I drafted them. Somebody else copied them out."

"Sure. In case I saw your handwriting it had to be different. And then what? Let me see. You got Dirk to set up the guy in Tijuana, who set up Prince. Then everything was ready, and you brought me in, and the whole crazy machine went into motion. Sending me down to TJ, getting me to stir things up. You needed the bug to connect the plot elements, but otherwise, the more confusing it was, the better, because by the time the smoke cleared, you'd be long gone. Where? Your hotel in the South Pacific?"

"Yes."

"And I was your protection. I was the way you were going to cover yourself, make sure Dirk didn't cross you. And maybe—if things went really well—I'd take the bastard out and you'd have everything."

She tried to smile. "It worked."

"You were cutting it kind of close, weren't you? I mean, I could've just said the hell with it and walked away."

"Oh, I was pretty confident that you wouldn't do that."

"Yeah, I guess you were. But suppose it had gone the other way, and they'd taken me out? Dirk would never have let you leave with half the dough."

"I had insurance—a letter saying what he'd done. If anything happened to me, it would go to the police."

"What *he'd* done? Wasn't that all part of your master plan?"

She shook her head. "Not in the beginning. I didn't think . . . all that . . . would be necessary."

"No? But Dirk did, didn't he? He wasn't very bright, but he was smart enough to realize that those were all connections back to him. Something I'm sure you were aware of."

She didn't say anything.

"And besides, you knew he liked it. He got off on doing those guys."

Natalie Orlov shrugged.

"Nice partner you picked."

"That's why I needed you. Like I said, I had a lot of confidence in you." She tried another smile.

"Save it, okay? Somehow I don't feel flattered." I shook my head. "Yeah, you had it all worked out, in complete control. But not quite, right? You did your job a little too well. I was working a little too hard for you. And things

started getting out of hand. I tell Demorest about you, and
he manages to get in touch with Pinkham, who wasn't out
of the country like you let me think, but in New York,
right where he always was. All of a sudden, the shit has hit
the fan. Pinkham is coming out here to find out what the
hell is going on. That was another little bit that didn't fit.
You said he was arriving in the evening, but he got in
much earlier. You must've been climbing the walls then. It
had worked, the whole scheme. You were just about to
score, and then everything was about to fall apart. Something had to be done. Dirk had taken care of the other loose
ends, but Pinkham was your responsibility. So, while you
stand me up for dinner, you go over to his place and blow
him away. It was a nice touch, making sure he went into
the pool. Makes it difficult to establish time of death."

Natalie Orlov nodded slowly.

"Meanwhile," I went on, "you've told Dirk where I'll be.
I'm becoming a complication myself, and it might be better
if I'm removed, so I meet his boys. Since the bug was just a
prop, you had to tell him where to find me. Only his boys
aren't very good, and I show up on your doorstep. I thought
you looked a little strange then, but I put it down to concern." I barked a terse laugh. "It was, but not for me. Still,
you covered very well, and you saw how you could use it.
You were very cool. Shit! I still can't believe how cool you
were. You'd only just gotten back from Pinkham's. But
there's nothing like a little sex to distract the old P.I. Lead
him around by his dick. Lady, you're really something
else. And the phone calls. What was it? You got somebody
to keep phoning you, so I think it's Pinkham, and I'm your
alibi?"

"Yes, yes, yes. You're right about everything. But it
wasn't that easy for me."

"Don't sell yourself short, lady. You make Dirk the rep-
tile look positively hot-blooded."

"Not entirely. I *was* surprised when you showed up. But
believe me, I was really glad you were okay. . . . And the
rest—that was real."

"If you say so. And as far as my being okay—well, that
just meant you put Plan B into effect. If I'd been taken out,
you would've dealt directly with the network. As it turned
out, there was the phony kidnapping, and I did the work.

You sure can think on your feet. I wish I did. I was so bothered about your being grabbed, I assumed I'd made a mistake, but in fact you either took a cab or made a phone
call."

"I made a phone call. They picked me up."

"And you screamed on cue over the phone. Cute. You
must really have liked the Hunter doll. You wind him up,
and he does whatever you fucking well want."

Natalie Orlov stared at me. Her eyes seemed very sad. I
thought that maybe she really was sorry. Or maybe not. It
didn't make a fuck of a lot of difference.

"Let's see—what else? Was it your idea to make the
tape?"

She sighed. "Again, yes. I knew we'd need something to
sell."

"Well," I said, "What difference did it make? Alana'd
sucked so many cocks, one more hardly mattered. Right?
And as for using her—you were just the latest on a long
list, and that's just life in the big city. Shit. You're really a
honey, aren't you. You were the right person, all right, to
run a mag called SLEAZE."

"Yes, I did all those things," Natalie Orlov said, "but I
didn't like myself very much for doing them. I didn't like
finding out that I was no different from the people I hate."

"Who the fuck is? The only distinction is how you show
it. What are you trying for? Sympathy because you feel
sorry you're an asshole?"

She shook her head. "No. No sympathy. My choice, my
responsibility. I started it, and I did what was necessary. I
accept that. And I only regret one thing—the way I used
you."

"Swell. Glad to hear it. But you still did it. That's the
bottom line."

"Then why are you here?"

I motioned behind her, to Alana Lanier who'd been
standing on the porch the whole time. She didn't have any
makeup on, and she was wearing an old work shirt and
faded cords, but she still looked like ten million bucks.
Also, for the first time, her eyes were clear and lively, and
it didn't seem like she was outside her luscious body, floating somewhere up on one of the moons of Jupiter.

"I came up here to get her out," I said. "I suppose I also wanted to play this to the end. I do what's necessary, too."

"And where is it going to come out?"

Good question. She looked straight at me, her green eyes holding mine, no glancing down, no flinching. Shit. Even with everything that had gone on, even knowing all that I did, she could still reach me. I didn't like her anymore, but that somehow seemed beside the point. I couldn't trust her, and I couldn't trust myself where she was concerned. From the beginning, I'd recognized that she was a dangerous woman for me, and nothing had changed. I came up here knowing that, and knowing that I didn't know what I wanted to have happen. So where was it going to come out?

Natalie Orlov had shown she could read me pretty well, and she read my indecision then. "I can try to make it up to you."

"How?"

"I've made a down payment on that hotel I was telling you about—the one a thousand miles from anything else. I've got a plane ticket leaving tonight. We can get another. We've got the money. We can get out, get clear, get free."

I knew that was coming, but until I felt my head shake, I didn't know what my answer would be.

"Why not?" she said. "It would be good."

"It probably would be."

"Then why not?"

I just shook my head. I couldn't explain it to her. Hell, I couldn't explain it to myself. I wanted to go, but I wouldn't. Maybe it was because we were both the same, and the only difference was where we ultimately drew the line. But if that was the only distinction, it was the only distinction that mattered.

"Then will you let me go?"

I shook my head again.

"Are you sure?"

"I'm sure."

"I'm sorry."

"I know," I said.

She reached in her purse and took out a gun. I'd known it was there, and I'd known all along it was coming. That empty feeling I had when I'd looked down at Dirk's body was back, only I was considering myself.

"I'm sorry," Natalie Orlov repeated.

There was a gunshot. Natalie Orlov's eyes opened wide in surprise, and she tilted her head to the side, as though listening for something. Then she glanced down, and brought her hand up to the red stain that was rapidly spreading across her chest. There was another shot, and it caught the side of her head, and she fell, and she died.

Alana Lanier walked over, looked at the body, and let the automatic drop from her hands. Then she looked up at me.

"Thank you," I said.

"She used me," she said. "Just like all the others. You were the only one who didn't."

She came over to me, putting her arms around me and burying her face in my chest. I held her as her body shook. After a while the sobs diminished, then ceased, and she looked up at me.

"You're out now," I said.

"Am I?"

"Sure. You're free, you're a star, you're at the top. You can do whatever you want."

She shook her head. "Not really. It's still the same. I don't want the show, I don't want the network, I don't want any of that."

"Then go. There's a bag full of money, a plane ticket, and an island in the Pacific."

She looked hopeful, then sadly shook her head again. "I'm too valuable. They won't let me go. So they're the ones who own me now."

I looked at her for a minute. She was probably right. If she walked, she'd just be going into courts and hassles and a whole lot of new shit that she didn't need.

"I can get you really out," I said, "if that's what you want most."

"How?"

"I made a copy of that tape before I sold it to the network. I can get it to somebody who'll put it onto film. In a week, it'll be in every porn house in the country. In eight days, no one at the network will even want to hear your name."

She looked at me, then slowly, her eyes brightened and her lips spread into a wide, radiant smile. I realized it was

the first time I'd ever seen her smile, really smile, and it
was like everything she'd been through had never been.

"That would do it, wouldn't it?" she said.

"It sure would."

She started to laugh, a joyful, free sound. I thought
about those guys in the three-piece suits at the network
popping their pills. It *was* pretty funny.

"It'll be a scandal for a while, you know."

She shrugged. "I'll be on that island."

"Then you'll go? Good."

"If you'll come with me."

I looked down at her. Alone with Alana Lanier on a desert island. It was a cartoon fantasy.

"I think you'll be better on your own," I finally said.

She shook her head, and I felt her shiny blond hair brush
my chest. "No. I feel like I'm just waking up from a very
long, very bad dream. I'm going to be okay now—I know
that—but I'm going to need some help. . . . And there's
something else."

"What?"

She hesitated, looking down, seeming almost embarrassed. "Before—at Malibu—you wouldn't let me. . . . No
one else ever did that. As much as anything you've done, I
appreciate that. When I do finally, really wake up, I'd like
you to be there."

She looked up at me and smiled, very seriously, very sol-
emnly. She brought her hand up and touched my chest,
very lightly. She smelled warm and sweet.

Well, shit. There were worse things, I supposed, than
being in a tropical paradise with her for a couple of
months.

Or a couple of decades.

I escorted her over to the Checker and opened the door
for her. She got in, and I shut the door.

I looked around. I figured I'd give Burroughs a call just
before we left. I grinned. It'd really make the bastard's
day.

I glanced at Natalie Orlov's body, then quickly turned
away. There was stuff there I had to work out. I felt Alana
put her hand on my arm. Fuck it. I'd deal with it later. A
lot later.

Down toward the barn, I saw a vulture make an awkward, heavy landing next to Dirk's body. I smiled again. For probably the only time in the asshole's whole unnatural existence, he would be of value to another creature.

The vulture hopped onto Dirk's chest, pecking away with his dark beak. I watched as the big ugly bird plucked out one of Dirk's yellow eyes.

Bon appétit, pal.